Keagans Crossing
By Jonathon Bernard

[Blue] [Murrey] Publishing
Salem, Oregon

From *Turning Paige* by Theresa Hatcher

The leather of the pilot's gloves creaked as he tightened his grip on the stick. He peered through the cockpit glass at the little black clouds exploding in the otherwise lovely late-autumn sky like rotten popcorn, like a mockery of the Fourth of July. *Eighty-eights,* Captain Edwards thought. *Those damn eighty-eights.*

"Control transfer," Edwards said out loud as he turned a switch on the left-hand side of the control panel. Knowing — no, never knowing; *hoping* — that the radio system was doing its job and effectively transmitting his voice, he added, "She's yours, Beacham. Let's make a fast job of it. This neighborhood has gone to hell."

Sgt. Jack Beacham's voice came through the captain's headphones. "Yessir, Cap'n," the nineteen-year-old kid said. "Clear skies should mean a quick, clean drop."

"Let's hope."

Edwards allowed himself a deep breath, one of the deepest, sucking oxygen in through his mask. The bomb run was always the best and the worst part of the mission for him. Flipping that Control Transfer switch gave much of the control of *Screaming Lucy* to whoever sat in the bombardier's seat. That usually was Lt. Ed Reminger, but today, he was serving as the navigator, positioned just a few feet behind the bombardier, which lessened the strain a bit. Beacham was a good kid, but that's what he was. He'd trained as a bombardier, but he usually manned one of the B-17's waist guns. Ear infections and stomachaches had brought on a minor mess of position transfers and stand-ins from other crews. All solid and well-trained men, Edwards was sure of that. But that didn't mean he liked it. He liked the familiar. He liked what he knew.

One of those swaps sat right beside Edwards: Capt. Marlowe, a man of twenty-six, which made him the oldest man on the crew. A bug of some sort had knocked him out of his regular crew's rotation once or twice, putting him short of his required missions. This mission he was logging today as *Screaming Lucy's* co-pilot, this run over the railyard in Cologne, Germany, would finally be his last one. As long as he made it back, he'd make it home. As long as he made it back.

Another of those damn eighty-eight millimeter shells exploded just to Marlowe's right, so close he saw the fire burning red and angry in its heart, so close the ship rocked almost like it had been hit. "Christ," he said as Edwards shouted something with fewer letters. "I think they're trying to make me miss this place."

"Hell of a send-off. You must have made an impression," Edwards said. Then, touching the small microphone at his throat, he said, "Jack? How are we looking?"

"Ah, you just about ruined the surprise, Cap'n," Beacham said. "Bombs away."

"Well, praise be," Edwards said, and he resumed control of the plane just in time to compensate for the sudden weight differential caused by the sudden loss of bombs, which totaled more than 4,000 pounds of weight. Naturally, *Lucy* tried to float upward. Skillfully, Edwards nudged her back down.

"Well, hell. It's done," Marlowe said, his exhilaration under control but detectable by Edwards. "Now all we have to do is make it back home."

"Well, that's right," Edwards said. "Nothing but that. It's just a little over 400 miles back to the airfield. That's practically a puddle jum —"

An incredible concussive force struck their seats, first ramming the captains into their seat backs and then sending each of them straight up into the air. Something like snow whirled in the cockpit: the batting from the destroyed instrument-panel. The captains' heads banged against the cockpit ceiling, and then they were dropped through that false snowstorm with no more courtesy. They fell roughly right back onto the thin cushions covering their metal chairs.

"We have a bomb blow in the bomb bay?" Marlowe asked, and then he repeated the question into his throat-mic.

"No," Edwards said flatly as he pushed in on the stick, not just dropping altitude but angling *Lucy* precariously toward the ground.

"Captain!"

"Save your air!" Edwards said as the front left side of the cockpit peeled open like a can, like an orange, as their instruments warped out of reach, out of sight, as the frigid air of five or six miles high rushed into the cockpit, rushed past them into the cabin, freezing the oxygen lines running to the captains' masks before hurrying to do the same to the lines running to the masks worn by the other crewmen.

Black rimmed Edwards's field of sight like a vignette on an old photograph. *This isn't old, this is now*, he thought with a curious mix of clarity and delirium, and he made that thought echo in his brain like a chant, like a spell, as he struggled to keep at least one hand on his consciousness, as he fought to level out that plane.

He allowed himself to breathe when he saw sky instead of "down." And he breathed again when he let himself believe that, while drastically adjusting *Lucy's* altitude and attitude, he'd managed to point her in the right direction. He still heard explosions of flak, of those eighty-eights, but those sounds of horror faded behind him. And he may have heard the engines of a sister B-17 flying near them, but that was hard to determine. It was impossible to confidently separate that potential sound from the cacophony surrounding him, the horrendous screech of wind torn by the gnarled metal fingers of the blasted fuselage, the same wind that gnashed at his face and his ears and that snagged through his hair.

I've lost my hat, he thought stupidly.

"All we have to do is make it back home," Marlowe said again but with much less excitement and even confidence this time.

Edwards leaned forward as far as he dared and made a quick survey of what had so recently been his instrument panel. He recognized the compass, but recognizable was all it was. Sitting back down and reasserting his grip on the stick, he asked, shouting to be heard above the din, "Capt. Marlowe, you didn't, by chance, pack a road atlas with you, did you?"

Just as loudly, and just as desperately, Marlowe said, "Not today, Capt. Edwards. At least, not one of Germany."

Something that couldn't have been a hand settled on Edwards's shoulder, sending an intense chill through every one of his shattered nerves. He glanced at Marlowe, who was looking at something just behind and just a little higher than Edwards. Marlowe's gaping mouth, wide blue eyes, and bloodless pallor told Edwards his reaction to the can't-be-a-hand wasn't an overreaction.

Edwards looked behind himself and saw a leather bomber jacket, which was natural enough, but then he looked up a little higher and saw something that threw him even more severely than the hand. It was the face of Lt. Ed Fenton, *Lucy's* usual bombardier and current navigator. Edwards had determined that a shell had struck right below the cockpit, directly hitting the nose section that housed his bombardier and navigator. At some point between those short seconds while dropping and leveling the plane — keeping them all alive, just *alive,* the rest they could figure out later — he had also determined that he'd lost both those men. His bombardier would have been positioned right at the point of impact, and the navigator would have been just a few feet behind him. But now, his surely dead navigator was standing right there, no more than a foot behind his chair. "Beacham?" Edwards said.

Fenton shook his head, and then he swiped at the blood running from the three-inch gash on his forehead, grumbled unintelligibly when it ran into his eyes again, and attempted to stanch the flow by shoving his right arm against his head. "Won't hold for long," he said, and Marlowe called back for an aid kit. Fenton nodded his thanks, and then he narrowed his eyes and looked through the cockpit into the open air, right through the space where the cockpit windows should have been. He muttered something to himself, nodded again, and then he said, "Well, I'm out of hands."

Edwards figured they were the babbled words of a man who had just had his bell rung by his proximity to the explosion that had done *this* to their plane. Marlowe caught on, though, and pulled the crumpled bundle out from under Fenton's left arm. He blinked, made sense of what he was holding, and then he blinked again. "Maps," he said. It was all he could say.

Fenton wiped his arm on the leg of his uniform pants and brought it back up to his forehead. "If I'm right, we're about to see Walcheren Island up there on our right."

"And if we do?" Edwards asked.

"Well," Fenton said, "then I'll be right."

Sgt. Boucher, one of the waist gunners, appeared with the aid kit and set to work wrapping Fenton's head.

Edwards faced forward and flexed his gloved fingers. He had no idea how Ed Fenton could be alive, let alone how he could be walking and talking, how he could have had the mental acuity to grab those magical, miraculous maps before he climbed up to the cockpit. In fact, the more Edwards tried to apply things like reason and logic and probability to it, the more certain he was that Ed Fenton was a ghost. But the ghost had maps, which meant the ghost offered their best and perhaps only chance to bring

Screaming Lucy and the surviving members of her crew back to England.

Whatever's going to happen is going to happen, Edwards knew, and he found a surprising amount of peace in the thought.

***

Screaming Lucy's horrendously distorted remains sat in the dark, resting on the grass 100 yards from the end of the 6,000-foot-long airstrip on which Edwards and Marlowe had tried to land her. She'd had just a little more life left in her, and she'd given every bit of that to them.

Life, Fenton thought, standing alone in front of the ruined B-17, looking up at the long crease in the nose section. He knew that marked the flak's impact point. Fenton had been looking over his maps at the time, but that did nothing to lessen his certainty that the eighty-eight had exploded right in Jack Beacham's lap.

Life, he thought again as he rapped his knuckles against plane's aluminum belly. *Life and luck.* He raised his head, wishing he could have seen Lucy, could have seen *her,* one last time, but the nose art had been obliterated, just like so much else.

Fenton heard a scuffling noise behind him and turned to see Vic Weider, who had been a fixture of *Lucy*'s ground crew.

"Vic," Fenton said.

"Hi, Lieutenant," Weider said, hanging back a bit. "I'm sorry. I'm probably interrupting you."

Fenton remembered that Weider was the man who had given the pin-up to the painter. "Lucy" was the name of the captain's girlfriend back at home, but the art had been courtesy of the ground crew. "She was yours as much as mine," Fenton said. "I've told you before, call me Ed. Especially a night like this."

"Smoke?"

"Yep."

Fenton pinched a cigarette out of Weider's offered pack and lit both of their smokes with his Zippo.

As Fenton ground the butt of his third cigarette beneath his heel, Weider said, "So, I thought it was you I saw standing out here, and I figured I should tell you something." It was the first thing either of them had said since "Love one."

"You did say something." Fenton shrugged. "Supposed you were just paying respects."

"Well, I did that. All of us on the ground crew, we … uh … we did that." Weider shifted from one foot to another, and he looked down at his feet, and then he glanced back over his shoulder toward the barracks. "We, uh … that's when you all were still out. You were still sleeping."

"We were out," Fenton said. "You were right the first time." Almost as soon as they'd stepped back on solid ground, the flight crew of *Screaming Lucy* had found themselves given sedatives by the base doctor. It had been a blessing. Edwards and Marlowe had already fallen to their knees, and neither of them seemed to see or even be aware of much of anything. Fenton, though, had seen Clowes deftly step in front of Col. Hoyle, who must have been intent on an immediate debrief.

"Well, what I mean is, we were out here, and we, uh … we wanted to, we wanted to take care of things for you. For in case you came out here like you are now."

Fenton frowned and tapped his temple. "Vic, I may still be a little foggy."

Weider exhaled loudly and said, "I mean, we wanted to put your bombardier to rest if there was … if he was still there."

If any of him was still there, Fenton knew he meant. He swallowed, clenched his jaw, and nodded. It wouldn't have been the first small box quietly, graciously buried alongside that airfield. "Thank you, Vic," he said hoarsely. "That was a kindness."

"Ed, there wasn't ... he wasn't there. There's not a trace. I saw some of what I figure is your blood at the back there, but it's like ... it's like Beacham, he just disappeared. Like he wasn't ever hurt but just vanished in an instant, and that's ... that's a blessing, right?"

"Well, I wonder," Fenton said, looking again at the crease, at *Screaming Lucy*'s gaping maw, at her ruined face. "I wonder if it is."

Nathan

We wound our way down Echo Creek Road, bouncing lightly on the bench seat of Grandpa Keagan's '61 Chevy pickup. "Flaxen Yellow," if I remember the paint chip right. The truck hadn't come with seatbelts, and Grandpa would never put them in. Keeping it original while stickin' it to the man — he won all around. The truck had entered our lives about a year before, and its restoration had dominated just about every Saturday and Sunday and more than a few weekdays since then. Cosmetically, it still needed some work, but under the hood, it was all there. The motor and tranny had come first. Like Grandpa said, he bought it so he could drive it. He'd work on making it pretty later.

His name sat all alone on the title, but that day, shockingly, he rode shotgun. He'd asked me if I felt like driving, which surprised the hell out of me, but I didn't ask any questions. When Grandpa gave, I took it.

I came around that last curve and saw the whitewashed wood of Keagans Crossing, the covered bridge that spans the southern leg of Echo Creek. It was named after my great-great someone, who had evidently put more stock in monuments than apostrophes. I stomped the brake pedal, maybe a little too hard — just a little — and whipped the truck onto the shoulder, spraying gravel from that little turnaround there. I put the truck into park and then, better late than never, I smacked the turn-signal lever. *Click-click. Click-click.* I sighed, shut the signal off, and thought, *Well, there you go. That's it. I'm the one who found this truck, but I'll never be touchin' these keys again.*

"Well, what the hell was that?" Grandpa asked. He laughed, though, and it was a big laugh, and it was free of most of what usually colored it. It was still early, though, and a full Coleman cooler waited in the bed of the truck.

"Yeah. Sorry about that," I said.

"Catch you daydreamin'?" He laughed again, slapped my back, and squeezed my shoulder. "Well, we're here now. Not how I woulda done it, but we're here."

I nodded and cleared my throat. It was all I could do. He threw me off more when he was nice than when he wasn't.

Grandpa gave my shoulder another squeeze, said, "Yep," and opened his door. With one leg out the door and his boot on the shoulder of the road, he said, "Y'know, you can probably shut that engine off now."

I did, and then I met him outside, and both of us peered down into the truck bed. Ignoring the cooler for a moment — there wasn't much for me in there anyway — I nodded at the metal detectors and asked, "Which one do you want me to use?"

"Oh, I don't know," Grandpa said. "Why don't you just grab the one that's closest to you?"

"Is there a difference?"

"Yeah," he said. "Only one of 'em's closest to you."

I reached over and took the nearest detector out of the bed. I scrutinized the controls, the fiddly wire, and even the handle as if I knew, as if I even kind of knew, what I was seeing.

"Somethin' wrong?" Grandpa asked, smirking as he opened his first beer.

"Nah," I said. "I'm just pretty sure you're keeping the more sensitive one for yourself."

Grandpa had the other detector in-hand. "Yeah, well, 'sensitive' is about right," he said. "This one's supposed to be able to pick up more, but it can be a little finicky. So who's to say? Hell, though, what do you think you'll find?"

"I actually have no idea," I said. "What kind of luck have you had out here?"

Grandpa shrugged, took a long drink, kept drinking, burped. "Oh, a whole lotta this and that," he said. "You'll find some coins. Some old Zippo lighters. I got a nice money clip down there once — think that's where I got that. People get down there, drinking and swimming and whatever else they wanna do, and they end up losin' all sorts of shit." He shrugged, brought his can back to his lips, and tilted his head back so far he wound up looking straight up at the sky.

"So it's new stuff," I said.

Grandpa glared at me down the length of the beer can. "No, none of it's 'new.'" He took another pull, slurped to get the last drops, and tossed the empty into the truck bed. He belched, gestured toward the creek with a calloused hand, and asked me, "You see any goddamn stores down there?"

I clenched my jaw, hoping he didn't notice and hoping my face didn't show anything else. *Just took him one beer,* I thought. *He's ahead of schedule.* "No, but what I meant was —"

He flapped the same hand he'd used to gesture at the creek. "Ah, you don't know what you meant. You think you do, but you don't. All I said, that's all on the shore. Ain't none of it new, but it's gonna be hard to find anything too old. You go other places, you'll find other things." He flipped the toggle switches on his metal detector and turned the knobs. He might have actually known what he was doing. "It all depends how much sweat you want to put in and how much you want to gamble. You get down by the berm, and it's all shell casings. Be hard to find anything else." He got back into the cooler, took out two more cans of beer, and shoved them into the pockets of his quilted vest. "Now, maybe you'll find some old belt buckles or rusted tools if you go back a little further into the woods, back to where them Indians and them other people used to live." He grinned, hoisted his metal detector, and rested it over his shoulder. "Now, me, I'm just here for the exercise."

"Them Indians and them other people," I thought. *Nice. Gonna be a great day.* I was mildly curious about who "them other folk" were this time around. There was no telling with Grandpa.

I grabbed a couple cans of Dr. Pepper for myself, and then I followed Grandpa's lead and used a carabiner to attach a trowel to one of my belt loops. We stepped down off the shoulder, navigated the weed-choked embankment, and made our way down to the creek. I got to listen to Grandpa grunt and puff and cuss the whole way. It was the perfect audio accompaniment to my view of the back of his graying dark-blond hair. The trek would have been sketchy for anyone, but Grandpa took a couple of hard, wobbling steps that scared the shit out of me. "Damn hip's trying to put in a half-day," he said at one point after I'd grabbed his arm just above the elbow to keep him upright. He shook off my hand. "Well, I'll show it. Come on."

We made it down. I wasn't entirely sure we'd make it back up, but hey, we made it down. We went a little further, stood in the mud, and looked out at what was left of the creek. We shouldn't have been able to stand there, not as far out as we were. I knew it had been a dry year, but I hadn't been down there in a while. The treeline was where it should have been, of course, then the bank of smooth rocks and scrubby tufts of grass. But then there was the mud, a good ten yards of it that wasn't usually exposed.

"Huh," Grandpa said.

That pretty much covered it, but I added, "Yeah, I didn't know it was this low."

"I didn't either," Grandpa said, actually sort of admitting he was wrong. It was a hell of a day. "Far cry from last year, isn't it? Even further from '64 and '75." He sucked his teeth, looking out at the water, and then he sighed and turned on his detector. "Well, let's get at it. Let's just follow the bend, see what we find."

I nodded, turned my machine on, and trudged behind him, knowing he was bound to find just about everything before I did. That was how it was. He'd say it wasn't always about me, but I often wondered when it was.

He said to follow him along the bend. The creek is sort of shaped like a horseshoe, and my hometown —Westley, Oregon — sits in the belly. Keagans Crossing gets you over one of the legs that heads out to the Willamette River, and Geary Bridge gets you over the one to the north.

That was early 1997, the start of the back half of my senior year. And it *had* been a dry year: dry summer, dry fall, dry winter. That was all relative, though, since the winter before had seen the Flood of 1996. You see that capital letter? It was a big one. Echo Creek swelled up over both bridges, caused a shitload of property damage, and even managed to drown some cows. A year later, and the town had just about recovered — as much as it would, anyway. There was another bad one in 2012, but not like that.

Doop. Doo-doop.

Grandpa's metal detector. As I'd predicted, he claimed the first catch of the day. It was a wristwatch, and it wasn't ticking, but the crystal didn't look too bad, and he was convinced the band had some silver in it. It didn't, but hey, he was happy, and that was the important thing. That was a good thing.

Doop. Doop. Doop doop doop.

Grandpa again. Coins.

I drained and then flattened my last can of Dr. Pepper and slid it into my pants pocket, nestling it right on top of its brother. I belched, and then I listed to the left, out to the ground that should have been beneath Echo Creek. My shoes went *smuck* in the mud as I ranged out toward the receded waterline. The scrunched soda-cans in my pocket jabbed into my legs with every other step. My feet were wet and cold, and I absolutely should not have worn Vans.

Brrraaap.

I blinked, took a step or two back, and swept the detector over what looked to me like a completely unremarkable stretch of mud.

Brrraaap.

"Hey, uh, Grandpa?" I called out. "What's this sound mean?"

I kept my position and kept my eyes on the ground as I listened to Grandpa's approach across the boggy ground. "What, did you find somethin'?" he asked.

"Well, I got a weird sound," I said.

"What sound?"

Brrraaap. "That one." I saw the look on Grandpa's face and I didn't know what to make of it. "It's not broken, is it? I'm using it just like you showed me."

"Check that again," Grandpa said.

"What?"

"Sweep it," Grandpa said. "I want to hear that. Check it again."

Brrraaap.

Grandpa cocked his head and smiled, but, you know, it wasn't really a smile. "Well, hell," he said. "I was happy with that wristwatch."

"Well, it seems like it's a nice watch," I said, not at all sure what was happening. "What? What did I find? You gonna help me dig it out?"

Grandpa smirked and crossed his arms over his slightly but definitely puffed-out chest. "Yeah, you know, I'll tell you what," he said. "If that thing ain't lyin' to you, then that sounds like gold. You can dig that shit out yourself."

By the time I said "What?" I was already down on my knees in the mud, and I had the trowel in the ground when I said, "No shit." I vaguely wondered what I'd done with the metal detector. Judging from the word-ish sounds emitting from Grandpa, I'd flung it aside on my way down. *That won't make him happy,* I thought. *But shit, if this is gold, I can buy him a new one.*

Yeah, key word being "could," I suggested to myself.

Oh, come on now, said the buzzkill, the truth-teller. *You know how this will end. And if there isn't any gold, you're —*

My mental conversation ended right then and right there. I yelled out, lurched to my feet, stepped back, and fell on my ass. Yeah, it was gold, which was cool. Real cool. It was a heavy gold ring set with an incredible green stone, and it was beautifully displayed on one of the human finger-bones I'd exposed just below the surface of the mud.

I looked up at Grandpa.

"Keep digging," he said. "Be careful." I'd heard his voice take on a lot of tones, but I'd never heard that one.

"Why?" I asked. "What could we —"

"Dig," he said. That tone I knew.

I held the trowel like a dagger and slowly drew it down from the ring, trying to find a balance between getting the job done and making minimal contact with whatever the hell I'd found. I revealed part of the hand, the wrist, and the long bones of a forearm.

"OK, that's enough," Grandpa said as he pulled his Motorola cell phone out of the holder clipped to his belt. He flipped down the mouthpiece, extended the antenna, and dialed. A moment later, he said, "Yeah, this is Jim Keagan. I'm calling from down here by the crick, and ... well, is the chief in?" He narrowed his eyes, listening, and then he grinned. "Oh, I think I can find him. Thank you."

He ended the call. As he dialed another number from memory, he said, "Shoulda known to call him at the diner. Don't know why I bothered with the station." He put the phone up to his ear, and then he said, "Hello. Yeah, this is Jim Keagan. I'm calling from down here by the crick. I hear the chief might be there."

Ten, maybe fifteen minutes later, and Echo Creek was treated to a visit from the entire six-person complement of the Westley Police Department. They rolled out the yellow tape, extracted a nearly complete skeleton from the mud, and clapped each other on their backs. God, there was a lot of back-clapping going on. Grandpa got in on it, too. I kept my distance and hung out back by the trees. *Let him have his moment,* I thought. A good day for Grandpa meant a better day for everyone.

Later that night, after dinner, Grandma thanked me for helping with the dishes but then almost immediately put her mug down and pushed me aside. She had her way. I never did learn what that was, I never could get it right, but she had her way.

I went upstairs, heading for my bedroom, but stopped as I often did to peruse the framed photos that covered the left-hand wall. Most were in color, but a few of them were in black-and-white. One of the black-and-white ones — one that always grabbed me — was at the very top, a little left of center. It was an eight-by-ten shot of a mangled-to-shit airplane from World War II. It was a B-17 called the *Tawny Terror*. Grandpa Keagan's brother, Thomas, had died on that plane. On that flight. I'd always thought it was a weird image to hold onto, to put up on the wall, and I said that to him once. What he said back was, "Well, so's a crucifix, and we have enough of those hanging up on our walls, too."

Together, the rest of the photos in the collection gave glimpses of at least three generations of Keagan goodness. My great-grandparents. Grandma and Grandpa's wedding picture. My dad, aunt and uncle. My dad in his senior photo, my uncle in his a few years later, my aunt in hers a couple of years after that. My dad in his Army dress-uniform.

I was up there, and so were my cousins. School photos, mostly, though there were one or two group shots. My sister, Tomlin, was only in one of those, and that was either because it was a great shot of everyone else or because Grandpa had simply missed it during the Great Purge after he heard rumors of her having a girlfriend.

I sighed and turned toward my room, but I stopped when I heard some noises from the bathroom. Running water and grumbling. There were two bedrooms upstairs, mine and a spare, with the bathroom between them. Grandma and Grandpa's bedroom and the main bathroom were downstairs. I'd left Grandma in the kitchen, and Grandpa avoided the stairs whenever he could. I was curious, so I knocked. The door, which hadn't totally been shut, swung open.

Grandpa stood hunched over the sink, using the toothbrush held in his right hand to scrub the small object clutched in his left. As he scrubbed, he shook his head and muttered, "Don't make sense ... don't make sense ..."

"Uh, what are you doing?" I asked.

He flinched, growled something profane, and said, "What does it look like?"

Ooh, it's a riddle, I was brave enough to think but too smart to say out loud. A small Tupperware bowl sat on the bathroom counter, and from the look and the smell of it, I could tell it was filled with Grandpa's DIY jewelry cleaner: warm water, Dawn dish-soap, and ammonia. "OK," I said, "so why are you doing it here?"

"Bristles of my toothbrush are too hard," Grandpa said. "You're gonna need a new one. I'll give you a couple bucks tomorrow. You can pick one up on your way to school."

I ran my tongue along my teeth and still tasted meatloaf. I shut my eyes and rubbed my forehead, but whatever. At least he'd offered to replace it.

I took a step into the bathroom, moved so I could see what he was working on, and saw the dead man's ring in Grandpa's left hand. Of course, that was an assumption. I didn't know if the bones belonged to a man. But that wasn't what was important right then.

"What the hell, Grandpa?" I said. "They let you take that?"

Grandpa stopped brushing but didn't look up. "I didn't ask."

"Grandpa."

"What?" Back to brushing. "Farrel said that body had probably been there for years. You know how unlikely it is something like this stayed with it?"

"But ... it did," I said.

He threw the toothbrush — *my* toothbrush — and the ring into the stoppered sink, straightened his back, and whirled to face me. I stayed standing where I was but leaned back at my waist, trying to move my face away from the index finger jabbing toward me. "You think you're smart, don't you? Well, there are more than 200 bones in the human body. Did you know that?"

Don't say yes, I thought. *Don't say yes.*

"More'n 200, and they pulled almost all of 'em out of that mud. Should be enough evidence for 'em, don't you think? I got bills to pay. What, you think I should be doing their job, too?"

"Nope," I said.

"'Nope,'" he repeated in a mocking, doofy voice. "Yeah, you're goddamn right, 'nope.' And you know what? You can forget what I said about the money. Go buy your own fuckin' toothbrush."

He punctuated that with a three-fingered thump to my sternum. I grunted and stepped back into the hall, and he slammed the bathroom door in my face.

I don't know how long I just stood there. It was always hard to say. It could have been five seconds, or it could have been five minutes. I know that Grandpa didn't come out, and I didn't move. Not at all.

Grandma broke the spell. She had a talent for that. Just her voice, climbing the stairs: "Jim? Nathan? I'm all done with the dishes."

I checked my watch. We'd missed *Jeopardy!*, which sucked, but there was still time for our standby. I nodded to no one and jogged down the stairs. "Grandpa's busy, Grandma," I said. "You wanna watch *Wheel of Fortune*?"

***

Years later and a mile away, I was cleaning the main glass showcase-counter at Keagan's Collections when the little bell at the top of the shop door went *ting ting*. I glanced up and gave the customer a nod, but I don't like to swoop in, so

I finished getting rid of that handprint before I went to see how I could help him.

He was the only customer in the store, so when the time came, he wasn't too hard to pick out. He'd turned right from the door and gone to that corner, taking a quick look at the typewriters and adding machines displayed in the window but paying more attention to the cameras, light meters, and shit sitting on an old bookshelf against the wall. He wore a long, light-brown coat over a dark-blue suit. It was a fancier look than I usually saw in the shop. Or in the town, for that matter. My guess was that he'd come down from the Portland area and was looking for some kind of a conversation piece to sit on a shelf and collect dust. Which I could handle, but everything I sell has been fixed up to working order, so it's nice to know the person is actually going to use the thing.

"Hey. Are you looking for something in particular?" I asked.

He put the camera he'd been holding back on the shelf. It was an Argus C3, which is more commonly known as the "Brick" for reasons that aren't too mysterious: except for the lens, there isn't a round-anything anywhere on that thing. "Oh, I don't know," he said. "I try not to be."

I hoped I hadn't come up on him too soon. "You took a look at the typewriters. Are you a collector?"

"Oh, I've owned a few," he said as he sort of drifted back toward the window.

"Yeah, they can be fun," I said, glad that he respected the functionality of the machines. "I'm just old enough that I learned how to type on one."

"Oh, is that right?" he said, smiling. I put him at around twenty-five years old, so about fifteen years younger than me. Learned to type on a typewriter? I may as well have told him I churned my own butter, too.

"Well, when we started typing at school, we used computers," I said, "but I had a head start because of the big ol' Underwood my grandma had at home. Huge thing. It has to weigh thirty pounds. Still have it at home."

"That's great," the man said, his smile heading toward a laugh. That seemed like a good sign.

"My favorite one, though," I said, standing beside him and looking down at the machines arrayed in the show window, "is probably that Remington Portable right there."

"Which one?"

"That one," I said, pointing at a relatively small typewriter that was attached to a covered black board that also served as the bottom of its carrying case. The strikers were supposed to be lowered when they weren't being used, and they had to be when the typewriter was closed up in its case, but it made a better display with them all raised, jutting up like metal teeth.

"Oh," he said. "I've seen one of those before. I think my parents had one."

"Is that right?" I said, and I thought, *Not a collector, my ass. Now we're talking generations.* "If I remember right, that one's from about 1926, '27."

"That sounds about right."

"You want to take a closer look at it?"

"Oh, no thank you," he said. "If I get something, it'll need to be smaller. I'm traveling."

"Got it. Shall we return to the cameras?" I said, gesturing broadly at the bookshelf, hamming up my salesman role.

The man chuckled. "Yes, let's do that," he said, and we returned to the photography section. I guess you'd call it a section. I had quite a few pieces over there and didn't have them anywhere else.

"You were looking at the Brick," I said.

"Yes, I was," the man said, "but what I'd like to find is a Kodak 35. The rangefinder."

"Ah. Which Kodak made in response to the Brick."

"Right," he said. "Yeah, I think that's how that worked out."

"Well, I don't have one of those now," I said, "but they do come through. I was actually planning on hitting some estate sales this weekend. If that's what you're settled on, let me get your name and number, and —"

"I'm, um ... between phone numbers," the man said. "That's strange. I really thought you'd have one." He brought his right hand up to rub his chin, and light caught the gemstone in the ring he was wearing on the third finger of that hand. Green, step-cut, and just like the one in the ring Grandpa Keagan had looted off a skeleton twenty-something years before and sold not too long after that.

And not just the gemstone. Except for its condition, the whole ring looked identical — the shape, the thickness, the etching on the sides, everything. But that "except" had to count for something. It couldn't be the same ring. The other one had never looked that good, not even after Grandpa finished polishing it with my damn toothbrush.

"It probably sounds like I'm brushing you off, but I'm not," the man said. "I'm just passing through, but I am likely to come by here again."

I blinked and tried to put my game face back on. I was glad he'd kept looking at the cameras on the shelves. "That's fine," I said. "I'll, uh ... I'll be here."

"Good," the man said. "Thank you. I'll let you get back to it then."

He strolled to the door and pulled it open.

I said, "Hey, uh ... I'm curious. If you've, uh ... if you've got the time."

He closed the door and shrugged. "I suppose I do."

He stayed by the door, just inside it, and I stayed back in that corner, all snugged up between the cameras and the typewriters. "I'm just a little curious about that ring," I said. "That stone, it's a tourmaline, isn't it?"

"Yes, it is. Good eye. Most people would probably call it an emerald."

"It's not an emerald."

"I agree."

"Well, it's a hell of a piece," I said.

"Thank you."

"What do you know about it?"

The man brought his hand up like he needed to get a closer look at the ring himself. "I was told it's one-of-a-kind. Well, as one-of-a-kind as anything is, anyway."

Mack

My world began to end on a Thursday in February during my senior year. I was just chilling in my room with the door shut, the miniblinds closed, and the lights off. Well, for the most part. Some lights were unavoidable, like the pale green numbers on the frequency dial of my old Kenwood receiver, or necessary for the vibe, like my lava lamp, which was getting its freak on and doing its lava-lamp thing.

I'm playing the same record now as I was then: *Aja* by Steely Dan. Tonight, it was a deliberate choice, but it was a totally random one then. Just the first one I grabbed. Then, just like now, I had the volume dial turned just a little past the halfway-point, and I fiddled with the thick, curly cord coiling from the receiver to the kickass vintage Koss headphones clamped to my head.

I closed my eyes. Even though the glowing radio dial and the lamp were pretty mild, they were too stimulating for what I wanted to do and where I wanted to go. They worked together to keep me grounded, to keep my ass planted in my beanbag and my feet on the laminate floor. But I needed to go somewhere else. I needed to go *in*. I shut my eyes to make sure the other door and those other windows would open. That's the What, and it's basically the limit of what I understood then. The Why and the How and All That Other Shit would come later.

I opened my eyes, though I really didn't, and I walked up to the ratty recliner, which wasn't really there. I know; I know. It's not meant for words, but I'm just going to roll with this.

The recliner squatted fifteen feet back from one of the walls of my Attic, which was filled with rows and rows and rows of tall shelves. They spread out to the left and the right of the chair and behind it, and they were loaded down with bags and bottles and boxes and other things that, you know, held stuff. In front of the chair spread a relatively open expanse of the scuffed hardwood floor that ran throughout the entire attic, as far as I knew, though I'd only seen one end of it for sure. That end was the wall in front of the chair, on the other side of that stretch of the floor: a wide wood-paneled wall that didn't hold anything I could see other than two tall, thin windows, each of which was covered with a dingy, once-white shade. I had no idea know how wide the wall was. I couldn't have even guessed. Like I said, that was the only limit I'd seen; I'd never been all the way to the left or right. Honestly, I'd never seen the point. The big show was always right through those windows, and that recliner provided the best seat in the house.

Something usually pulled me up to the Attic, and whatever that was would be sitting on the floor exactly halfway between the chair and the windows. Most of the time, it was a box, which makes sense. Most of what was up there was boxed-up. When it wasn't a box, it was another container that had migrated from one of the shelves.

And it was a box this time, which was nice. Predictable. Easy. Sweet. The folded flaps had been taped shut at one point: ripped and raggedy shreds of packing tape curled and puckered along their edges. I took the box back to the chair, sat down, and set the box on my lap. It didn't feel heavy, but that didn't mean it wasn't.

I opened the flaps. Inside the box, there was a white travel mug, a library book (face down), and a report card from my elementary school. I could only see the letterhead because of the way it was folded, but I knew which one it had to be. I couldn't think of another report card that would've made the cut. Second grade. First-semester progress report. The book, too: there was only one it could have been.

The shades snapped up. Through the glass, I saw the decorated wall across the hallway from Mrs. Goodall's classroom door. It was covered with projects from my class and the three other second-grade classes. It was November, so we're talking construction-paper hand-turkeys and other Thanksgiving shit.

The perspective shifted, twisting to the left and tilting up slightly. I was ready for it, so it didn't make my stomach lurch or give me the spins like it sometimes did. Now the window on the left framed the shoulders and head of one of my moms, Tomlin, who was sitting on one of the short plastic classroom-chairs they'd put out there for the occasion. She lightly, absently scratched her knuckles, shifted her weight, and sighed. She has always had trouble sitting still.

The view shifted again, tilting down this time, and I saw another pair of hands and another set of twiddling fingers. They belonged to Mackenzie Keagan Hatcher, age seven, who was suddenly worried about their dirty nails and who started to rub, rub, rub their sweaty hands on their blue jeans.

Another pair of hands entered the shot and settled on Mackenzie's, and the POV changed again. This time, it featured Mackenzie's other mom, sitting on the little plastic chair to Mackenzie's right. Tessa smiled and said, "It's OK. And if it's not, it will be. Remember: we'll be talking about you, but we're here *for* you."

"Not everyone," Mackenzie said.

Tessa's smile stayed, but it tightened. She glanced past Mackenzie toward Tomlin — I saw that from the Attic, but Mackenzie didn't notice it then — and then she looked back at their child, and said, "Well, *we* are here for you. I can promise that. Do you understand me?"

"Yes."

"I said it's a promise."

"I know. I heard you."

"Do you believe me?" Tessa asked.

The scene shifted in a way that I didn't exactly see and still can't describe, but which I felt. I smiled, and I knew that

Mackenzie was smiling now, too. "Yes," they said. "I believe you, Mom. Both of you."

Tessa nodded, took a sip from her white travel-mug, and patted Mackenzie's leg.

Tomlin patted Mackenzie's other leg and sighed.

A few minutes of forever later, the classroom door opened, and Melanie Cochran came out with her mom and dad and Mrs. Goodall. They exchanged smiles and said their good-byes, and then Mrs. Goodall ushered Mackenzie, Tessa, and Tomlin into the classroom.

This is tricky. I don't want to body-shame Mrs. Goodall, especially since there are so many other and more respectful ways to shame her, but I feel like I have to describe her. Maybe I already have. Well, she also wore rhinestone-studded glasses, and she had brown hair, so there you go. Let's work with that.

Tomlin, Tessa, and Mackenzie traded the three plastic chairs by the door for three plastic chairs on the you're-in-trouble side of Mrs. Goodall's desk. They sat in the same configuration, too, with Mackenzie in the middle, Tomlin to their left, and Tessa to the right.

Mrs. Goodall sat in her cushy chair on the other side of the desk. She looked from Tomlin to Tessa, and then she looked back at Tomlin, and then she gazed at something that must have been hovering just over Tomlin's head. "Well, hi. I'm Mrs. Goodall, Mackenzie's teacher, and it's ... so nice to meet both of you."

Tessa took a sip of coffee from her travel mug.

"You too," Tomlin said. "It's nice to put a face to all the emails."

"Oh, isn't it?" Mrs. Goodall said. "I was just thinking that. Now, Mrs. .... uh ..." She blinked, shuffled a few papers, and then said, "Oh, I'm sorry. You probably prefer Ms., don't you?"

"I'm Tessa, that's Tomlin, and I hope you're getting to know Mackenzie," Tessa said.

"Yeah, let's just go with first names," Tomlin said. "That might be easier for you."

"Well, for everyone," Tessa said. She took a long drink of coffee, draining her mug, and then she put her mug on Mrs. Goodall's desk. From my spot on the recliner in the Attic, I remembered what Mackenzie had realized then, sitting between Tomlin and Tessa on that side of the teacher's desk. The image on the mug perfectly faced Mrs. Goodall, and it was an illustration of Zippy the Pinhead asking, "Are we having FUN yet?" A sort of shimmer passed over the windows. Mackenzie smiled again, and so did I.

Mrs. Goodall didn't do any damn thing for a few moments, and then she cleared her throat and said, "Well, if that's what you'd like. My first name is Janis."

"Cool," Tessa said. "Let's talk about Mackenzie."

"Right," Janis said as she shuffled some papers. "Of course. That's why we're all here." She looked at Mackenzie and gave them a smile they'd seen an awful, awful lot. "And we're all on the same team."

Shift. Mackenzie looked at Tomlin, who smiled and said, "Well, that's nice."

Shift again. Mackenzie looked at Tessa, who said, "Hm."

"Now, grade-wise, Mackenzie is doing pretty well."

"Uh, she sure is," Tomlin said. "As and Bs. One C, but that's in PE."

"Well, that's true," Janis Goodall said, "but I don't think we should overlook that. With its focuses on teamwork and collaboration and —"

"I don't like P.E.," Mackenzie said, and in the Attic, I smiled at the force packed into those four words. Each one hit like its own sentence: *I. Don't. Like. P.E.* That feeling wouldn't change.

Mrs. Goodall cleared her throat and moved like she was going to shuffle those papers again. She caught herself, but she didn't look up from them, either. "Well, and you've made that very clear, haven't you? And as we've talked about a few times, I think, there might be a connection between your difficulties there and —”

“I want to know about the book,” Tessa said.

This startled Mrs. Goodall into looking up and meeting Tessa Hatcher’s hard stare. Both seven-year-old Mackenzie and the eighteen-year-old observer in the Attic knew that look very well. “Book?” Mrs. Goodall said.

“Oh, is there more than one we should be talking about?” Tessa asked. “If so, we’ll take them one at a time. The one I’m talking about is *Heather Has Two Mommies*.”

Mrs. Goodall responded with this weird sound that was probably supposed to be a chuckle. She flattened her palms on her desk, and she didn’t move her head, but her eyes flitted from Tessa to Tomlin and then back up to that odd spot above their heads. “Well, that is a book carried in our school library, and —”

“And one of Mack’s precious little classmates checked that book out from the library, threw it down on her desk, and said, ‘Is this about you? Is your name really Heather?’ And all the other little rays of sunshine in the class laughed, and then they kept laughing.” Tomlin said. “I’m sorry. I think I interrupted you. But that’s what you were going to say, right?”

“Well,” Janis said, “I don’t remember that she *threw* it ...”

“Don’t,” Tessa said.

In the Attic, I looked down at my lap and realized I’d scooted forward in the chair. I was literally on the edge of my seat. I thought, *Huh. People actually do that.*

“I understand how that could have been ... upsetting to ... Mackenzie,” Mrs. Goodall said, slapping on that damn smile again but trying it on Tomlin and Tessa this time. She seemed like she was having trouble looking at Tessa for too long. “And I know it’s difficult sometimes, but these are children, and they —”

“Right. They’re blank slates,” Tessa said.

"To a point. and the times have changed, and they are changing, but your living —"

"They're blank slates until someone —"

Tomlin stood, knocking her little chair over, and yelled, "Our 'living situation' isn't any of their fucking business!"

Mrs. Goodall's eyes bulged, and her jaw dropped right the hell open.

In the classroom, Mackenzie laughed.

In the Attic, I laughed, too, and I clapped my damn hands.

Tomlin righted her chair, sat back down, and said, "Oh, I just used a grown-up word, didn't I? I *do* know it's difficult sometimes, but we can deal with that, can't we?"

I've been trying for more than ten years, and I don't think I'll ever have the word for the sound that rumbled and grumbled out of Mrs. Goodall's throat.

"My relationship with Tomlin is a detail, and it shouldn't figure into any of the relationships in this classroom," Tessa said. "It shouldn't, and it can't, any more than the domestic situation of any other student in this class. Mackenzie sits down for dinner at night, and two women happen to also be sitting at the dining-room table or setting up TV trays in the front room, OK? That's it. That's the situation. o you understand me?"

"Yes, I do, Tessa, and let me just say that —"

Tessa snatched her mug off the desk and got to her feet. Tomlin and Mackenzie quickly followed suit. "Now that we're familiar with each other, you can call me *Ms.* Hatcher, OK?" she said. "And that is my partner, *Ms.* Keagan."

Mrs. Goodall swallowed, and then she nodded, and then she reshuffled those papers on her desk.

"Good talk," Tomlin said. "This was a good talk. I think we covered a lot of really good ground."

"Was there anything you wanted to say, Mackenzie?" Tessa asked.

Mackenzie said, "No, I'm good." I'd forgotten that part, but I loved it.

"Very good," Mrs. Goodall said. "Yes, that's nice. It was good to meet you both."

"OK. Say 'Good-bye,' Mackenzie," Tessa said.

"'Bye, Mrs. Goodall," Mackenzie said cheerily. "See you tomorrow."

God, I loved that kid.

The blinds rolled down, and the Attic went dark.

I rubbed my temples and opened my eyes. My lava lamp still gurgled, and the radio dial still glowed, but the only sound coming from the speakers was the *skt thup ... skt thup ... skt thup* of the stylus trying to play the runout. I leaned forward, returned the tone arm to its dock, and shut the stereo off. Now the lava lamp was the only light on in my room. I wobbled to my feet, and then I groaned as I waited for the feeling to return to my ass and legs. The pins and needles came pretty quickly. I made my way to the door, walking with just a little bit more grace than a newborn deer.

I strolled on down the hall, following the sound of click-clacking typewriter keys to the office. I say "the" office, and Tomlin and I did technically have access to it whenever we wanted, but we all knew it was really Tessa's office. And that was cool. She'd turned it into a pretty sweet place to write, and it was always better for all of us when she could get that shit out of her head.

The room was filled with all sorts of stuff specially chosen to either help her focus or totally distract her. Most of the objects could have done either of those things, depending on her mood and whichever way her world happened to be turning. Among other things, there was a stereo, a TV, an XBox, and a stash of edibles that I absolutely didn't know anything about.

An old oak rolltop-desk took up a good chunk of the space, and an even older Royal typewriter, a big honkin' office model, squatted on top of it. Other typewriters, smaller portable ones, sat on floating shelves staggered all over two of the walls. Blow-ups of the cover art for each of

Mom's books were interspersed with those shelves. Also in the mix was a framed black-and-white photo of a beat-to-shit airplane parked on the grass just past the runway somewhere in England. I know I knew that much, and I knew that her grandpa, Henry Clairvaux, had served on that plane and had survived that landing, but I don't think I knew anything else. It didn't seem like it fit up there, but then again, it kind of did, if only because of the ages of some of the typewriters.

Every once in a while, Mom would decide that one those machines would work better for whatever she was doing, so she'd lug the Royal over and pull one of the other typewriters down. I know she had a 1930s Underwood and a Corona from the 1920s. Those both got a lot of use, but the Royal was her favorite. She didn't own a computer until she was in her twenties, and she couldn't always read her own handwriting, so she'd typed the first couple of drafts of her first book with that Royal. Even after she bought a PC, she always drafted with a typewriter so she could focus on getting the damn thing done. That's how she put it. For her, computers were for finalizing things, for making them look pretty, when the actual, messy creating was already done.

I waited in the doorway because I knew it wouldn't do any good to say "Mom" or "Tessa" or any other damn thing. She was in her space, and I respected that.

The typewriter went *ding,* she typed a little more, then she pulled the paper from the roller and went over the page with her favorite pen. It was a Cross, and it was loaded with blue ink.

She flipped the paper and put it face-down on the remarkable stack to the left of the typewriter. A stack of blank sheets sat to the right. I thought she'd load another one, but instead, she looked at the machine's empty roller, took a deep breath, and said, "Yeah, I'm about due for a break. It's probably good you broke the spell."

I nodded at the stack of finished pages and said, "It looks like it's going OK."

"It's going somewhere," she said.

"Is Sgt. Beacham giving you trouble?"

She exhaled deeply. "A bit more than usual, yeah. But some things need to happen."

"Well, you gotta be getting close to the end." The pages of her manuscripts all rose to about the same height.

"Maybe," she said. "With this one, it's hard to tell." Then she sort of folded her hands on her lap, smiled, looked up at me, and said, "So. Hi. You came back."

I frowned and said, "I've been here. I've just been in my room."

"Yeah, I know," Mom said. "I peeked in on you, and you were … somewhere else."

My cheeks got hot. I knew my moms knew about my Attic, but we never talked about it. Like masturbation. Or the stash in the desk drawer, and how there were sometimes fewer gummies than the moms remembered. "Yeah, I … yeah," I said.

"Is everything OK?" she asked.

"I don't know about everything, but yeah. I'm good."

"Yeah?"

"Yeah," I said, and then I shrugged. "Second grade. That parent-teacher conference with Goodall. You remember that, right?"

Her expression tightened. "Of course I do," she said. "Why'd you go there?"

I frowned. "Feldman called you, right? He said he was going to."

"Yeah, he called me. I let it go to voicemail."

"Did you listen to the voicemail?"

"Yes."

"Then why are you asking me?"

"I don't know. I guess I'm trying to make it casual," Mom said, and then she shrugged. "So what happened? Honestly,

I didn't get much from the voicemail. I was hoping you'd tell me."

I shrugged. "Oh, you know. Same phobic shit, different day."

"Are we talking student-shit, teacher-shit, or administration-shit?"

I shook my head and tried to wave her off. "Don't worry about it. I handled it. Like I've been handling it."

"Should I call him back?"

"What, Feldman?" I said. "That won't help anyone. I've got this. I've had this. It's only a couple of months until I'm out of that damn place."

Tessa stood and squeezed my shoulder. "I'm sorry, Mack. We should have moved ten years ago."

"Yeah, at least," I said. "But ... we didn't."

"No, we didn't," Mom said. She took a deep breath. "You want to skip school tomorrow?"

"Fucking sold. What are we doing?"

Mom laughed and said, "Well, I don't know. Tomlin's expecting us to see her show on Saturday, but maybe we can surprise her tomorrow for opening night."

"Well, that won't take all day."

"Right, but we could spend the day in Seattle."

"Ooh."

"And then that'll open up our whole weekend — if you're OK with that. Me and you."

My cheeks flushed again, but I was OK with it that time. "You don't have to write?"

"Of course I do. But you come first." She patted my back and moved past me into the hall. "Come on. I need some coffee."

I cleared my throat and wiped my eyes, and then I joined my mom in the kitchen. She'd filled two cups with water and put them both in the microwave. "Works better one at a time," I said.

"Yeah, you're probably right." She took one out, shut the door, and set the timer for a minute and a half. She found the little jar of Medaglia d'Oro instant coffee in the cupboard, got a couple of spoons from the silverware drawer and the creamer from the fridge, and she leaned against the kitchen counter as the microwave did its thing. And she looked at me.

"What?" I said.

"Nothin'," she said. "I love you, kid."

"Love you, too," I said, the words sounding a little froggy. I heard it, and she heard it, and I fucking lost it, standing there like an idiot in the archway leading into the kitchen.

She hugged me, and like always, she waited for me to let go. Then she tore two paper towels off the roll, and as we wiped our eyes, she said, "One more thing."

"Jesus, what now?" I said, and I managed to follow that with a laugh. Well, a chuckle. Kind of.

"You're handling dinner tonight," she said.

"I can do that," I said.

"So probably spaghetti?"

I laughed. "Yeah, it'll be spaghetti. I make good spaghetti."

"That'll be fine," Mom said. "That sounds good."

It *was* good. And it was also the last dinner we ate together at that house.

Tomlin

Two hours into opening night, I stared into the bathroom mirror and tried working up the motivation to get back out to the gallery floor. I couldn't do it. All those tiny, blurry photos, the tangled-wire abstract bullshit, the half-assed sketches being passed off as some profound artistic statement, the pretentious artistes themselves ... Jesus.

Yeah, they were horrible, petty thoughts, and I knew that. Shit, I'd been a pretentious artiste once. I'd had write-ups in arts sections and campus papers. I'd loved recognizing familiar faces, attendees from previous shows. I really loved trying to play it cool when I saw some of those people lingering in front of one of my pieces. Maybe it was a piece they'd seen the last time, or maybe it was a new one. I tried not to get too close, but I wanted to hear what they were saying to each other. I wanted to know what they saw. I've never been very good at keeping anything subtle, but in that case, it was actually fun to be so bad at something.

God, though, just look at all that past-tense. My ship had sailed, or maybe it had never even had a sail, and I'd drifted too far from the shore.

The bathroom door opened, and James walked in, wearing a three-piece burgundy suit and looking amazing. I looked at the restroom's stalls reflected in the mirror and saw feet beneath two of the doors. "Uh, I don't think this is gender neutral," I said.

James said, "Neither am I."

I smiled despite a lot of things. "Thanks, James. I needed that."

"Oh, I know. I also know that you need to get back to your show."

"'My' show?" I said. "Come on. You're probably the only person out there who even realized I was gone. I could totally just duck out now. Let's do that. Let's go and get drinks somewhere."

James stepped to the side as one of the recent occupants of one of the stalls washed her hands. He stepped back when she left, put a hand on my shoulder, and gently turned me to face him. "We can do that later," he said. "Maybe. But you're on the clock now, girl. Let's *go*."

"OK. I'll give you five minutes," I said.

James rolled his eyes. "Just get out there and sip some champagne. It'll get you started. It will help."

"Champagne gives me a headache."

"I said *sip*," he insisted. "Alternate. Work some water in there every now and then. What's your problem?"

He moved closer to me as the other recent stall-dweller did her thing at the sink. He still had his hand on my shoulder, so we almost looked like we were dancing. He looked deep into my eyes, dropped his voice about an octave, and said, "They really need more sinks in this place."

The woman laughed, and I smiled a little wider. Just a little. Then the woman left, and James and I were alone again. His hand dropped down to hold mine. Our skin colors contrasted beautifully. I felt a sort of warm tingle just behind my eyes: the seed of a new painting.

"Shall we?" James asked.

"We shall," I said, and we exited the bathroom together, still holding hands.

The Oster-Shelton Gallery is in an increasingly trendy part of Seattle. Now, a totally hypothetical person could say "increasingly gentrified," especially if she clearly remembered when the building that housed the gallery had been a sketchy concert venue. And, you know, that would be a shame, and it would probably even be a damn shame, because she would also remember all she'd seen going on and all the people she'd seen going down throughout that venue, and she would be pathologically unable to eat hors d'oeuvres when they set up the catering table in the southwest corner of the building. Which would be sad. But she digresses.

The crowd had thinned some, but there were still people in the gallery, so it could have been cooler. Call it a funk, call it a mood, call it a crisis, I don't care. I just knew I wanted the night to be over. I'd try again on Saturday. Plus, the plan was that Tessa and Mack would be there on Saturday. That would help.

I felt like a visitor to the gallery, confronted by all the art that surrounded mine. That drowned mine out. I mean, my pieces fit the show's theme (*For the Boys? Pin-Up Art from Diverse Perspectives*), but that's all it did. When I mentioned "tangled-wire abstract bullshit," that was a specific snipe at one of Cortney May's pieces. That sculpture was a mass of barbed wire bent into a voluptuous feminine form: thighs, breasts, shoulder-length hair. It had *hair,* or at least the representation of it. There was even a suggestion of Bettie Page bangs, just from the way the wire in that section was formed and spaced. Goddammit. It was brilliant.

Cortney smiled at James and me as we passed by her spot, and then she went back to dazzling the five or six people who had gathered around her.

Good for her.

Then we approached my shit. I'd submitted six pieces, and four had been selected for the show. None of them had titles. I've always been terrible with titles. They were all mixed-media collages with some common elements, like "Genesis 6:4." Just that — just the name of the chapter and the chapter and verse number, not the verse itself. For years, I'd worked that phrase into almost everything I made, hiding it in a sun ray or wrapping it around the edge of a flower petal or letting it ride an ocean wave. I loved the challenge, and I loved the verse. I'd picked it up from Tessa's books: the sons of God, the daughters of men, and their misfit children, who "were the mighty men that were of old, the men of renown." So odd and ominous. I liked it.

The other recurring component was a 1940s pin-up girl, rendered and placed differently but always dominating the piece. In one, it was a black-and-white copy-of-a-copy of her face placed at the center of a sun I'd shaped with lines from the poem "Dulce et Decorum Est":

Bent double, like old beggars under sacks,
Knock-kneed, coughing like hags, we cursed through sludge,
Till on the haunting flares we turned our backs,
And towards our distant rest began to trudge.
Men marched asleep. Many had lost their boots,
But limped on, blood-shod. All went lame; all blind;
Drunk with fatigue; deaf even to the hoots
Of gas-shells dropping softly behind.

In another one, I'd gone with a psychedelic sky, filled a line drawing of her with Ben Day dots, and placed her in a field of poppies. And so on. I've never learned the name of the original 1940s model, but I've never been able to get away from her. Even when I use an actual, breathing model to create a piece, I know the poses or expressions or hairstyles I ask for are based on images I've seen of that '40s bombshell.

She's like a family friend. Well, she's a friend of Tessa's family, at least. An image of her was painted on the nose of the *Tawny Terror,* one of the B-17s Tessa's grandpa served on during World War II. It's the plane that served as the basis for the *Screaming Lucy* in her books. One of my relatives served on it, too. The photo I'd grown up with — a copy of which hung on the wall in Tessa's office — was taken after the plane was "removed from service," which is a really nice way of saying "got all 'sploded and ain't gonna fly no more." It's an amazing image, but you can't see the lady. It took a lot of digging to find a picture of the *Terror* from before that mission. In that one, my friend is right there behind the nose bubble, just underneath a small square window that has a machine-gun barrel sticking out of it. She is straddling a bomb, and she's covering her boobs with one arm and catching her blown-off shirt with the other. Her mouth is in a perfect "O" shape, that classic "Uh-oh!" expression that no one actually, naturally makes in real life. But there's more to her than that silly expression. There's something about her raised eyebrows and her big, gorgeous eyes. I feel like if it came down to choosing between keeping her grip on her shirt or staying on that bomb, she would let that shirt fly and see the battle to the end, whooping all the way to the ground like Major Kong in *Dr. Strangelove*.

This is a whole lot more than I wound up saying about her that night. No one had hung around long enough for that kind of chat, plus there was that whole hiding-in-the-bathroom thing. But as James and I completed our Green Mile-walk to my area, I thought I might have the chance. A tall man stood alone, looking over my work. He seemed especially transfixed by the field of poppies. James squeezed my hand, and I grumbled, "I know. I got it."

"I want his coat," James said in a whisper that was so loud it defeated the point of whispering.

Honestly, it *was* a nice coat. It was a light-brown overcoat — camel, to be specific — worn over a pinstriped navy-blue suit; I could see a few inches of the pant legs between the hem of the man's coat and his cognac-colored dress shoes. Still, though, I squeezed James's hand and said, "*Shh.*"

James opened his mouth to say something back, but we were there. I freed my hand from my friend's grasp, wiped my sweaty palms on my thighs in a very discreet way and completed the approach to my newest — and, at the moment, my only — fan. "Hey. Hi," I said, already hating my awkwardness. But it was too late to turn back. "I don't want to interrupt you, but I just wanted to ... introduce myself."

He was totally still except for his eyes, which kept moving from the poppies to the sun and back again, and his hand, which lightly rubbed his chin. He wore a large ring on that hand. Its beautiful stone glittered in the gallery's megawatt lights. I wasn't sure if he'd heard me, but then he said, "No, it's fine. It's fine." He turned to look at me and asked, "Are you the artist?"

I said, "I am."

The man smiled, and something brightened either in his eyes or right behind them. "That's very burning-bush" he said. "What does your mother call you?"

His eyes were such an odd color — light green. Seafoam. They were distracting, but I'm used to that. Whether I want to or not, I'm always picking up ideas for a new piece. "Tomlin," I said, and I shook his hand. "And what does your mom call you?"

"Jacob," he said. "At least, she did."

Shit, I thought. *Well, that's great. Remind the guy of his dead mom.*

James, wonderful James, stepped forward then and introduced himself to Jacob as my best friend and booking manager, usually in that order. It was a pretty accurate description.

The three of us rearranged ourselves so we could all get a good view of the piece that had grabbed Jacob's attention. I do remember a few other people milling around us, but I'm pretty sure I ignored them. Why? What was I picking up about that guy? For these last several months — shoot, it's been more than two years now — I've been trying to figure that out. What did I know from the start versus what did I just "know," and what have I only plugged in since then? Retrospect, man. Memory is a shapeshifting bitch.

"This is amazing. You've really done something here," Jacob said. He took a half-step back and gestured at all the pieces on display. "The woman and the war and ... and all of this."

"Did you ... I'm sorry, but did you serve?" James asked.

Jacob nodded slowly, and his eyes dimmed. "I did. Briefly," he said.

James put up his hands. "I am so sorry. I shouldn't have gone there. It's none of my business."

"Well, it's someone's, and that's one of the problems, isn't it?" Jacob said, and then he sighed. "No worries. You asked me a question, and I gave you an answer. From most places I stand, it was a long time ago. Then again, from others, it was only yesterday."

The din of the gallery around us — the conversations, the laughter, the clinking glasses, gasps at a comment or a striking piece — somehow both faded and got louder, too. It was almost nauseating, and I'd never had that glass of champagne. I don't know if that would have hurt or helped.

"I'm sorry," Jacob said, and I flinched a little at the sudden sound. "I'm taking too much of your time."

"No, it's totally fine. You —"

Jacob shook James's hand first. "Pleasure to meet you, James."

"You too," James said. "And I love that coat."

"I think I heard that," Jacob said, and then he grinned at James's blinking, stammering, and totally ineffective attempt to respond. "Tomlin, thank you for the time," he said to me.

"No worries," I said.

He turned and headed toward the door. I started to follow him to ask ... what? What was I going to ask? To exchange business cards or something. I don't know. But then I was surprised by my wife and our kid smiling and waving and coming toward me, and I switched gears.

***

I was in a field of poppies, like in my picture, but I sort of pranced through them, so it was kind of like *The Wizard of Oz,* too. I've hated that movie since I was four or five and saw it for the first time on a nine-inch black-and-white TV in my brother's room. Even then, it scared the shit out of me. And I've never really been into drugs or Pink Floyd, so I couldn't enjoy it via those routes, either. And I'm not a prancer. It was just a weird dream.

So I pranced through those damn flowers, but then I stopped prancing because there was something like an earthquake in front of me. The poppies shook, then they rose up in a kind of hill that I knew wasn't a hill. Not really. Especially not when it got up to about six feet tall and spread out to a couple feet wide and stopped. Then the not-hill shook, and because it was a dream, I wasn't surprised at all when the poppies shrugged away to reveal a person. And if it's possible to be less surprised than totally unsurprised, then that's what I felt when I saw who the person was: my new maybe-friend, Jacob, wearing the same suit and coat he'd been wearing at the gallery. I was glad. I was really, really glad. I mean, thank God he wasn't naked under all those flowers. I couldn't have handled that. This shit was weird enough.

I knew — I mean, I just *knew* — that he was about to say something profound.

So I waited.

And he smiled his smile, and he said: "Chutu hoes ... chutu hoes ... gotta get the chutu hoes."

Don't bother. Don't even try. It means nothing. I was wrong.

I woke up, and I knew I wouldn't be getting back to sleep any time soon. I tried not to wake Tessa as I rummaged around in the dark and found one of my favorite flannel shirts on the floor. I put it on over the T-shirt and shorts I'd worn to bed. It didn't matter that it was February. I run hot when I'm sleeping even when I have to layer up to walk around. It's weird. I'm weird. I know.

In the kitchen, I thought some spiked tea would help me relax and increase the chances of actually going back to bed. I arranged all the ingredients on the counter, but then I wound up skipping the lemon and honey and the tea bag and even the water and just poured a couple of glugs of bourbon into the mug instead. I took it to the dining-room table and planned on just cruising the internet on my phone as I got a nice buzz on, but I'd left it charging on the table next to my side of the bed. On the table, though, was one of the Chromebooks that always seemed to be floating around the house. Tessa, Mack, and I each had our own phones and computers, but we also had this legion of Chromebooks and tablets of various vintages and levels of dependability. We always got the new models, but we never got rid of the old ones. Pack rats on the cutting edge.

This one was a white Acer, and it was several years old, but it usually did what I wanted it to. I opened it up, logged into my account, and checked the battery. Twenty-four percent. I consulted the clock and my mug and looked back over my shoulder at the bottle on the kitchen counter, and I figured I'd be fine.

I didn't know what I was looking for. Well, that's a lie. At first, it was nothing. I was just killing time. But as my "tea" kicked in, my memory of that weird-ass poppy-dream got sharper. Then it wasn't the dream but the conversation I'd had with James and Jacob at the gallery. As it replayed in my head, I went to Google, typed "Jacob," and had to laugh. He hadn't given me his last name. What the hell was I supposed to do with just the first one?

I needed more whiskey.

I really didn't need any more whiskey.

I poured some more whiskey.

I reminded myself to work in a glass of water at some point and then saw that I'd mysteriously, magically wound up at the gallery's website. I don't remember typing the address, and I sure as hell don't know what I expected to find, but I immediately saw that I was in luck: they'd already posted a slideshow of pictures from opening night.

I clicked through a dozen or so pictures of artwork and artists and champagne-sipping donors and miscellaneous muckety-mucks. I think I was somewhere around image twenty (of sixty-six — don't ask me how I remember that) when I stopped. There he was. It was a cool shot: from a bit of a distance, James, Jacob, and I and a couple of my works in sharp focus, rising over the blurred shoulders and heads of who-knows-who in the foreground.

It was a clear profile-shot of Jacob, and it was even clearer when I blew it up. Camel overcoat, navy-blue suit, dark hair, green eyes ...

I blinked and thought, *No. Wait.* Even embiggened, I couldn't make out the color of his eyes. How or why had I remembered it?

I dumped the last bit of bourbon into the sink, rinsed the mug, filled it with water, and sat back down at the table. And I closed my eyes. *Don't fall asleep,* I told myself. *Please don't do it.*

I let my mind drift into the sort of a half-guided daydream that I knew could turn into a real dream if my hands slipped off the controls. It's what I've always done to zero in on a new idea or to refine a current one. It flushes out or at least dilutes all the bullshit swirling around in my head and often leads me to places I wouldn't have found if I'd been completely and totally conscious. I think that makes sense. I hope it does. And if it doesn't make sense, well, that's all I have.

This is how I first saw the poppies and blazing sun before I even started on that piece, and it's what I had in mind when Tessa and Dr. Hill and I tried to come up with something to help Mack when they started having their troubles — or at least when they told us about them. I'm pretty sure Mack tried to white-knuckle their way through on their own for a while. But anyway. My suggestion, Tessa's agreement, and Mack and Dr. Hill's collaboration, and that's how you get an Attic. Or find one. Whatever. It seemed to work and to help, but we didn't talk about it much.

Anyway. I put myself back in the poppy field, and then I just let it happen. I *hoped* it would happen, and before too long, something did. There he was. No rising poppy-monster, none of that bullshit. Just him, and a fully-dressed him (again, thank God). He was just there, still smiling, like we were rejoining my dream in-progress. He said something, and I don't know if it was about those damn chutu hoes again or something else because it was drowned out by the sound of an airplane engine. I looked up, he looked up, *we* looked up — it was a looking-up party! — and sure enough, there was a plane up there, high in the sky. Too high, actually, for its engines to deafen us with their sounds, but that's why they call it a daydream.

Then the sound changed. It became ... wrong. It became all there was. Not even an engine sound, not the sound of any engine, but a horrendous screeching —

No. More than that. More specific than that.

"Like someone gave a kid a flute but didn't teach him how to play it."

That was a new voice, but it wasn't, and it was all coming together. It was too much, though. Too soon. The edges of the field faded, and I knew I'd come out of it if I didn't hold on a little longer. I needed to focus on something, but I couldn't focus on the fading field or Jacob or even the *fact* that it was fading. I had to reach out and grab onto whatever was on the other side of the change.

It worked. Jacob and the poppy field and the screaming airplane went wherever expired daydreams go, and another scene resolved itself in that place. High-shine concrete floors, windows — no — walls that were *mainly* windows, and then the walls pushed out, expanding the floor and making room for the airplanes and helicopters and space capsules that now populated the floor, and I knew where I was: my middle-school field trip to the DeLancey Air Museum.

I looked down at my hands, which was a trick I'd played with both while working through these daydream-adventures and while trying to get a grip on lucid dreaming.

My hands were solid, detailed, but not as lined as the hands that rested on a kitchen table in Batchley, Oregon. I saw little scratches, the scar on my right hand from something when I was five, even a couple of hangnails (one on each hand). But I didn't see the knife-nick on my left middle finger from the only time we hosted Thanksgiving, when the red potatoes got a little too red. There wasn't the slight but definite burn-scar on the back of my right hand, from the one and only time I tried to smoke a chicken. These were my hands, but they weren't *mine*-mine. These hands belonged to Tomlin Keagan, yeah, but Tomlin Keagan, age thirteen.

Hands: solid. The din of the tour groups: suitably din-ny. Even the smell of the oil pattering from many of the planes onto the dingy drop-cloths placed beneath them.

Dammit, I thought. *I think I fell asleep.*

But it all was solid, and it felt like it would hold for a while. *Use this,* I told both myself and the avatar in the dream. And I drew back and gave thirteen-year-old Tomlin the controls. *I'm here but just to watch. Just show me.*

We looked down at the itinerary in our hands:

    9:00 - 10:00: Guided tour

    11:00-11:30: B-17 Presentation — E.C. (Summary required)

    12:00-12:30: Lunch

And some other stuff. Lunch took us far enough. A quick look at our watch: 11:05. We felt kinda scared and totally lost, knowing that we were a little late for the extra-credit opportunity but hoping we weren't *too* late. A summary? Easy. That was so much better than the regular credit, with which we had probably (definitely) irreversibly fallen behind. But where the hell was the presentation?

We glanced around and saw quite a few students, but only some of whom we recognized. Our school wasn't the only one there that day. But they weren't heading toward anything that rhymed with "presentation." Instead, they'd realized that "E.C." meant they could hit up the snack bar or gift shop or little theater early. Not because they actually wanted to see a ten-minute documentary on World War I aviation but because they *really* dug the dark.

Finally, we spotted a couple-dozen people settling into folding chairs in front of a folding table in front of a plane that might have been a B-17. The dreamer knew what it was, of course, but li'l me wasn't quite as sure. She would be pretty soon, though.

We sat at the end of one row, close to the back of the cluster of chairs and right by Jenny Goldstein and Becca Wentz. Both of them were in our grade. Becca was in our Social Studies class. She was also kind of a bitch.

In front of all the chairs and standing behind the folding table was an old dude wearing a button-spangled volunteer's vest and a mesh-backed ballcap that said WORLD WAR II VETERAN. He was in his seventies then but could have passed for ten years older. That was just based on looks, though, and not on his bearing. In that department, there was still quite a lot there. He couldn't have been more than five-seven, maybe five-eight, but he was built like a bulldog, and he sort of carried himself like one, too.

Right next to him was his young assistant. Li'l Tomlin figured she was a freshman or sophomore in high school and wondered what she was doing there. Li'l Tomlin had a few other questions, too, but she was a couple of years away from fully formulating them, let alone being able to deal with the answers. And even then, there'd be confusing and awkward moments, like the veteran's assistant saying, "Well, I'm bi," and Slightly Less Li'l Tomlin looking to her left and right and asking, "You're by what?"

The veteran and his assistant made some minor adjustments to the brochures, maps, and laminated photos covering the folding table. Then he set up a projection screen next to the table and in front of the plane, and his assistant took her spot at the old-school slide projector, which was in back of all of the chairs, right in the middle.

Li'l Tomlin figured that she hadn't missed much but wondered when they were going to start. Neither her schoolmates or the kids from the other groups showed any sign of shutting up. None of the teachers or parent-chaperones posted at the four corners of the seated area looked especially "ready," either. They rolled their necks, sighed, shifted from foot to foot ...

The assistant switched on the projector, casting a glowing rectangle onto the screen. No effect on the crowd. She clicked the button and flipped to a slide that said:

ON WINGS AND PRAYERS
LT. HENRY CLAIRVAUX (RET.)

The old dude — Li'l Tomlin guessed he was Lt. Henry Clairvaux, Ret. — scruffed a hand over his white buzzcut and loudly cleared his throat. Still, there wasn't a shred of attention from the kids. Talk talk talk talk talk.

The assistant clicked to the next slide: a painting of a formation of B-17s flying through wispy clouds in a pale-blue sky. And still, the assembled teenagers quieted down not-at-all. This time, though, there was no try at another slide. Instead, the old vet roared, "Now, I have been blessed by twelve kids and twenty-seven grandkids, and I can *clearly* see that not a *one* of you is one of them 'cause even the *worst* of 'em would know it's time to shut up and listen, dammit!"

That did it: instant silence. Several of the kids looked toward the teachers and chaperones for help, but they didn't get any help there. Every one of the grown-ups was grinning, and one of them — Adelita Ramírez's dad, Domingo — popped a thumbs-up.

I'd forgotten about that. Another thing I'd forgotten was how quickly Li'l Tomlin's attention had drifted from the kids and the chaperones to the old man's assistant standing behind the slide projector. She didn't look *that* long at her — really, she didn't — but the assistant caught Li'l Tomlin's gaze, smiled at her, and Li'l Tomlin snapped her head right the hell back to look at Lt. Henry Clairvaux, Ret., as he formally fired up his presentation.

"Now, this is a little closer to how I want it," Henry said. "Maybe we can forget that other stuff and start right here. If you read that first slide, you know I'm Henry Clairvaux, and during WWII, I spent a few years on a few planes a lot like this one creeping up behind me." There were some cautious, quiet laughs at that. "Now. I served as a togglier — probably easier to remember bombardier — or a navigator, depending on the day. You know what a navigator is, don't ya?"

Mumbles, few of them confident.

"Hm. Maybe you don't." He chuckled, which turned into an alarming smoker's cough. He got it under control and said, "Navigator reads the maps, makes the calculations, draws the lines, and tells everyone else where to go."

He rumbled on, describing the differences between the B-17A, B, C, D, E, F, and G. When Henry got to the B-17G, which he'd already said was the last of the series, he didn't end the presentation there. Instead, he dropped his head, pressed his thick hands to the table, and took a deep breath. And then he took another one. And then he looked back at his assistant and nodded.

She pressed her button, and the slide switched to a black-and-white photo that was captioned "BATTLE DAMAGED B-17G (*TAWNY TERROR*)." Its nose and cockpit looked like they'd been peeled open with a can opener, but there was grass beneath it, and its landing gears were down. Miraculously, the thing had somehow landed. Eventually, everyone in the crowd figured that part out. Henry was quiet until that happened. Li'l Tomlin didn't know, but I did, that the delay was as much for Henry's benefit as the crowd's.

Bells clanged in Li'l Tomlin's brain and echoed back to me. The cacophony almost knocked me out of the dream, but I held on. I tried to. I caught snippets of the rest of the presentation:

The *Tawny Terror*.

One casualty: the bombardier, Sgt. Thomas L. Keagan.

Thomas Lynne Keagan.

Tom Lynne.

Someone we'd never met. The man we were named after.

Li'l Tomlin gasped, slammed her eyes shut, and that was it. I lost my grip, but I still refused to go. I don't know how to describe the feeling, but I knew I was waking up. I yelled "No!" and who knows; maybe I yelled it in my sleep, slumped over the dining-room table.

I heard the fridge. I felt the table and chair. But I kept my eyes shut. I forced myself to fall back. I begged for it.

No fridge. No table or chairs. Just ... nothing. But shit flew past me. Memories, phantoms, fairies ... I don't know. I didn't know what they were. But I grabbed for them, hoping one of them would keep me there. I couldn't leave yet.

I caught one, held it tight, snapped it like a bedsheet, and I was back at the museum, though it was a few minutes later. I didn't care. That was close enough. Li'l Tomlin and I, we elbowed our way up to the table, where Henry's assistant was doing her best to answer questions about the maps and photos and whatever other things were up there in front of her. We lurched to the front, slapped the table both to steady ourselves and to keep from knocking it over, and we wound up catching the assistant's attention.

"Hi. Can I help you?" the assistant said, smiling a smile that I would never get tired of seeing. But that was the first time for Li'l Tomlin. She would always hold onto that moment, and I got to experience it again.

"Yeah," Li'l Tomlin said. "I was kinda hoping to talk to, uh ..."

"Oh, my grandpa?" the assistant said. "Yeah, I don't know. You and everyone else here. He always ends with that story, but he usually doesn't ditch me here, like, right afterward. But I guess he saw someone he knew and wanted to grab a cup of coffee with him." She shrugged. "I doubt there's anything *I* could help you with, but ... is there anything I could help you with?"

"I don't know," Li'l Tomlin said, and it was true: she didn't know. Not yet. She managed to say another three words — the three words that, I knew, would make all the other ones possible: "My name's Tomlin."

"Ooh. That is a cool name," the assistant said. "I'm Tessa. Not as cool as yours, but it's what I have."

Fade. Nothing.

Another bedsheet. *Snap.*

Back at the museum. *Leaving* the museum. Dark, vignette edges — already. I knew I wouldn't hold onto this one for long. Our classmates bonked and stumbled toward and through the museum doors in a formation that was called a line but only resembled one in the loosest of senses.

Someone banged into us from the right. It was only an elbow or shoulder, but it felt like a truck, and it knocked us out of the dubious line. We fell to the polished concrete floor and dropped our itinerary and souvenir bag.

It was fading. *Hold on,* I thought, and I grabbed the edges and snapped it, and the scene moved forward a few seconds. Thin. Moth-eaten. I knew this would be the last one.

Students, laughing.

Someone helped us up. Not from our school. The cuff of his suit-jacket shot out of his light-brown coat as he gave us our bag. He still had our itinerary, though. He looked at the back.

Camel, I tried to tell Li'l Tomlin. *Not just light brown. The color of that coat is camel.*

"Thanks for helping me up, but I, uh ... I need that," Li'l Tomlin said. "I wrote some notes on the back."

"Yes, you did," our helper said. He returned the sheet to us, holding it upside-down, displaying our notes, yes, but also the sketched airplane flying through them. As we took the sheet, our hand brushed against the smooth metal of his ring. "You drew the *Terror*," he said.

"Y-yeah. I did," Li'l Tomlin said as we made our way back toward the exiting throng (assholes, every one of them). "It was an incredible story."

"This is amazing. You've really done something here," the man said, and his smile reached his pale-green eyes.

***

I was standing at the table, gripping the edge of it. My mug lay on its side on the floor. So did my chair. I had to have caused a hell of a racket, but both my wife and kid were ridiculously heavy sleepers, so they had no idea. My night was still my own.

"Holy shit," I said. "Holy, holy shit."

***

Tessa woke up as I miserably failed to quietly slip back into bed. A toppled bedside lamp might have been involved. "You OK?" she asked groggily.

"No, I don't think I am," I said, staring wide-eyed at the time displayed on my charging cell phone. Well, I was at least staring in that direction. I couldn't tell you what I saw.

"Somethin' wrong?" Tessa asked drowsily.

"I don't know," I said. "Probably not."

"'S OK. Tell me." The sheets rustled and tugged lightly at me as Tessa repositioned herself. "Whas wrong?"

"Nothing," I said. "Just had a weird dream."

"Hm. Y'sure?"

"Yeah," I said, and I don't know; maybe I believed it. What was the other option? "Don't worry about it. Go back to sleep."

"OK ... g'night ..."

"Yeah. Good night, honey."

It didn't take her long to get back to where she'd been. I closed my eyes, and I tried, I *tried,* to get there, too.

At the time, it was a miserable, sleepless three or four hours that I spent grumbling and tossing and turning, kept awake by both the din of my wandering thoughts and Tessa's light snoring. Now, it's one of my most treasured memories.

That was the last night Tessa slept beside me.

Nathan

I had my mornings down to a pretty solid routine. It followed your basic three-act structure. First, I'd wake up around 8:00 in the same room I'd been waking up in since I was twelve years old. After the Waking Up, there was the Staring at the Ceiling, then the Sighing, then the Rubbing of the Face.

The second act took place in the bathroom. Shit, shower, shave. Three short scenes. Compact. Efficient.

The denouement involved a breakfast of two pieces of barely toasted toast and a couple cups of coffee at the dining-room table while I scrolled through Twitter and Instagram on my cell phone. If I was feeling nasty, I'd browse through the headlines on a couple of news apps. And that was it. That was all that varied. It was a hell of a life.

That Saturday, the changes hit almost from the start. Twitter didn't hold my attention for too long before I looked up from my phone, across the table, and through the half-open door to what used to be Grandma and Grandpa's bedroom. I'd turned it into an office. The house had been "mine" for almost fifteen years, but I still couldn't get my head around the idea of that being "my" bedroom. So an office it became and an office it stayed.

These days, I keep most of the shop's records electronically. I tried making that change toward the end of Grandpa's reign, but some battles just aren't worth it. I'd kept all his old shit, his filing cabinets and boxes and even some *really* old-school ledgers, and I'd put them all the office. In my office. My space. Mine.

I walked my breakfast into the office and put my plate and mug on the desk. I sat in the chair, wheeled over to one of the four-drawer cabinets, and wandered through Grandpa's haphazard records until I found my way to the mid-1990s. I'd been working full-time for him by then, so that was where the files started to make sense, but I was careful not to get too optimistic.

Grandpa Keagan was a grandmaster of being cash-rich but appearing paper-poor. Dealing with antiques and other collectibles gave him a lot of opportunities for cash sales and for items to pass through the shop without leaving any sort of a paper trail. All I remembered about the tourmaline ring was that we'd sold it. But it wouldn't have been the easiest thing to sell due to its value, and Grandpa would have tried to squeeze every dollar out of something like that, so I thought there was a solid chance there'd be some paperwork for it.

And boom. I found it. November 1997 to Sharon Carey. Paid with a check.

I shoved the drawer shut, put the sales receipt next to my tragically cold coffee and forgotten toast, and called her. We're talking more than twenty years later, sure, but she was a local. People die in Westley, but they rarely move.

"Hello."

"Good morning," I said. "Is this Sharon Carey?"

"Who's calling?" she asked, her telemarketer-sense clearly tingling.

"Oh, I'm sorry. This is Nathan Keagan, from Keagan's — "

"Oh, I know who you are, Nathan. I think you went to school with my daughter, Robin."

Robin Carey, I thought, remembering pompoms, short skirts, and cold shoulders. "Oh, yeah," I said. "Robin was ... in my class."

"I thought so. Well, that's nice. What can I do for you, Nathan? Or wasn't it Nate?"

"Either one's fine," I said, marveling that even after a number of decades, my classmates' parents likely knew me better than most of my classmates did. "Well, I was just looking through some of the old paperwork at the shop, and I see that you got a ring from us way back in '97. By any chance, do you remember that?"

There was a pause. When Sharon spoke again, her tone was different. Subdued. It didn't sound like we were friends anymore. "Yes, I do," she said. "I hope you don't want it back."

"Well, no, not necessarily," I said. "I —"

"I bought that as a thirtieth anniversary present for my husband, Mark. We buried him with it last November. Just before Thanksgiving." There was a sniff.

"Oh, Mrs. Carey, I'm —"

"I'm sorry I couldn't help you."

"No, it's fine, I'm —"

"Was there something else you needed?"

"No. No, that is totally all."

"OK. I should go now, Nathan. Thank you for calling. I'll tell Robin you said hi."

"OK. That would be great. Thank you, Mrs. Carey. Good-bye."

"Mm-hm."

Well. That was that. At first, I did nothing. Not a damn thing.

Then I finished my toast.

***

It's only a mile from the house to the shop, so I could've walked it. Sometimes, I do. It was cold, though, dammit, and it had rained the night before, and it was working on raining again. I can do cold, and I can do wet, but I can't hack it when they come at me at once.

So I drove, truly turning only once. That was the left out of my gravel driveway and onto the two-lane rural highway that calls itself Main Street when it gets to town. It's a straight shot, but there is one steep, son-of-a-bitching hill toward the end. Just past the summit is the hand-carved, hand-painted sign that says

Welcome to
Westley, Oregon

Population 1,634
You're only a stranger once!
I parked my car just on the other side of that, up against
the curb in front of the feed store. Polly Rodgers had already
set the A-frame specials board out on the sidewalk, which
told me that while I might not be late, I couldn't really call
myself early, either. The car's heater finally, fully woke up
and blasted out some blessed warmth. *Neat. Right on
schedule,* I thought as I shut the engine off. At least I was
dry.

I crossed the street to the shop. To *my* shop. It had been
mine on paper for as long as the house, but I still had to
remind myself of that. Turned out there was a difference
between having legal ownership of something and feeling
like it's "mine." I figured I could probably reconcile all that
in another fifteen years.

As I stepped up onto the sidewalk, I looked up at the sky.
There were the right kinds of clouds and the right kind of
chill for me to think the forecasted thirty-percent chance of
precipitation would pay off. Sunlight poked through the
clouds in a few places and glinted off the gold highlights of
the lettering on the windows. The one on the left side said
"KEAGAN'S COLLECTIONS" and "Est. 1947," which was a
bit of a cheat. My great-grandpa bought the building in '47,
but he converted it from a failed bank into a dry-goods store.
The change to Keagan's Collections, with the antiques and
such, was my grandpa's doing about twenty years later.

The words "We BUY We SELL We TRADE" arced at the
top of the right-hand window. The shop's phone number
and hours ran below that.

I opened the door, cupping the little bell at the top not to
be sneaky but because I knew I'd be hearing enough of that
sound throughout the day, thank you very much. The shop
was dim. Murky. The only natural light came from those
front windows and the glass set into the door, but the
lettering and displays blocked a lot of it. Most of the items I

57

had out for sale just looked like poorly defined shapes. Blobs. But I could have identified every one of them.

I flipped the sign so OPEN faced out, turned on the lights, and strolled through the store. Past the Zippos and fountain pens and coins and pocketknives in the slowly spinning cases, past the uranium glass glowing under black light, the toys, furniture, the record bins, turntables, stereos …

I prepped the till, and then I decided I had some work to do in the back. I propped the door open with a wastebasket so I'd be able to hear if someone came in.

I sat at the makeshift workbench, which Grandpa had made by setting a sheet of plywood on top of two two-drawer file cabinets. That was it. That's the bench. Three small plastic toolboxes sat on the shelves above the bench, one red, one blue, and one yellow. I brought down the yellow one along with a few other items to set up my workstation, like a couple of small bowls to hold parts, a bottle of rubbing alcohol, lighter fluid, cotton balls, and so on. And three Argus C3s in a shoebox. My conversation with the man with the tourmaline ring hadn't been totally fruitless. I hadn't found a Kodak 35 for him, but I had remembered the grungy and/or seized-up Bricks I'd picked up at a flea market a month or two before. Even when those things work, they're kind of funky pains in the ass, and they're not worth a whole hell of a lot. I've always liked them, though. I had a couple of them back in my film-shooting days. Tessa introduced me to them.

I used a cotton ball and just a little bit of water to soften the black leatherette covering the first patient. I took off the shutter-cocking lever, focusing coupler, and the lens, which is easy enough, and then I got my set of little screwdrivers out of the yellow toolbox. I carefully worked the tip of the two-millimeter flathead under the leatherette in six places and found the screws — one in each of the corners, one at the top-middle, and straight down from that at the bottom. The faceplate lifted right off, and a minute later, I had the frozen speed-mechanism soaking in a Ronsonol lighter-fluid bath in one of those little bowls. Easy peasy. I reached for Camera Number Two.

Ting ting.

A purse sat on the counter. A pair of perfectly manicured hands clutched the purse, the hands positioned next to each other on the strap, keeping each other safe. The hands led to wrists that led to the sleeves of a sequin-studded sweatshirt that announced IT'S WINE O'CLOCK SOMEWHERE! Skipping up to the head, a pair of tortoiseshell-framed eyeglasses shielded and slightly magnified a pair of brown eyes. Topping the whole shebang was hair that was dyed, obviously but tastefully, and teased and poofed in a way that looked fresh from the salon. She looked familiar, but I couldn't place her.

"Hi. How can I help you?" I said.

"Hi. You're Nate, right?"

That was all it took. Shit, I'd heard her voice on my phone maybe an hour before. "Mrs. Carey," I said. "Hi. Yes, I'm Nate. Look, I'm sorry about —"

"Oh, you don't have to be sorry. November was just three months ago, and some days are ... well, they're days. Some days are days." There was a breathy sort of sound that was supposed to be a laugh, but God, it was weak. "But you know how that goes. I remembered that ... well, I'm sure you know how it can be."

I clenched my jaw but tried not to look like I was clenching my jaw. "Yeah, and it hits everyone differently. And some days hit different than others," I said.

Mrs. Carey exhaled deeply. "Oh, isn't that the truth ..."

I didn't wake up that morning thinking I needed another friend, and I sure as hell wasn't in the market for a friend in misery. But it wasn't my first time down that road. I thought I could redirect her. "Mrs. Carey, look. No worries. I just started thinking about that ring for some reason, and I remembered it was an interesting piece, and ... I'm sorry I started your day like this. I hadn't heard about your husband."

"It was sudden."

"Yeah," I said. I've always had a way with words. It surprises me sometimes.

"Well, speaking of Mark," Mrs. Carey said.

I really don't want to talk about Mark, I thought. *I don't have anything I want to add to that conversation.*

"He found this old typewriter," she said, "and I saw that you had a few typewriters in your window. And some old adding-machines, too."

I shrugged and said, "I buy them because I like them, not because I can sell them."

"Oh, is that right?"

"There can be some interest in the *really* old ones," I said. "Pre-World War II. Glass keys. Though a lot of the time, I wonder if the people who buy them are just going to break them down and make earrings or cufflinks and shit."

"Oh, that's terrible."

"I try not to think about it. Who knows what happens to something when it leaves here? And I'm ... sorry about the 'shit.'" God, I hate writing that down. How the hell had I forgotten how to, well, how to be a person? And why wouldn't she just wrap it up and leave?

She smirked, hoisted her purse onto her shoulder, and said, "'They way I see it, you got to say shit, but don't forget to drop me a line.'"

"Is that Aerosmith?" I said, now slightly glad she'd hung out that long. A seventy-year-old woman quoting 1970s hard-rock poetry — that didn't happen too much. Not in my shop, at least.

She glanced over her shoulder and then leaned forward, and her purse sort of went *plop* on the glass counter. She said, like it was a big secret, "I saw them in '73 on their first big tour. I grew up back East. They opened for Mott the Hoople."

"Oh, Mott the *Hoople*," I said. "*That* Mott."

"Yes. And that Hoople."

We laughed, and then I pointed at my record bins. "You know, I have a decent copy of *All the Young Dudes* over there."

She waved me off. "Oh, I have that on my Spotify playlist. You young kids can get into records if you want. I did all that. I like streaming now."

I laughed at that, too, and then I said, "Typewriter."

"Oh. Yes. Do you think you might be interested in it?"

"Well, it depends. Is it pre-war, do you think?"

"No, no, it's not that old."

"Plastic keys?" I asked, already disappointed.

"Yes, but I think it's from Germany. I think that's what Mark said. It's an Adler. Does that sound right?"

"Ooh. That could be interesting," I said.

"Do you think so? Even if it's newer?"

"Adlers are cool," I said. "That's what Jack Nicholson typed on in the *Shining*. 'All work and no play makes Jack a dull boy.'"

Mrs. Carey shuddered. "Oh, I don't watch those movies. Do you want me to bring it down?"

"You could," I said, "Or I could come by. Whichever is easier for you." I briefly rummaged through some of the dustier files in my memory. "Do you still live out there off of Echo Creek?"

Mrs. Carey smiled. "Almost fifty years," she said.

"Wow. Well, I can come by whenever works for you."

"OK, well, I don't know your hours," Mrs. Carey said.

"Any time," I said again. "I know the owner."

She smiled and said, "Well, yes, I suppose you do. Well, how about 4:00 this afternoon? Or maybe 4:30? I'll be back home around then."

"Sold," I said, and then I shrugged. "Or maybe. In any case, that's when I'll stop by."

"Good," Mrs. Carey said. "That's nice. I'm glad you called me this morning, Nate. I'll see you then."

I nodded, she left, and I got back to the cameras in the back. After an iffy start, it seemed like it was turning into a good day.

It really, really did.

***

I flipped the sign and locked the door at about 4:10. There'd been a bit of a rush after lunchtime, but it had been slow as hell since a little after three. I doubted I'd lose much business by closing up early, and I thought that closing that deal with Mrs. Carey would be a nice way to cap off the day. I'd left her with "maybe," but I knew I'd wind up buying the machine from her. It seemed like the thing to do after ruining her morning. Plus, if it did turn out to look like the one used in *The Shining,* that would be cool as hell. I was already thinking about how to dress up the window display — hexagonal carpet and everything.

It actually seemed colder than it had been that morning. Either that, or the seven hours I'd spent in the nicely warm shop had softened me up. Or it could have been a little of both. I shut my car door, turned the engine on, and huffed and puffed and rubbed my hands together until the heater came on. Finally satisfied with that, I made a U-turn on Main Street and headed back out of town.

The first few snowflakes fluttered down to the windshield as I dropped down that son-of-a-bitching hill. They lasted just long enough for me to say "Huh," and then they melted to nothing. Others followed, and then some others fluttered down after those. They all vanished the same way, though it took longer each time. "Huh," I said again.

I pulled over for the first set of emergency vehicles just a little ways past my house. There was a Westley PD car, a fire truck, and an ambulance. All three. Shit, shower, and shave. I just about made it to the turnoff before I had to pull over for the next set.

Something had happened, and that was rare enough for a Saturday morning on the outskirts of Westley. Could have been a house fire. It was February, and it had gotten crazy cold, so I knew the wood stoves and pellet stoves would be in heavy use. More likely, though, I figured someone had blown the stop where Echo Creek Road met the highway. Drivers on the highway have always had the right of way, and drivers on Echo Creek have always treated that red sign as a suggestion.

The snarl wasn't at the intersection, but it wasn't too far past it. I made the left turn onto Echo Creek without a problem, but when I took that bend right before the west end of the bridge, I swore, slammed the brake, and narrowly missed the mid-'90s Taurus parked in front of me. Parked right there in the road, right around that blind corner, not moving even a little and with no brake lights on, either. I shut off my engine, too, and I tried to make sense of what I was seeing.

At least ten other vehicles sat between the Taurus and the entrance to Keagans Crossing. After I learned all I could from counting the cars, I unbuckled my seatbelt, opened the door, and stood on the frame so I could get a broader and further view. There were several fresh tire-tracks, some of them heavy, on the dirt shoulder. I craned my neck to see past the jammed-up cars and made out all of those emergency vehicles that had passed me, sirens off but their lights still spinning. The fire trucks had pulled over to the left, the ambulances to the right, and the squad cars were dead-center, parked sideways and nose-to-nose to block access to the bridge. They also obstructed my view of the road running through it.

I drummed my fingers on the roof of the car. I looked behind me. Only one other vehicle had pulled up since my arrival. I could have easily flipped my car around and rescheduled with Mrs. Carey, but I didn't. Instead, I hopped down off the car, shut the door, and strolled past everyone queued up in front of the crossing. I stopped at the police cars and smiled when I saw Officer Angélica Morales standing by the back bumper of one of them, her back to me, talking into her shoulder-mounted radio.

I took one step further and immediately slipped on a patch of ice just short of the mouth of the bridge. Because of course I did. pinwheeled my arms, regained my balance, and managed to keep everything but my dignity intact. *It's cold, but it's not* that *cold,* I thought, remembering the snowflakes that had all tried to linger before they melted my windshield.

I flicked one of the strands of POLICE LINE DO NOT CROSS tape stretched over the entrance of the bridge. I saw a similar "X" of bright-yellow tape blocking the other end. Past that was another police car — that one was from Burwell — parked between the bridge and another line of backed-up vehicles. I was so caught up in that looking-glass effect that it took me a while to realize I wasn't seeing a wrecked car or *any* car — any*thing* — on the bridge itself.

"Nathan. Hey. What do you think you're doing?"

I flinched and looked over at Angie as she came up to me. She didn't seem especially happy to see me. "Well, hello, Officer," I said, not meaning to sound nearly as smart-assed as I immediately realized I did. "I'm just, you know, wondering what the hell is going on over here."

"Single-car MVA," Angie said. "Now come on. Go back to your car. Please. I can't have all these people following your example and glomming up on this side of the bridge."

Right on cue, a door opened and shut about six cars down the line.

Angie heard it, sighed, and said, "Come on. Let's go." She patted my elbow with the back of her hand, and I dutifully followed her away from the bridge. "You know how this works. You'll hear all about this around town by the end of the day. Probably multiple versions of it. Some will be pretty cool. One might even be true."

"Multiple versions of *what*?" I said, stopping at the first car. "Don't know if you noticed, Angie, but it looks like you've lost the single car that was involved in your single-car accident."

She stood beside me and jerked her head toward the crossing.

"What?" I asked. "You telling me there's a car there?"

"Nope. But there's something," Angie said. "Abra los ojos."

Open my eyes. Look. I did as I was told.

Angie told someone, probably the same someone who had just opened and shut her car door, to return to her vehicle, please.

There still clearly wasn't a car on the bridge — I hadn't missed that — but now I saw the effects of one. There was a definite jagged, automobile-sized gap in the wooden guardrail on the northern side of the bridge, opening onto the twenty-foot drop down to Echo Creek. I walked over to the shoulder and peered through the space between the trees and the edge of the bridge.

"Well, what about him?"

"Yes, ma'am, I'm on it. Let me worry about him. Go back to your car, please."

It hadn't clicked that Angie was the sole person working crowd-control on that side of the bridge, but now I saw how she'd wound up alone. Two other WPD officers were down along the creek, one of them taking photos of the crumpled metallic mess that had wound up half-in and half-out of the water. I pulled out my cell phone and snapped some shots of my own, zooming in on a few to get a better view of the car. It was a 1960s something, and it was definitely blue, but that was about as far as I could go. I can talk your ear off about cameras and typewriters, and I love a good wood-paneled stereo receiver, and I guess I know a little bit about early- to mid-'60s Chevy pickups, but there are significant gaps in my identification-and-appraisal skills when it comes to cars.

The car's front end had settled in the creek. Tongues of flame still licked out from beneath the ruined hood and hissed on the surface of the muddy water. Several other small fires dotted the water like tea candles burning on lily pads. Some of those floating fires drifted toward the western shore, getting precariously close to the needles and leaves that stretched from the creek to more than a few back-ends of more than a few properties, which meant trees, wooden fences, barns, and out-buildings. I figured the wet ground would help a bit, but bad was bad.

For the moment, the fires seemed to be under control thanks to the small crews wielding the hoses they'd extended from the engines parked on the shoulder. Four paramedics milled about, not doing much at that point besides satisfying their own curiosity. There was no one left in that car for them to help.

That car, though. There was something about that car.

"Nathan! Nathan Keagan, goddammit, get back to your car *now*!"

I looked down at Angie's hand, which had suddenly and very assertively grabbed onto my arm, her fingers digging in beneath my bicep. "Yeah, you know what?" I said. "I do believe I'll be getting back to my car now."

Angie yanked me away from the shoulder and took me for a walk down the line of cars. "Oh, do you think?" she said. "Do you know what *I* think? I think I should arrest you just so I don't have to deal with a week's worth of phone calls from people like Anna Allman."

Ah. So Anna Allman was the woman Angie had asked to return to her car. I knew Anna Allman. Everyone in the fine town of Westley, Oregon, population 1,634, knew Anna Allman. "Oh, I don't think you'll have to worry about that," I said. "That's too direct for her. She'll probably just write a tersely worded letter to the paper."

"Yeah, calling me a minority hire and accusing me of playing favorites with a former man-friend. That's probably how she'd put it."

"So it'll be a Wednesday."

"Yeah, you're not helping yourself," Angie said.

"Hey. I'm still a man. And I'd like to think we're still friends."

"Well, today you can show me that." She stopped and let go of my arm. "Car. Now. And stay there. Stay."

"Woof," I said, and I went.

Another half-dozen cars had stacked up behind mine. I opened my driver-side door but didn't get in. Standing beside the car, leaning on the door, I unlocked my phone, opened the gallery, and flipped through the photos I'd taken. Snow fell again and put a more concerted effort into falling this time. Several flakes gathered on my phone screen before I wiped them off with the side of my hand.

I found one of the pictures I'd zoomed-in on, and I embiggened it some more. There was something about that car, but what did that mean? "It's a car," I muttered to myself. "Just a car. And it's ... blue."

Then a certainty exploded in my head. Not like a firework — more like a mental belch. *Blue. Blue. Fathom Blue.*

And another one. *It's a '68 Nova.*

And hell. Why stop there? *That's Tessa's car.*

I blinked, I looked up, and I blinked some more. Things were blurry. I was too stunned to realize I was weeping.

There was an odd percussion, a drumbeat of car doors opening between me and the bridge, and the scene resolved back into horrible focus.

I pocketed my phone and joined the crowd. Drivers and passengers swarmed all around me, filling that gap between the trees and the bridge, glomming up exactly as Angie hadn't wanted them to do. She didn't do a thing to stop me or anyone else. She'd stepped off the shoulder and was making her way down to the shore. I was glad for my height but still needed to stand on my toes to get a clear view of the new commotion down by the creek.

It looked like the fires were out, but the firefighters were still hosing the shore to make sure they stayed out. That was good. But not a single one of them was looking at the hose running through their thickly gloved hands or the water or the shore or even each other. Instead, every one of them looked toward the tree line, which was where all the cops and paramedics had gathered. Angie jogged their way.

A tall teenager with short, matted hair — dyed electric green, or maybe teal — had emerged from the trees and now stood, dazed, on the creekside. Clothes soaked and torn, an arm that didn't hang right, and no apparent awareness of that injury or the assembled emergency personnel. The teen just stared past them, through them, first at the smoldering car, then at the hole in the side of the bridge, then at the gawking throng.

Stupidly, I waved. Then, before I consciously thought, *You know, I'm going to scramble down to the shore,* I'd scrambled down to the shore, partly on my feet and partly on my ass.

I passed Angie. She reached out for me, tried to pull me back. She missed. "Nate!" she said. "What are you doing?"

"That's Mackenzie!" I hollered back, not stopping, not slowing down. "That's my kid!"

Tomlin

That phone call from my brother opened every single one of my locks, and I came undone.

I tried to put myself back together, but I didn't do it right. I was ten years old, barely. Ten and a couple of months. It was morning, but I still had my pajamas on: those baby-blue one-piece footed things. I usually liked them, but I'd snagged the skin of my chest in the zipper the night before. It still kinda stung, but it didn't bother me as much as the mystery I saw from where I stood, at the end of the hall. Still groggy, I looked out into the living room, and I thought, *Why are all these people here?* I mean, I knew every one of them — there were aunts and uncles and uncles and some of my cousins and some family friends — but it wasn't Easter yet, and Christmas had already happened. That's when people came over. This wasn't how we did things.

The bathroom door opened to my right, and Nate came out. He was only two years older than me, but he already had his day-clothes on, so I knew he knew something. "Why's everyone here?" I asked.

He sniffed and rubbed his eyes. He almost looked like he'd been crying, but that didn't seem right. "Go back to your room. You need to get dressed," he said.

Such a boring answer, such a boring non-answer, and so bossy, which was so typical of him. Now, it's clear that's why it scared me. It didn't fit at all with the unscheduled holiday in the front of the house. "What's going on, Nate?" I asked. "Why is everyone here?"

Nate opened and closed his mouth, and then he shook his head. He looked out at the living room, and he shook his head again, and he said, "No, no I don't want to. I don't want to. Go back and get dressed, Tomlin. I'll bring you something to eat for breakfast in your room."

Now I knew something wasn't just wrong, but it was terribly wrong. "We're not supposed to eat in our rooms," I said. "Remember, it brings ants."

"No one's worried about ants today," he said. He already had his back to me, and he was already leaving the hall. "It'll be OK."

Somehow, even at age ten, I knew it wouldn't.

***

Some time after that, I came together at my friend James's kitchen table. My purse sat on the table. It was open, and three traffic tickets curled out of it. I looked at them. At their shapes. They looked like snakes, like flat white snakes. Not paper. No, they weren't paper. I heard them hiss, and I fell apart again.

***

Ten again. I sat at the antique school-desk in the corner of my bedroom, which was at the corner of our house, which was on the corner of our street. Sunlight came in through the window to my right and the other one behind me. I usually liked that light. That day, it shone down on the sheet of paper on the desk. I'd drawn a superhero. I was still drawing him. I colored him in with smelly markers, not "smelly" like they got me high but "smelly" like they were supposed to smell like different kinds of fruit.

Nate lay on my bottom bunk, reading a comic book. Our cousins Tyler, Bryce, and Ethan moved around on the floor, playing with a mixture of my stuff and Nathan's stuff. Nathan never hung out in my room. We never mixed our stuff. Something was wrong. I kept drawing.

The door opened, and three grown-ups came into my room. I kept drawing. I didn't look up, but I figured out who the grown-ups were because of where they'd stopped. Bryce and Tyler's mom stood next to them, and Ethan's mom kneeled beside him. No one was playing.

"Tomlin?"

70

That was my mom, next to me. Way too close to me. My brother abandoned his comic and stood to her left, just a little behind her.

"Tomlin, honey, stop coloring for a second."

I didn't.

Her hand plopped on top of mine and screwed up my superhero's boot.

I looked up and read the news in her eyes. I told myself not not to scream, and at that moment, I managed to listen.

"Your dad is gone," she said. "He died, honey."

Both her hands flew up and covered her mouth, freeing my hand to try and fix my superhero's boot. Then I moved on to his shoulders. His shoulders weren't right, either, but that was my fault.

"Say something!" my mom said.

"What do you want me to say?" shouted a voice that shouldn't have been mine.

I was dimly aware of movement, and then of the sound of footsteps walking out of my room. My aunts and my cousins left.

Then my mom left, and then my brother did. He'd leave again a few months later. Either that, or he stayed, and I was the one who left. I've never been totally clear on who did what or on who left who. It didn't matter, though. The effect was the same.

***

I put my pieces back together, and, there I was, a pathetic Humpty Dumpty nodding off on James's couch. "I need to take my meds," I said.

"You took your medicine," his voice said. Then, with a whole lot of exhaustion and relief, his voice added, "Finally."

"Bring me my phone," I said thickly. "I want to call Mack."

"Girl, you just need to rest now," he told me. "I don't think you should —"

I shoved my hands, my stinging, throbbing wrists, into my armpits, and clamped down on them. "Bring me my

71

phone," I said to him again. "Please. I need to tell them I'm sorry."

James sighed, and then his chair creaked, and his footsteps took him away. And I was alone.

I was alone.

Mack

They weren't flashes. That's too bright. Too gentle.
Chunks. They hit me in chunks. They came in a mixed-up
order, and I knew on some level that they were memories,
but I also remember wondering if my *now* was fractured.
Each one of the chunks hit like a singularity, like a first
awareness. Like those dreams where you're just going
around, doing your thing somewhere, and then you stop and
wonder, *Wait. How'd I get here? There's this room, and I
see the door, but I don't remember walking on the sidewalk
outside.* That's what it was like: being born into a new
dream, a new dream, a new dream.

The first one was the ambulance's metal ceiling.

Then running. Running. *I can't. Stop. Running.*

Who was that? Who the hell was that?

Woods.

Reeling in the Attic, gripping the recliner for support.

Snow?

A sign: Keagans Crossing.

Another one that said The 45th Parallel. *But wait — that
happened first.*

The bare bulb in the Attic, swinging on its cord over the
chair, splashing light, bending shadows.

Boxes, falling.

"Sir Duke," playing from my Stevie Wonder playlist.

On the gurney and staring up at the metal ceiling of the
ambulance, thinking, *How'd I get here? What happened
before this? Is this my first Now?*

More Stevie. Sweet. "Superstition."

Impact. A hole punched in the bridge. In the world.

That sign: KEAGANS CROSSING. *That should have an
apostrophe.*

Two snowflakes melting on the windshield.

"Geez. I hope it's not icy." My mom.

Impact.

The ambulance.

My cell phone smacking my forehead, then landing beside me. Earbuds popping out of my ears, out of the phone, flying into the front.

Ambulance.

My floating backpack.

Running.

Gagging. *Oh. I'm drowning.*

IMPACT.

My earbuds dangling from the mirror.

A scuffing sound. On hardwood.

The bare bulb in the Attic, swinging on its cord.

Ambulance.

"I hope it's not icy."

Mom. Screaming.

Mom. A crimson spiderweb on the glass of the driver-side door. *Just like her book. But that's the wrong character.* It's a stupid thought. It's an instant. It's less than that. *She's not screaming.*

Ambulance.

Cell phone.

Blanket. A paperback book. Scraps of paper, receipts, jettisoned from the cupholders.

Dragging, scuffing sounds. From where? *Something's moving in the Attic.*

Toppled boxes, spilling onto the Attic floor.

My backpack, sitting so calmly and sweetly on my lap.

I can't stop running.

KEAGANS CROSSING.

"Where's the apostrophe?"

Running.

Lying on a gurney, staring up at the ambulance's metal ceiling. The ambulance. An ambulance.

I'm in an ambulance.

Yeah, you are. Now, I thought. *This is Now.* I was almost sure.

"What is your name?" the paramedic asked. "Do you remember your name?"

"Mack," I said. Was that me? Was that my voice? I didn't seem close enough.

"Mack? Hi, Mack. What's your full name?"

"Mackenzie," I said again, but he was looking for something else, wasn't he? "It's Mackenzie. Mackenzie Keagan Hatcher."

"Good. Cool. That's cool. I'm Nolan. Do you know what day it is, Mackenzie?"

Damn. No — maybe. Dammit. Wait. "I think it's Friday. No, it's Thursday." *Is it?* "It happened on a Thursday."

"OK. Mackenzie, do you—"

"Did you find my backpack?" I asked, still looking at the ceiling of the ambulance because I couldn't look at anything else. Something was holding onto my neck. I saw part of Nolan's knee when he pulled some straps or something, but I don't think I ever saw his face.

"Backpack? No, no backpack," Nolan the paramedic said. "You did drop something when we found you, though. Well, when you found us."

I couldn't move my head, so I just moved my eyes and strained to look down over my chin and my chest as he set my favorite damn ballcap on my stomach. Tom Peterson grinned at me from the stained and crumpled crown and declared, "FREE is a VERY good price!"

"Thank you," I said. My throat hurt. Something was in it. "Thank you." *I sound like I'm crying,* I thought. Then I thought, *Am I crying?*

"Don't mention it. I remember him. I loved those commercials. That's a little before your time, though, isn't it?"

"I ..." Cleared my throat. "I, uh ..."

"Don't worry about it," Nolan said. "I was just thinking."

Someone knocked, and even in the state I was in, I knew that was strange. Nolan's knee moved out of my limited field of view as Nolan moved to open the ambulance doors.

There was some talking. I made out almost none of it. But then Nolan's knee came back, and Nolan said, "There's someone here who says he wants to talk to you. He says his name is Nathan. He says he's your dad."

"We're meeting him for lunch," I said, and for a few seconds, everything made sense. But then I thought about it some more, especially the "we," and everything stopped being OK.

"Well, I told him he'd have to meet us at the hospital. Does that sound OK, Mackenzie?" Nolan said. "You might still make lunchtime, or else maybe the two of you can grab an early dinner."

"Hospital food," I said.

"Yep. Probably hospital food," Nolan said.

"Dinner for two," I said, and I understood things again, but I didn't want to. My eyes got hot, the ceiling blurred, and I smiled so widely that my cheeks ached. Actually, all can say is that I tried to smile. I don't know if I pulled it off. No one but Nolan the Paramedic could say what actually wound up happening.

He said, "Do you want me to — "

"Let's go," I said roughly. "Probably gonna be hungry."

***

The Attic looked ransacked. A few of the shelves still held some boxes, but the rest of them were, well, everywhere else, knocked over, burst open, contents spilling out. And several of the shelves were gone, too ... then they were there ... then they were gone ... then there ...

What the shit? I thought. *I didn't make this.*

One of the blinds was up, like the windows had winked and got stuck that way. Overlapping images flashed on the other side of the glass. Same with the sounds that went along with them: they bumped into each other and ricocheted around the Attic. Some of them seemed familiar, but whenever I tried to look or listen a little closer, all I could make out were flickers and splashes and noise.

I kicked a couple of boxes and some spilled-out shit aside, then I made my way through, sighed, and sat on the floor in front of the chair. I didn't know where to start. I didn't even know what I wanted to do. I pulled a nearby box toward me and flipped it upright. It was empty. *Cool,* I thought. *Awesome.* With my other hand and without really looking, I swiped the closest random object off the floor. It wound up being a bookmark from a new-and-used bookstore in downtown Salem. At first, it looked identical to all the other bookmarks the clerks stuck inside the front cover of a purchase. But only at first.

The Attic recognized it, too. The second blind snapped up, and outside the windows, a set of images struggled to stand out from the rest. First, they lasted longer before they flickered out, and then they lasted longer and longer and longer. Then they sort of pulsed, and with each beat, they gained more color and saturation, more everything, than the images projected by the other spilled items. Eventually, that one picture, that scene, was all I could see through the glass. All because of that damn bookmark.

Up closest to the panes was a bitchin' tie-dyed T-shirt that Mackenzie had made a week before in the garage. I missed that shirt. I remembered wearing the shit out of it.
Below the shirt was a pair of jean shorts, then a couple of legs stretched out on our old leather couch. They were the legs of Mackenzie Keagan Hatcher, age ten, who had almost exactly two months to go until they started the fifth grade. On the feet at the end of Mackenzie's legs was a pair of black-and-white checkerboard Vans, and they tapped together, swung apart, tapped together, swung apart. And that was it for a good minute. That was the show. Then a book rose into view, blocking my view of the feet. The first pages of *A*

Woman Called Kidd filled the window, and both Mackenzie and I read:

> It snowed the night Eleanor Kidd helped kill an angel and met Jack Beacham.
>
> She tore down River Road South in her '68 Cougar, taking a 25 mph corner at 50 and kicking up a torrent of needles and leaves in her wake. In the passenger seat, Taija grabbed the armrest with her right hand and the Cougar's center console with her left. "Ellie, slow down!" Taija said.

A finger entered the frame, dropping in from the top, and gently pulled down the book. The perspective tilted up slightly and focused on Tessa's smiling face. She was younger then, too. "*A Woman Called Kidd,*" she said. "Where'd you find this?"

"Gwen's mom took us to … what's it called? That big bookstore in downtown Salem. And I bought it," Mackenzie said rapidly. A slight tremor passed through their words.

Our mom nodded, and then she pulled up the footstool that matched the couch and sat down. Mackenzie turned their head a little to look at Tessa, which perfectly framed her in the left-hand window. Seven years younger. Beautiful and alive.

Tessa held out her hand. Mackenzie sighed and handed over the book. Tessa examined the front cover, and then she flipped the book over, checked out the back, and said, "Huh. This is an early printing. And it's well-read, which I love to see. You know, I'm sure I still have a box of these in the closet in the office. Or maybe they're in the shed. They're somewhere."

"Yeah, but I didn't know if —"

"Oh, you knew," Tessa said. "You did. Tomlin told you she didn't think you were old enough to get into these yet. She said that pretty recently, actually. Did you think buying it would change her mind?"

The perspective lowered a bit. "I didn't ..." A sigh. "I don't know. I didn't really think it out," Mackenzie said. "You'll help me, right?"

Tessa blinked, and then she slowly shook her head. "Oh, you are playing a dangerous game, kid."

Then she laughed, and I wanted her to keep laughing. I wanted to hear that. I wanted to hear *her*. But the scene dimmed, and all those other sounds and images instantly came on back — if they'd ever really left. They fizzled and flickered and popped, fighting for the front but burning up their own fuel in the process.

I stood up and kicked the box. It tumbled across the floor and banged into the wall below the windows. "Dammit!" I said, and "Dammit!" I said again, lying there in the hospital bed with my splinted arm resting on my chest. It didn't change anything, but it was easy, and it felt good, so I stared up at the ceiling tiles and kept right on saying it: "Dammit, dammit, god*dammit*!"

***

I had the incredible pleasure of staying overnight at the hospital. My sole-surviving mother had won three tickets in her first forty-five miles out of Seattle, so she was back in that city, chilling with her friend James until he felt comfy giving her keys back. So I was alone — I thought. I was surprised to see my dad by the gurney, talking to the surgeon when I came out of the anesthetic.

I spent most of the ride from Salem to Westley with my eyes closed, but I don't know much that helped. Every lurch or swerve, even the littlest ones, tossed one of those chunks right up in front of my mind's eye. I don't remember flinching, squirming, or whimpering too much, but judging from how often my dad apologized or straight-up asked if I was OK, what I remember probably doesn't amount for shit.

After forever, gravel crunched under the tires of his Corolla. "Well, we're here," he said. I dared to open my eyes even though we hadn't stopped moving, and I saw that we'd just turned down the long gravel driveway that ran alongside his house and then sort of crept along the back of it. A single tall, skinny window looked out from the exact middle of the front of the second floor. Below it and to the left was the front door, which he'd painted red since the last time I was there. To the right of the door was the living room's big picture window. The house had a covered porch and a half-acre of grass in front of it, which meant it was a field as far as I was concerned. Get right on out of here with that "front lawn" bullshit.

I'd been there before, of course, but I also kinda hadn't. I felt totally raw and blank and completely unconnected to anything. Just sort of … I don't know. Drifting. So basically, I had the weird experience of looking at that should-have-been-familiar place for the first time.

We didn't go into the house through the front door. We never did that. Honestly, I didn't even know if the front door worked. Dad parked his car around back, right up in front of the outbuilding that he'd always called the "workshop," but which I'd always just known as a sort of catch-all space. We went up the steps to the back deck, and Dad pulled open the sliding door that opened into the kitchen. We walked without talking through the kitchen, the dining room, and the living room. Those last two flowed into each other, and two doors opened off of them, leading to my dad's office and the downstairs bathroom. And actually, there was another door between those, going from the office directly to the crapper.

We took a right past the TV and stepped into the house's official, on-the-blueprints entryway. There was a coat closet and the stairs up to the second floor. The high window I'd seen from the outside was set way up there in the wall. It didn't look into anything but the dead space above the stairway.

When we got upstairs, I continued my little self-directed tour of a place I sort of knew but really didn't. The stairs ended at the upstairs hall, and the hall ended at a door. There were three more doors to my right. To the left, there was technically just a wall, but it wasn't just any wall. Oh no. It was totally, and I mean *totally* covered, with dozens of framed pictures. Most of them were in color, but only most of them. There were so many of them, and they'd been hung so closely together, that the wallpaper only peeked through in a couple of spaces.

I stepped away from my dad and got up close to the Wall-o'-Photos. Dad stood behind me and waited for me to finish doing whatever the hell I was doing. I spotted the picture of the *Tawny Terror* right off. It was the same shot that blessed the wall of Tessa's office. That *had* blessed, maybe? Shit. Anyway. The rest of the pictures had people, and I recognized some of them. I saw Nana Ronnie and Grandpa Keagan, though the "together" pics stopped somewhere close to their fortieth birthdays. I never met my grandpa — my dad's dad. My great-grandparents were up there, too, which made sense because it had been their house for years before it was my dad's. Dad featured pretty prominently in the gallery. My mom — Tomlin — was only in a couple of the pics. At least that I could see.

One of those was a candid picture, and it grabbed me. It was a relatively recent one, but it still had to be twenty years old. It featured five teenagers hanging out on the muddy shore of Echo Creek. I adjusted the sling on my left arm, and I brought my right hand up to touch the frame. I definitely recognized three of the people in the photo: they were younger versions of my dad and both my moms. I thought I'd met the other people before. Their future-ized versions, anyway.

"That's you and the moms," I said without turning around from the wall. I hadn't talked in a while, and my voice sounded like it was someone else's.

"Yep," Dad said.

"Who're the other people?"

"That's Caleb Geary and Angélica Morales," Dad said behind me. "We're all still teenagers in that. That wasn't too long before, uh ..." He blinked and shook his head like something had just hit him. "Shit. That was right before a lot. Anyway."

"Yeah, I thought so," I said. "Are you still friends with, uh ... with them?" I'd already forgotten their names.

"Yeah, sort of. Caleb moved down to California, and I get a message from him now and then. We aren't *not*-friends. Angie and I dated for a while, a couple of times. She actually sort of led me to you the, uh ... the other day. She's a police officer now. Here in town."

"Oh. Small world."

"Small town," he said. "You know, when that picture was taken, she was going out with Caleb."

"Oh. Well ... shit," I said.

"Yeah, it's always been a pretty limited dating-pool," my dad said.

"Cool," I said. "This is a lot of pictures. I know I've seen them before, but ... I mean ... this is a *lot* of pictures."

"You know, most of the time, I don't even notice them. Sometimes, I guess. And I've added a few in the last fifteen years or so. But when they've been up there as long as most of them have been up there, they sort of become the wallpaper."

"I can't even see the wallpaper."

"Oh, it's there," Dad said. "I remember it. Little roses and shit. You're not missing much."

I smiled, and I nodded, and then I suddenly realized how heavy my eyelids were, and I let out a breath that seemed to last forever. "OK," I said.

"You've gotta be tired. Let me show you your room."

"Yeah, and I think that last dose of pain meds is kicking in," I told him. "Some rest sounds great right now." That didn't quite capture it. I didn't want to 'rest.' I wanted to pass right the hell out. I wanted to slide out of the world for a bit.

Dad resumed his journey down the hall, and I followed close behind him. "You probably remember this, but the bathroom's to your right, in the middle over there," he said. "Both those other rooms are technically bedrooms. The one on the right's mine. The other one, the one on the left, is mainly just holding boxes right now."

"Boxes," I said.

"Yep," he said. "That's where the boxes sleep."

I didn't like that. I know what he didn't mean, but I I didn't like that at all.

"They're sort of like those pictures," he said. "A lot of 'em have been in there since this was my grandparents' place. I don't know, maybe since my dad and my aunt and uncle were kids. The rest of them, though, are what I moved out of the attic to make room for you."

I scratched the back of my neck. Something tickled back there. "Attic," I said.

We stopped in front of that door at the end of the hall. It was a little shorter than the other three, and it looked like it had ever been varnished, let alone painted. It was a scabbed and scrappy misfit. I dug it.

"Yeah, I mean, I could have pulled the boxes and crap out of that room and moved them into here," Dad said, "but what's the fun in that? Besides, that other one's just a *room*. This is … well, it seemed more like you." He turned the knob and gave the door a little shove, and from there, it creaked open on its own. "Yeah, it's never quite hung right. But there you go. It was a late night last night, and I spent some time with it today, and I think it turned out OK. Light switch to your right. Go ahead. Check it out."

I stepped forward and reached into the dark. I basically felt up the wall, and then I flipped the light switch and went into the room. Slowly. Very slowly. Each step carried something else with it. Sadness, apprehension, outright fear, appreciation, some relief, confusion, love …

A lot. It was a lot.

Once I was in the attic, I knew I'd never been there before. There is no way I would have forgotten it. It was a finished space only in the sense that someone had "finished" it by slapping some wood paneling over the angled rafters and stubby wall studs. The walls were even shorter than the door. They came up maybe four feet before they connected with the sharply angled ceiling. I stooped less and less as I moved further into the room. A few yards in, I could stand totally upright. The peak in the middle must have been ten feet up.

He said he wanted me to see how he'd set it up. At first, I thought he'd meant the paneling, like he'd totally redone the place while I chilled out at the hospital, waiting for my discharge. There wouldn't have been enough time, though. It didn't make any sense. But it also didn't make sense for me to find my bed in that room — my *actual* bed from my *actual* house. But there it was, up against the far wall, just to the left of the room's only window.

A banged-up dresser squatted to my right, as close to that wall as it could get while still respecting the plummeting ceiling. For a second, I was incredibly relieved that the dresser and I were strangers to each other. But then I opened the drawers and found my T-shirts, my socks, and a whole lot of my et ceteras.

"This is my shit," I said.

Still on the other side of the doorway, my dad sighed. "Yeah. I wondered if you'd think it was weird."

I shook my head. Hard. It felt like it was packed with cotton. I didn't know if that was because of the Percocet or literally everything else, but it was like I couldn't form a single coherent thought. Finally, I managed, "Yeah, you know, a sleeping bag would have worked."

"Oh, I thought you deserved more than that." He forced a smile, trying for humor. For friendliness. It felt off. I don't know. Like I said, maybe I wasn't totally thinking straight.

"OK, you have a pretty sweet couch, too" I said.

His smile started to move into a confused frown. "You want to sleep on the couch?" he asked. "If you want to, you can sleep on the couch."

"It's what I've done before," I said.

"Well, that's just because you —"

He stopped himself, but I thought, *Because I've never had a bed here. Never stayed more than a night at a time.* I wanted to hear him say it. I wanted him to finally say why. Also, I kind of didn't.

Never stayed more than a night at a time, I thought again. It echoed. I asked him, "How long am I staying here?"

"You know, uh ... I don't know the answer to that," he said. "They said they were keeping you overnight, and then Tomlin had her, uh ... her difficulties getting down here, and ... I don't know. That friend of mine, Angie, she has a truck, so ... we gave it a shot." He scratched at the door frame, sort of picking at the paint. "Tomlin, uh, your mom — she gave me the code for the garage, but she didn't really have to. That's the same number she used for her PIN back when we were in high school."

"It's ..." Nope. That was it. That was all I had.

"I'm sorry," he said. "I'd tell you it made sense at the time, but it didn't. I didn't know what else to do, though."

I nodded, opened the underwear drawer, and closed it again.

The floor creaked, and my dad talked to me again, and his voice was closer than it had been. "Look, Mackenzie, you just tell me what works for you. You want to go back to your house, I'll pack up all this shit and take you there right now. I'll sleep on the couch, and Tomlin will ..." He nodded. "She'll get back down here tomorrow. It just ... staying in that house, right now, without either of your moms ... I don't know. I tried to think of what I'd want to do in this situation, but I don't know *what* I'd do in this situation. Because this is an incredibly fucked-up situation."

I opened another drawer, one of the full-width ones, just for something to do. And then I opened the one under that. The top one was filled with my shirts, and the second one had my pants and shorts and skirts. There were basic 501s, printed slacks, and even my favorite pair of fitted jeans, with the fancy shiny shit on the pockets. And there were some of my T-shirts, and cardigans, and even a cropped hoody.

I shoved the drawers shut with my hip.

A pretty even assortment. A little of everything. Which was great, because I rarely knew at night how I'd present in the morning. And my dad had packed all that for me — picked all that. Dad and Angie, his maybe-girlfriend with the pick-em-up truck.

I turned around, and I surprised myself by pressing my face into my dad's shoulder. He hugged me, and I threw my good arm around his back. Through my damn sobs, I said, "Thank you. That's badass."

"Hey, OK … hey …"

"She's gone," I blubbered, and I gasped. That was the first time I'd said it out loud. "I already miss her so much, and sometimes I don't think I even acted like I liked her."

"OK," he said. "OK. OK. Shit. Tessa and I didn't always, uh … well, we used to be friends. We were close. You know that. And sometimes … well, it wasn't always good. But she knew you loved her. I *know* she loved you, and I *know* she knew you loved her. I'm sure. I'm positive about that, OK?"

He said some other shit, and all of that was totally predictable and trite, too. But that was fine. That was good. Some of it was perfect.

"And hey, maybe we shouldn't rush into this past-tense," he said. "We don't know. There's always a —"

I pulled back and glared at him. I don't know what all was in my face, but it totally and completely shut him up. His eyes shined, and his cheeks were wet. "No, don't do that," I said. "She's gone. It might take 'em a while to find her in that muddy fucking water, or maybe they never will, but she's gone."

Dad nodded. "Yeah, OK," he said. "OK. You're right. I know better. I know how it feels to lose a parent, and how much it sucks to deal with bullshit attempts to pick you up. And my sister's heart is broken, and I won't ever see one of my oldest friends again, and I don't know if I'll ever wrap my head around all that. I kind of hope I won't."

I nodded. I got that.

He smiled weakly and sort of squeezed my good shoulder. "You still want some time to rest?" he asked.

"Yeah, I think I should," I told him. "I'll make sure to come down for dinner or ... whatever."

"Good. OK. I'll be right downstairs."

"I know," I said. "Thanks, uh ... thanks, Dad."

He clenched his jaw, nodded, and left the room. He shut the door behind him.

I flopped back onto the bed — onto *my* bed — and stared up at the sharply angled ceiling. *Just a minute. I just need a minute,* I thought, and I closed my eyes. At first, I just listened to the occasional traffic passing by on the highway in front of the house, and I gazed at the red glow of my eyelids because I hadn't shut off the light.

Then I heard and saw a whole beautiful bunch of nothing.

***

I woke up gasping, totally sure that my left arm weighed a thousand pounds and was crushing my chest. I got off the bed and loosened the strap of the goddamn sling.

I stepped over to the attic window, waited for my heart to quit racing, and looked out at the dark sky. I wondered how long I'd been sleeping. I checked the time on my cell phone: 8:34. So I'd probably missed the official dinner-time, but I wasn't worried. I figured there was bound to be some sort of food in the fridge. Then again, it had been a while since I'd stayed over at my dad's house, and I couldn't really remember how things worked.

I decided to head downstairs and take my chances in the kitchen, but then I looked again at my phone's display and saw I'd missed more than a few calls and messages. A lot of calls *and* texts from my friend Sera, one call from a number I didn't recognize, and four missed calls from Tomlin — from my mom, from my *only mom*. She'd left me voicemails, and both of them were exceedingly apologetic and insanely heartbreaking. She'd failed me, she hated herself because she hadn't been there for me, did I want her to come and pick me up tonight, what were we going to do? I'm tearing up right now as I write this, but nothing happened then. I thought I'd cry, but I didn't. It sort of felt like a blessing.

She'd texted me, too. A lot. I scanned them, opted against calling her back, and just sent her a quick text back. Actually, I sent her a few, like:

> *Mom I love you. You're good. You're as good as you could be.*

and

> *This is nuts. No rules to break.*

and

> *I'm good here for now. Call you tomorrow.*

and

> *Love ya.*

I sighed and slid my phone back into my pants pocket. If I'd had any appetite when I'd woken up, it was totally gone now, so I thought I'd take a little to explore my new digs, temporary though they'd probably be. I was over the clothes, though it still seemed weird that my bed was there. I'd gotten used to him not having an extra bed lying around, and I guess he had to do something, but still: my bed. None of my books or music were there, though. Not my stereo or my records and not even a Bluetooth speaker. We'd need to pick something like that up. But would we? I figured my bed and I would probably go back home, back to my *actual* home, the next day. I was too numb and too drained to know for sure if that would help me, but I thought it might help Mom.

Mom, I remember thinking again. *My* only *mom.*

I didn't know how else we could hope to get back to normal or to whatever new best-worst reality would wind up taking the place of normal. The old Op Ivy song "Knowledge" blasted in my head, and once it hit the chorus, it just repeated that part over and over and over. Which made sense because all I knew at that point was that I didn't know nothin'.

I stared at the carpet. I don't know for how long. Most of it was matted, which I guessed was from the weight of all the boxes over the years. But there was one spot that was a little perkier than the rest. It was roughly a three-foot by three-foot square with little flattened circles at each of its corners. I felt that tickle again at the back of my neck, and this time, it sort of slithered down and danced along my shoulders. I checked out where I was in the room and how far I was from the window. I knew what had made that shape. It wasn't possible, but I *knew* it, and I knew it wasn't a damn box.

I stopped in front of the door to the room that Dad had said was holding boxes. I looked toward the stairs and listened. The TV was on in the living room, but I couldn't hear anything else, which meant no one was coming.

I opened the door.

Yes indeedy, it was a room full of boxes. Not quite hoarder-level, but someone definitely needed a garage sale. There was almost like a path between them, so I made my way through, though I had to remind myself that I only had one functioning arm and would basically be screwed if one of the stacks came tumbling down.

I got to the end of the path and stopped thinking about boxes. Instead, one hundred percent of my attention focused on the ratty tweed recliner that could *not* have been lurking in the far corner of that room. But there it was, surrounded by boxes and quilts and definitely looking back at me. It was impossible. It made zero sense. I was sure I'd never been in the attic before, and I was even *more* sure I'd never been in the room-of-boxes, either. Why would I have been? Kinda starting to freak out, I thought back, and I tried to remember who it was who had come up with the idea of the Attic and especially who had decided on its furniture when we worked out that space. But I didn't know. It had all been such a part of my life for so long. I couldn't remember the last time I'd thought to think about it.

I needed to get out of there, I really did, and I *knew* I did, but then I was sitting in that chair and half-consciously drumming my fingers on its raggedy arms. Every bit of it felt totally familiar, but at the same time, it was completely alien and so. Very. Wrong.

I stood up, but then I caught my foot on the carpet, and I pitched forward and banged into a pillar of boxes. There it was: my nightmare coming true. The top box fell and spilled on the way down. Its load of picture frames clattered to the floor. Frames chipped. Glass broke. Mass hysteria.

The faces of J.C. and the Virgin Mary looked up at me from under the shards of glass. Their halos were glorious; their complexions were European. Beneath those fine examples of Catholic Chic and peeking out between them was a painting of two Hansel-and-Gretel-looking kids crossing a sketchy wooden bridge. A giant angel loomed right behind them.

"Hm. They looked like feathers."

I stumbled back into the chair and picked at a frayed thread on the left arm. I blinked, and I was still in the chair, surrounded by boxes, but the rest of the scenery had changed. No room, no open door, no hallway or muffled TV beyond it. I didn't see what box had opened up there, but I could guess its contents. There'd be a tangled set of earbuds, splinters of whitewashed wood, and maybe even two snowflakes, somehow perfectly preserved. But hey, would that really be the weirdest part of my Attic?

The blinds were up. Through the windows, trees whizzed by at a solid sixty miles per hour.

"Hey." That was my voice, but it was on the other side of the glass. "Did I miss the —"

"Hey, look who decided to wake up," Tessa said.

My breath hitched, and my throat seized up. *Mom*, I thought. I was immediately paralyzed in the chair, both by grief and by the certainty that I was about to lose her again. By the fucking *knowledge*.

The other Mack paused the playlist they'd fallen asleep to and pulled out their earbuds. Mack yawned and stretched, their long arms crossing in front of the Attic windows and then resting on the top of the Nova's empty passenger-side bucket seat. Mack usually opted for the back of whatever car they were riding in. Of course it was a given when both of their moms were in the car, but there'd been so many other times when something like a manuscript or a box of research materials or a new-old typewriter needed to ride shotgun that it had become locked in as a habit.

"Yeah, I'm awake," Mack said. "Did I miss the bridge?"

"Nope, you're just in time," Tessa said. "See? There you go." She slowed down a bit and took a hand off the steering wheel to point at a small road-sign that said KEAGANS CROSSING 3.

"Where's the apostrophe?" Mack asked her.

"*Every* time!" Tessa said. "Do you know what Tomlin would say?"

"Yep: 'Really? That's your takeaway?'" Mack said. Then, shifting to a shitty Brando impression, they added, "'We coulda been a contender! We used to *be* somebody.'"

Tessa cracked up. "Has she heard you do that?" Tessa asked.

"Yeah, I think I tried it the last time we passed through here."

"How'd that work?"

"She wasn't amused."

"Yeah, I'll bet." Then, startling Mack, she said, "Whoa! Did you see that?"

"What?" Mack turned their head, shifting the angle and perfectly setting the Nova's windshield within the frames of the Attic windows. A single snowflake sat on the glass. A second one drifted down to join it, landing just as the first one melted.

Then the second one melted, too.

"Hm. They looked like feathers," Mack said, and then they put their earbuds back in.

I had two good arms up in the Attic, and I used the hands at the ends of them to clutch the recliner.

"Geez. I hope it's not icy," Tessa said.

"Hm." Mack pressed the play button, resuming their Stevie Wonder playlist.

In the Attic, I gritted my teeth.

The car hit the patch of black ice, and everything reeled.

Tessa swore, and I thought, *That's her last word.*

Tessa screamed. No words. Just a scream.

Mack's arm broke against the cooler.

My mom's head hit the glass.

Then something like a light-brown shadow waved on the other side of the windows, like it was caught on a breeze.

In the Attic, I leaned forward. The chair creaked.

Then a muffled *pop*, and the Attic windows were under water.

I tightened my hold on the arms of the chair. The earbuds hanging from the mirror, the running through the woods — I'd already had those pieces. Those chunks. But this was new. The weird shadow, the water ...

Mack flailed, tried to scream, but just made bubbles. I felt them panic, but I didn't remember it. I told myself I didn't want to. *What else will I see?* I thought. *What else is hiding in the spaces between the chunks?*

A hand entered the scene from above, grabbed onto Mack's wrist.

In the Attic, I said, "What the shit?"

Pop.

Mack fell on their ass, splashed into the shallow water at the edge of the creek. They got to their knees, puked water, stood, looked around wildly. For me, it was nauseating, like they whipped a camera around, gave me just glimpses of their feet, the open backpack floating in the water, the papers all around, turning clear, smeared ink still visible on some of them.

A Tom Peterson ballcap calmly rode the ripples of the creek. Mack grabbed it, put it on, then heard something or saw something or *something*. The "camera" quickly tilted up and focused on the Nova peeking through that hole in the bridge, teetering over a thirty-foot drop to the creek below.

"No!" both of us yelled, but the car fell.

Mack looked down as that hand grabbed their wrist again. *Pop*.

Mack gasped, stumbled, and braced against a tree. A tree. They looked down, which showed both of us that they were standing on solid ground. A cushion of needles. Could have been pine or fir, maybe spruce, but neither of us gave a shit. And it was in a clearing somewhere in the woods surrounding Echo Creek. Mack knew that because they could still smell the wreck.

"Mack knows," I mumbled deliriously. "All they know is that they don't know ... All they know is that they don't know nothin'."

Odors. Stenches of automotive fluids and burning ... things. We both tried very hard not to identify those smells. But the breeze kept carrying those smells into the woods, and it reeked in the Attic, too.

Sirens. Distant now but coming closer.

A voice, closer than the sirens: "God, this is so much worse from here."

Mack whirled toward the voice, and the movement almost made both of us puke.

"The *fuck!*" I yelled in the Attic.

At the edge of the clearing, back to us, head pressed to arm, arm pressed to tree. Wearing a long brown coat that would probably have been a whole lot lighter if it wasn't soaked.

"Hey!" Mack said.

The person took a step back, away from the tree, but didn't turn to face us.

Mack said, "Who —"

"I'm sorry. I mean that. I am ... so sorry."

The figure briskly walked into the woods.

Mack lurched forward. "No, wait!" they said. "*Wait!*"

They stopped and leaned against that same tree at the edge of the clearing and looked into the woods. No coat. No person. Just trees.

Mack wailed, but deafening sirens drowned them out.

***

Wailing. No — keening. Is that the right word? Was that what I was doing? My hands hurt. I knew that. My fingers and my knuckles hurt, and they felt hot. Slick.

I blinked at the shards of glass glittering around me on the floor. Some of them were speckled with red, and sprinkled throughout them were torn pieces of something. I picked through the scraps and found the face of the angel.

That terrible sound started up again. Maybe it hadn't even stopped.

A hand closed over the fist I'd evidently made. "Mack, hey. Hey, hey," my dad said as he kneeled down in front of me. He gently but firmly pulled my fist down. "Listen. Hey. Listen to me. Can you hear me? You only have two hands, OK? You only have two hands."

Nathan

I shut off the TV on my way through the living room, tossed the clicker onto my recliner, and continued on through the dining room and into the kitchen. From somewhere behind me, Mackenzie said, "Yeah, so ... you don't need to do this."

"I don't have to do what?" I asked as I got the coffee can and a fresh filter down from the cupboard.

"I don't know. Act like you're not pissed I trashed your box-room."

I ran some water, filling up the coffee maker's tank, and looked out of the window above the kitchen sink. I looked out across the driveway that runs along my house, and at the Ortegas' field, which runs up to their house. Pretty exciting stuff. "What if I'm not pissed?"

"Come on," Mackenzie said.

"They're boxes. The sound startled the shit out of me. I didn't know you'd woken up, and then I heard that noise, and all I knew was that *something* had come crashing down." I scooped the coffee and flipped the switch. I ran out of things I could easily use for distractions, so I leaned back against the counter and looked at the completely overwhelmed teenager standing in the archway that led into the kitchen. Just a kid. *My* kid. I could almost hear the doors creaking open in my head and my heart. That sounds cheesy as shit, but I'm serious. Doors I'd slammed shut and blockaded years before. "I broke plenty of shit when my dad died, and I broke plenty more when I moved in here," I said. "It's like there was a toggle switch that flipped between being totally numb and feeling every fucking thing. If you have the same, it'll flip on its own for a long time. Unpredictably." I shrugged. "At least, that's how it happened with me."

Mackenzie blinked, and then they swallowed and nodded. "Yeah, so far, that's not too far off."

That blink had covered a hesitation, like there was something they'd decided against saying. Maybe they didn't want to say it out loud, or maybe they didn't have the words for it yet. Whatever. I didn't want to push. "Anyway," I said, "it's not too hard for me to handle it differently than my grandpa did. But maybe try to take it easy on the place. A bit. Please."

Mackenzie smiled, adjusted their sling, and walked into the kitchen. "I'll try," they said. "And I'll, uh, I'll clean it up later. I promise."

"Cool. I'll help."

"You don't have to."

"I know. I'll help."

"Really, it's kind of making me sick how cool you're being."

"That could be the Percocet. That shit always makes me feel pukey," I said. "What, would you rather I was yelling at you?"

"I don't know. Kind of. But it's probably good that you're not," Mackenzie said. "How did your grandparents handle it?"

I took a deep breath, wanting to keep it as light as I could, but I only had so much to work with. "Well, that depends," I said. "Grandma drank." I rapped a knuckle against the coffee pot, which was half-full and quite hot. "Not much coffee, though she usually sipped from a coffee mug. That wasn't because of me, though. My shit probably didn't help, but that particular habit wasn't because of me."

"What about your grandpa?"

"Do you remember him?" I asked, remembering one afternoon in particular and thinking, *Shit, I hope not.*

"Yeah, a little. I don't know. Not too much."

I nodded and thought that maybe I *could* keep it light. But then I thought, *How?* "There was some drinking there, too," I said. That's what I settled on — generalities. "And yelling. A lot of yelling. He was big on volume. He had a pretty solid slap when it came to it. Forehand and backhand. Shit, man could've been a tennis player."

"Jesus Christ," Mackenzie said.

"It wasn't all bad. I mean, not every day was bad," I said, and then I shrugged. "But hey — it was a long time ago. I think the coffee's done." My voice had gone low, and somehow, it sounded both far away and too damn close. I turned and opened the cupboard and looked at my informal collection of mismatched mugs. "Did I even ask if you wanted any coffee?"

"Coffee's fine," Mackenzie said. "Yeah, that sounds great."

"You drink coffee?"

"Yeah, at home, we usually drink instant."

"That sounds terrible."

"This might be a treat."

"Maybe. I usually drink it black, but there's some milk in the fridge, and I think I have some sugar in that skinny cupboard by the stove."

"Black's cool. I think I can hack it."

I smiled and took my time filling the cups, wanting to switch the topic but grudgingly accepting that we weren't quite there yet. "I don't know why he was like that — just so bitter and so goddamn mad so much of the time. It'd be easy to blame it on his generation, but, you know, I've met a lot of people that old. That just doesn't explain all of it." I gave Mackenzie one of the mugs and said, "I don't know. He was who he was."

"Still," Mackenzie said.

"Still." And really, that was it. I took a sip of coffee, and then I asked, "Well, do you want to keep standing here, or do you want to watch something?"

"Watching something sounds good," Mackenzie said. "Especially now that I'm wide awake. Yeah. Let's do that."

***

I snorted myself awake in my favorite chair somewhere around 11:30, just as the camera pulled back through the big-ass warehouse at the end of *Raiders of the Lost Ark*. Despite the coffee, I'd evidently slept through about a third of the movie. I narrowed my eyes, looked across the dim living-room, and saw that Mackenzie was all conked-out on the couch. I thought, *Well, maybe it's a wash.* We'd found the movie on TV, but I knew I had the Blu-Ray set around somewhere. We could give it another shot later.

Could we, though? What did that mean? I had no idea how long Mackenzie would be staying. Shit, at that point, I didn't know a whole hell of a lot about anything.

I shut off the TV and turned on the faux-Tiffany lamp that sat on the little table between the recliners. The lamp's twin bulbs were the only lights in the room, and there wasn't a sound besides my and Mackenzie's breathing, but it still seemed like too much. I got up from my chair and went out to the deck.

Light pollution will never be a problem for Westley, but even considering that, it was an exceptionally clear night. All the regular stars were out, and it seemed like there were some extra ones, too. I held onto the deck railing and took a long, deep breath, and then I took another one, and I kept that going for a bit.

I'd just about decided to go back inside when a vehicle crunched its way down my gravel driveway and parked up close to the workshop, right next to my Corolla. It was Angie's red F-150. The woman herself got out of the truck and waved. I waved back and gestured for her to come on up, and she joined me on the deck.

"Hey," she said. "Just getting off of work and passing by. I saw your light on."

"Just the lamp," I said. "You could see that from the road?"

"Maybe." She shrugged. "Or maybe I just thought I'd take my chances that you were up and go tap-tap-tap on that sliding door."

"Well, I'm up," I said. "Thanks for helping last night."

"No problem," Angie said. "And like I said, I could have helped you here."

"I know. I just felt like it needed to be a me-thing."

"I get that. You get it all set up?"

"Mackenzie's room? Yep."

"How'd it go over?"

"Pretty well. Little bit of weirdness. Probably about as well as you could expect."

"That's good. No, that's good. Have you heard anything from your sister? Or about her?"

I sighed. It seemed like I'd been doing a lot of that. "Yeah, I actually got a hold of her, I don't know, right around dinnertime. Mackenzie was upstairs taking a nap, so I took the chance." I shrugged. "She's spending another night up in Seattle with her friend, James. He's a cool guy."

"I think I've met him," Angie said.

"You may have. They've worked together for a long time, and they were friends for a while before that. Anyway, she said she was doing better, but she also said she was doing *really* bad before."

"And ... what does that mean?"

I knocked on the deck railing. "I don't know, but I know," I said. "I'm closing the shop again tomorrow. I'm hoping she gets down here tomorrow afternoon or evening. We'll figure out our next steps from there."

Angie nodded, and then she rubbed her arms and said, "It's cold tonight."

"Hey, it's over forty. Compared to the past few days, it's practically tropical." I idly scratched at the railing for at least a minute. Maybe more. "I'm guessing you haven't, uh ... you haven't found her."

"No, we haven't," Angie said. "It's *really* murky. You know how it can get."

"Yeah," I said, but I thought, *Except when it isn't,* and I pictured a mud-caked skeletal hand displaying a gleaming ring. "How much longer they gonna look?"

"I don't know."

"Yeah, you do, Officer. Educated guess."

Angie said, "They'll look all day tomorrow. I'm sure about that. Maybe Tuesday. But with these conditions, if there's nothing by then ..."

"Yeah, I get it," I said. "You wanna come in? Have a drink?"

Angie smiled, put her arm around my waist, and pressed her head against my shoulder. "Nate, you've had a crazy couple of days."

"I concur."

"It's just ... I don't want to get you confused. There's what you think you want, and there's what you need, and —"

"'And in between are the doors,'" I said.

She patted me on the back. "There you go. That's how you turn a girl on. Interrupt her with some Aldous Huxley."

"Ooh," I said, "you recognized the quote."

"That's what I'm saying. I've known you for a long time. And occasionally, I've known you really well, for about a six-month stretch at a time."

"Hey. There have been a few of those stretches."

"There have." She gave me a little squeeze, and then she pulled away. "I should go. Today's my Friday."

"I know that," I said.

"I just mean, after the last couple of days, I think I'm just going to turn in."

"Well, *I'm* going to have a drink," I said. "Hell, I might even have three. I'm just saying, I have those sweet recliners in the living room, and my bedroom is all the way upstairs. You don't want to drive home, I'll sleep wherever you're not. Your choice."

Angie stopped on the second step down to the lawn and looked back at me. "You'd give up your bed?"

I spread my hands and said, "Hey. It's just the kind of guy I am."

Angie nodded slowly and looked out at her pickup, weighing her choices. "Hijo le," She said, and then she turned back toward me and asked, "So what are we talking about? Do you just have a big jug of Ezra Brooks? Not that I couldn't give that a nice home."

"Actually, it's a fifth of Old Forrester," I said. "I think I even have some Four Roses Small Batch left over from my birthday."

Angie sighed and stepped back onto the deck. "OK, get out of the way," she said.

***

The winter of my junior year, so about a year before Grandpa and I found the bones at the creek, Westley High School set up tours at Oregon colleges for its soon-to-be seniors. They weren't required, but they were highly recommended. Between the trek to the University of Oregon and the overnighter to the Oregon Institute of Technology, they took us to Western Oregon University in Monmouth. It was about the same size as OIT, but it was quite a bit closer and focused more on the Humanities. Cost about the same, too, though the survivor benefit from my dad meant I didn't have to worry too much about that. But I didn't know what I wanted to do. Grandpa's already unstellar health was slipping, and he'd started talking about wanting to make sure Keagan's Collections kept our name on the window. I did not like the idea of having that big of an anchor pinning me down to Westley, but then again, getting set up in a business I already knew sounded kinda sweet. So I didn't know, and the tours weren't helping, but they were field trips, so I went on every one of them.

I'd ditched the WOU tour and was sitting in a steel patio-chair outside the coffee shop at the front corner of the student center, playing a little game of make-believe and trying to see myself as a college student. I can't remember what I'd ordered. It wouldn't have been anything too daring. It was probably whatever had been on the specials board, ordered with totally false confidence. I'd heard of Starbucks by then, but I doubt I'd been inside one.

Let's call it a white mocha. That'll work.

So there I was, sitting all by my lonesome and pretending I belonged there, sipping a white mocha and wondering if I liked it. I checked my watch, saw it said 12:15, and turned my hand over to see what I'd written on my palm. "12:30" was scrawled there in blue ink, underlined three times for shits and giggles. According to the official campus-tour itinerary, that was the beginning of the LUNCH ON YOUR OWN period. We were supposed to load the bus for home by 1:15, so I still had a little window in which to finish doing whatever the hell I was doing.

I drank my coffee. My mocha, maybe. I know I didn't mind it.

"Hey. Are you Nathan?"

My coffee cup hovered at my lips. I looked over the edge of the plastic lid and saw only a Green Day T-shirt, which didn't help much, so I put the cup down and looked up at the face of the college student who had, for some astounding reason, spoken to me. Naturally curly reddish-brown hair fell to the shoulders of that T-shirt, and then there were a couple of dark-brown eyes and an interesting smirk. I didn't object to any of that, but none of it gave me a clue as to what was happening. "Yes, I am Nathan," I said. "Nathan I am."

Her smirk instantly turned into a full grin "OK, awesome. I thought you were you. I've seen pictures of you, and Tomlin said you'd be here today."

"Tomlin."

"Yeah. Your sister."

"I'm aware she's my sister."

"Is this weird?"

"Yeah, a little bit," I said, "but I think I'm liking it." At the very least, I figured I'd have a cool story to tell on the long bus-ride back to Westley.

She laughed and sat across from me. She shrugged off her woven bag and set it against one of the table legs. "I'm Tessa," she said. "Tomlin's a good friend of mine."

"Ah," I said. That was the first time we'd met, but I'd been hearing about her for a couple of years. She came up in conversation every now and again whenever Tomlin and I hung out, so birthdays, holidays, occasional vacations, things like that. Whenever Mom and Tomlin came down to Westley or whenever we made the drive up to Seattle, which wasn't as often.

Anyway. Tessa. "It's cool that I finally get to meet you," she said. "Small world."

"Well, it's no smaller than when you met Tomlin," I said. "I mean, what are the chances that she'd see that presentation?"

"Or that my grandpa served with — "

"With our great-uncle, yeah, I said. It's crazy."

"Yeah, it seems like it, but I know my grandpa wanted to volunteer and share some stories, and there's only so many museums around here, and only one of them has a B-17, so ... yeah."

"I guess that makes the world a little less small," I said. "But still."

"Right," Tessa said.

"So what are *you* doing here today?" I asked. "Is your school here, too?"

"Well, sort of," she said, smirking again. "This is my school. I'm just about halfway through my first year."

Ooh, now I get to be awkward, I thought. *That's cool.* "Oh. Shit," I said. "I'm sorry. I thought Tomlin said you were just a year older than me."

"Yeah, I think I was. Am. I think I am. But I graduated a year early, so ... yeah."

"Ah."

"Actually, when I met Tomlin, I was working on some of the, like, community-service requirements to get that done.

It was cool. I got to hang out with my grandpa and meet a lot of people while I did my research.”

“Research?” I said.

Tessa nodded, and she blushed, and she looked down at her fingernails, and then sheer damn pride broke through all her reluctance and her shyness. She grinned, and her eyes lit up, and the sun even kicked up some of the coppery highlights in her hair. She didn’t have anything to do with that last one, but it happened at the perfect time. “It was for my senior project,” she said. “I, um ... I wrote a book.”

“What? Like, is it about your grandpa’s plane? That’s awesome.” I was truly impressed. I mean, come on.

“Yeah, it builds off of that,” she said. “Thank you.”

“Can I read it?”

Tessa said, “Ha!” and slapped the metal table. “Oh no. There is not a chance. If it ever gets published, and you find it in, like, a bookstore all by yourself, and I don’t know about it, then maybe. Maybe then. I think I’ve read a paragraph to Tomlin, and I let my grandpa read a chapter or two. That’s it. And that was hard.”

I put up my hands, and I hoped to hell I wasn’t blushing. I didn’t know why I would be, but it sure felt like I was. “OK. I got it. Don’t worry about it,” I said. “I —”

“*There* he is! Hey, look! It’s Skipper McDitcherson!”

That time, it wasn’t Tessa that interrupted me but Caleb Geary, holding Angie’s hand as they came up the concrete steps toward the coffee shop’s seating area. I looked at my watch, saw it said 12:33, and muttered, “Dammit.”

Angie broke away from Caleb and said she was going to check out the coffee shop.

Tessa dipped into her bag, took out a pen, and uncapped it.

Caleb clapped me on the back — quite a bit harder than was necessary, but that wasn’t unusual — crouched beside me, and said, “Hey, I think Butler noticed you skipped, but we covered for you. Who’s this?”

Tessa capped the pen and dropped it back into her bag.

"Uh, Caleb," I said, "this is —"

Tessa folded her hands on the table, batted her eyelashes, and said, "Oh, I'm just a lonely college girl looking for hot high-school boys."

A solid five seconds passed with no talking, no movement, no anything from the three of us.

Then Tessa said, in that same ridiculous but definitely effective voice, "Guess I'll keep looking." She slung her bag over her shoulder, stood up, and nudged my coffee cup toward me. "Don't forget your drink," she said.

Caleb watched her leave, and then he took her seat and said, "OK. Dude. What was *that*?"

"I don't know," I said.

"No, I'm serious," Caleb said. "I need to know this. What the hell was that?"

I rotated my empty cup, saw the phone number written on it, and I said it again. "Uh ... yeah. I don't know."

*****

Tomlin and James showed up around 1:30. The most any of us had eaten was a bowl of cereal (Mackenzie), so we worked together to make a sort of big breakfast for lunch. James made a fresh pot of coffee, Mackenzie did a cheesy-egg thing, Angie and I cooked up some sausage and ham, and Tomlin made the hashbrowns, which were fantastic. Mine usually wind up edible, but they're always at least a little gray and soggy. Tomlin has a "technique," as she likes to say, and she loved using one of our grandma's old cast-iron pans. Considering everything, she seemed to be doing alright. I did notice her a couple of times, pulling at the cuffs of her long-sleeved shirt. I tried not to notice anything else.

After breakfast, we all sort of spread out through the living room. James and I wound up in the dueling recliners, Tomlin and Mackenzie took the couch, and Angie set on the flagstone hearth. Above her head, two folded memorial-flags sat on the mantel in their triangular cases. One was my dad's

— Captain Benjamin Thomas Keagan, KIA 1991. The other was my grandpa's — Sergeant James Benjamin Keagan. Of all his ailments, it was kidney failure that finally did him in. He died fifteen years after his son, almost to the day.

My clicker-finger itched. Usually, my ass hit that chair, and the TV went on. That was the routine. But I resisted the urge, the TV stayed off, and I just listened to the conversations flowing through that space instead. And it was nice. At times, even if it was just for a minute or two, I actually managed to forget why we were all there.

At some point, I brought down the footrest, got up out of my chair, and went upstairs to take a leak. I don't know why I didn't use the downstairs bathroom. Someone could have been using that one, or maybe I didn't want any of my company listening to my stream.

Whatever the case, I went upstairs, and I did what people tend to do in bathrooms, and then I wound up standing outside the box room, looking down at and into the stuffed paper bag sitting outside the door. Books. It was full of books. Angie, Mackenzie, and I had done a quick clean-up that morning. For some reason, the contents of that bag hadn't found their way either back into boxes or into the trash. I took a knee and picked through the books, and I saw that most of them were Bibles. I recognized the well-read Revised Standard Version - Catholic Edition. That one was Grandma's. The Hebrew-English TANAKH from the Jewish Publication Society threw me. The TANAKH and every one of the Christian Bibles were marked with Post-Its, business cards, scraps of paper, even a shoelace in one case. One of the Bibles was only marked in a single spot, and I took that one out of the bag.

The stairs creaked, and I looked over my shoulder to see James stepping into the hall. "Hey," I said.

"Well, hey," James said back, and then he stopped and looked at the wall with all the pictures. "Well. Now, that is a shitload of photographs."

"Yeah, it is." I opened the Bible to its single marked page, which was near the beginning. Only one verse was highlighted.

"Have I interrupted you at a moment of prayer or contemplation?" James asked.

"No. This is just weird." I went to a couple of the other Bibles and the Jewish book and flipped through them. They all shared a mark in common — Genesis 6:4. "The Nephilim were on the earth in those days ... These were the heroes of old and the men of renown." Just like *Star Trek* eventually changed "where no man has gone before" to "where no *one,*" Tessa had changed the "men of renown" to the "Righteous Ones." That's how I knew it. I knew it as *her* verse, and I said so as I handed one of the Bibles to James.

"Your sister uses it, too," he said.

"Yeah, I know, but she got it from Tessa, right?" I asked.

James shrugged and gave me the book back. "Maybe someone was just a good *Chrustian.*"

I smiled, recognizing the pronunciation from a Flannery O'Connor story, and returned the book to the paper bag. "Well, Grandma was," I said. "I know at least one of these is hers. But why that verse? I mean, out of all of them?"

James glanced toward the stairs, and then he looked back at the wall and said, "Yeah, it's a little strange, but you know it's not the biggest thing we should be worried about." He moved closer to me, dropped his voice, and asked, "Be truthful with me, now. You think you can make this work?"

"With Tomlin? I'm ... not sure," I said, matching his volume. "But what's the choice?"

"Your sister is going to need some help. Probably Mack, too. But just talking about Tomlin, I've seen her bad before, but this was *bad.*"

"Well, James, that's probably because this is pretty fucking bad," I said.

"Come on. Don't do that," he said. "Right now, no one in this world cares for Tomlin or for Mack more than we do.

But last night was touch-and-go, man. She can *not* go back to that house yet. She can't be around anything that's Tessa's."

"Come on."

"Hey, I'm just telling you, man — I was with *all* of that last night."

I took a deep breath and nodded, suddenly feeling very, very tired. I couldn't help thinking, *I want to go home.* I knew where I was. I thought it again. "Yeah, we talked a little as we were making breakfast," I said. "She's putting on a brave face, but I know that's what it is." I actually knew more than that. Tomlin was my sister. Standing next to her at the stove, I could feel the wires sparking and storms howling under her mask. But James was her best friend, not mine. "She and Mackenzie are both welcome to stay here as long as they need to."

"Do they know that?"

I took another breath and nodded. James's heart was in the right place, but his nose was pushing a little further than it needed to. On the other hand, I knew that little quirk of his had helped my sister more than once. Maybe saved her. "Yeah, we hit on that, too," I said. "She said she'd be fine with an air mattress in my office, but I really don't want to lose my office." I put my hands up before James could verbally express how disgusted he was by that statement. His face said enough. "Not how I meant that. The box room, that extra room over there would work out better. It would work out great. And it would put her that much closer to Mackenzie." I pointed at the weird little door to the somewhat-converted attic. "Mackenzie," I said, and then I pointed at the box room. "Tomlin."

James pointed at the remaining bedroom door. "And that's you?"

"Yep," I said. "That's me. And the shitter's right between us."

"Well, that counts for something," James said. "OK. And you have my number, right?"

"I do," I said.

James brought his hands together. "Good. Sorry if I'm — "

"No worries. It's coming from a good place."

"It is," James said. "Thank you. Now, if you'll excuse me, I came up here to do something that wasn't this, and you are neglecting your guests."

"Fair enough," I said. James went into the bathroom, and I went back downstairs to deal with those who populated my changed and changing household.

***

I woke up in my recliner again, which wasn't unusual, but then I heard Mackenzie and/or Tomlin moving around upstairs. That was still very new.

I went into the kitchen, got a bottle and glass, and kept going. Physically, I was plenty alone out on the deck, but it wasn't quite there. I needed more. Or less. I crossed the back lawn, stepped onto the gravel, and unlocked the door of the larger of the two outbuildings I have at the back end of the property. I still thought of it as Grandpa's workshop, and I probably always will, even though it's just used for storage. Long-term, too. The smaller outbuilding is really just a shed, and that's where I keep the lawn mower and yard tools and other shit I need to get to with some regularity.

The workshop wasn't just for my stuff. Plenty of Grandpa's was still there, too. Table saws and sanders, a big metal Craftsman toolbox, drills and shit in plastic cases, those were all more-or-less arranged up against one wall. Then boxes, and more boxes, and Rubbermaid totes, and even more boxes, and in the back-right corner, a careless assortment of tarps that hinted at the edged-and-angled heap slouching underneath them.

There were two other items of note in there, and they both dated from Grandpa's era, too: Grandpa's much-dented steel desk and his creaking wheely-chair. They sat in a relatively open space just to the right of the door. The workshop's only window, and it was a small one, was behind the chair.

I flipped on the interior lights, pulled the door shut, and dropped into that horrendously creaky chair. I put the whiskey bottle and glass on the desk. The desk had officially been mine, I guess, for about a decade and a half, and it had been Grandpa's for decades before that, so that was absolutely not the first time a liquor bottle had sat on the surface of the desk. I narrowed my eyes, rotated the bottle for a better look at the label, and saw that I'd grabbed some rye instead of bourbon. *Well, whoops,* I thought, but that was followed very shortly after by *It'll do.*

I poured a drink, and I drank. And I winced. It was the type of booze that Grandpa would have called a "mixer" rather than a "sipper." I consulted the label again and wondered if it could still have been one of his. I couldn't remember ever buying rye. I twisted off the cap and filled the glass to the halfway point.

It got easier.

I leaned back in the incredibly noisy chair, blinked, drank, blinked and drank some more, and then I saw the same desk in the same workshop, though it looked like an actual, gen-u-wine workshop now, the toolbox and all the saws and shit arranged differently. Scrap iron and PVC and plexiglass and who knows what else had been leaned and piled and shoved in the back corner.

And there was me. Freshly eighteen, sitting at the desk with a mechanical pencil in my hand and a spiral-bound notebook and a physics textbook in front of me. And a bottle of Dr. Pepper to drink. The booze would have been inside the house on the dining-room table, and it would have been surrounded by my grandma and grandpa and a half-dozen or so of their increasingly intoxicated friends. Hence my self-exile to the workshop. It was just better out there.

A little cassette-player/radio combo sat on the windowsill, plugged into the outlet below it. I had the radio tuned to 94.7, but I would be sure to turn it back to country before I left.

The DJ announced a station break. The first commercial was for Tom Peterson's (and Gloria's Too!).

There was a knock at the door, and I tensed, but then I realized that neither Grandpa or Grandma or even any of their friends would have bothered to knock. I wheeled the squealing chair over to the door and opened it.

Tessa stood outside, her head lowered so that much of her hair fell over the front of her T-shirt. It was a Rocket From the Crypt concert-shit this time. Her left hand clutched the strap of her woven bag, pinning it to her shoulder. Her right hand, probably the one she'd knocked with, clenched and flexed, clenched and flexed. "Hey. Good," she said. "I hoped I wouldn't have to deal with the house."

"Yeah, I hope that about every day," I said. "What's going on?"

"Is Tomlin still here?" She still hadn't looked up. I still hadn't seen her eyes.

"No," I said. "No, she was, but she's gone. She unloaded a bunch of mysterious shit —" I pointed a thumb at the scraps in the corner. "— probably about an hour ago, and then she left."

Tessa nodded. Little nods. Rapid ones. And she kept clenching and flexing that hand.

"Come on," I said. "Come in."

I stepped aside, and she came into the workshop. I shut the door, let her have the chair, and I sat on the edge of the desk. She stopped nodding, and her hand stopped doing its clenching thing, but neither of us said anything. I didn't know what to say. I still didn't really know her. We'd talked on the phone, but I'd only seen her a couple of times in the year or so since we'd met at WOU.

Eventually, I went with the brilliant and incisive, "Is ... something wrong?"

She nodded again, just as fast as before, but it didn't last as long. She pushed her hand through her long, curly hair, and when it got to the back of her head, she finally looked up at me. I was instantly so sure of what she was about to say that I heard a sort of out-of-sync echo in my head when she said it.

"My grandpa died. He dozed off in his chair right after lunch, and he just went away."

"Oh, Tessa. I'm sorry." I knew I should say something else, but I just repeated myself. "I'm sorry."

She waved me off, shook her head, and raked her fingers through her hair again. She looked off toward the corner, sort of gazing in the vague direction of Tomlin's scrap collection, and she said, "You know, he survived something he shouldn't have fifty years ago, and he smoked — he smoked a lot — and he liked to drink, and he ate whatever the hell he wanted."

"I've heard worse eulogies," I said.

She laughed hoarsely but smiled warmly. I can still see and hear of all that. I can feel it. "He almost made it to eighty, and he hasn't spent a night in a hospital for three years." She shrugged. "This is the best it could be."

It was my turn to nod. Another silence stretched between us, but it didn't feel wrong. I'm not saying it felt right, but it didn't feel wrong.

Then I said, "Do you ... um. Do you want a hug or something?"

"Not usually," Tessa said. "But yeah, I think that would feel good right now."

She stood, I slid off the desk, and we hugged. Eventually. First, we very clumsily negotiated the arrangement of the arms. But that awkwardness eased a lot of the tension. We settled on her arms high, my arms low.

And we just stood there. Hugging.

On the radio, they went to another commercial break. I'd missed the entire music block. The DJ came back on and played "Novocaine for the Soul" by Eels. Tessa swayed, brought her arms up higher, and laced her fingers behind my neck. I dropped my hands to her hips and moved with the music. Moved with her.

Then she kissed me. It wasn't my first, but it's still my favorite. I said, "Are you —"

"Shh," she said.

I remember hearing something by STP and "Follow You Down" by Gin Blossoms, and then the music wasn't important anymore.

Later, I stood in the doorway of Grandpa's workshop, watching Tessa's primer-gray '68 Nova sputter down the driveway. It needed work, but it was getting there. Five other vehicles still remained parked behind the house: my car, Grandma's car, Grandpa's truck, and Doug and Anna Allman's Oldsmobile.

I went back into the workshop, and I saw something new on the desk. Right there, just to the left of my physics book, was a stack of twenty or so printed pages that must have been hiding inside Tessa's bag. I figured she'd originally intended to give them to Tomlin, but she had clearly left them for me, and I was OK with that.

I pushed my notebook and textbook aside and sat down to read what turned out to be the first draft of the first chapter of *Fenton's Runaways*, Tessa's second book. She still hadn't let me read a word of the first, so that was my intro to the world she was creating — to the Prometheus Project, to the Righteous Ones. And to Sgt. Jack Beacham, who was clearly based on Tom Keagan, my grandpa's favorite and forever-mourned brother. My face ached. I gingerly touched my cheek and discovered I was grinning. That I'd been grinning. I didn't stop grinning.

I still remember how that chapter originally ended, word-for-word:

Sgt. Jack Beacham tightened the belt of his overcoat, turned his back to the airfield, and strode toward the setting sun.

He "strode." I love that word. "Strode."

Twenty-two years later, I banged my knees against the metal desk, stumbled to my feet either like a newborn fawn or a drunk middle-aged man, and managed not only to get around the desk but also to plod through the workshop and stand in front of the tarp-covered pile in the corner.

I looked down. The bottle of rye dangled from my hand. *Neat,* I thought. Even through the fog, I could see it was a bad idea, but I took a drink straight from the bottle. Then I did it again.

Fragments, half-seen and half-heard through the booze and fatigue.

"Ninety-four seven, KNRK. Your alternative-rock station."

Tessa's fingers, coming together behind my neck.

Angie, smiling, nudging her empty glass toward me for a refill.

"It's Tessa. We need to, uh … we need to talk."

A ring on a skeleton's finger.

"Tessa and I didn't always, uh … talk."

Grandpa: "Well, so's a crucifix, and we have enough of those hanging up on our walls, too."

Mackenzie: "Yeah, you know, a sleeping bag would have worked."

I sniffed, and I sighed, and I set the nearly empty whiskey bottle on the desk. I must have put it down a little too hard. It wobbled for a bit, but then it stopped. It was fine.

I curled up on the workshop's dusty floor, and I shut my eyes.

"Author presumed dead in Echo Creek crash" by Cole Stevens, from The Westley *Monitor*, Feb. 12, 2019

Search and rescue efforts for Theresa Hatcher, 40, of Batchley were officially halted on Monday night.

At approximately 4:00 p.m. Saturday, Hatcher's 1968 Chevrolet Nova apparently broke through the wooden sidewall and damaged a structural support beam on the north side of Keagans Crossing before plunging into Echo Creek.

Authorities have not officially determined the cause of the accident but say that icy conditions on the bridge may have been a factor.

According to Chief Greg Murdock of the Westley Police Department, "The water level's real high, probably higher than it's been outside the big floods of '96 and the '70s and '60s."

Murdock added that cold temperatures and cloudy water hampered search efforts from the start.

Hatcher first gained fame in 1999 as the author of the science-fiction novel *A Woman Called Kidd*. The book has since become a staple of many high school and college reading lists.

Hatcher wrote several additional novels, most in the science-fiction genre, including two follow-ups to *A Woman Called Kidd*: *Fenton's Runaways*, published in 2004, and *Turning Paige*, published in 2009.

According to sources, Hatcher was writing a fourth book in the series, to be titled *Beachams Bridge*, at the time of her death.

In 2016, Hatcher married Tomlin Keagan, the sister of Nathan Keagan, Westley resident and owner of Keagan's Collections.

Hatcher and Keagan's child, Mackenzie, 18, was a passenger in the car at the time of the crash and was transported to Salem General Hospital to be treated for a broken arm, numerous contusions and lacerations, and to be observed for potential further injuries, such as a possible concussion.

Keagans Crossing is currently closed as it undergoes structural repairs.

Tomlin

We just dragged the air mattress into the attic that first night. I doubt I got two hours of sleep, and that's in total. Definitely no dreaming and only the worst kind of drifting. I spent most of the night doing one of two things. One of them was looking up at the weird, pointy ceiling and trying not to be freaked out by the shadows pooling up there. The other thing, which usually happened when the shadows *did* freak me out, just involved sitting up on the mattress, arranging the fleece blanket over my legs, and watching Mack sleep. Even when they were asleep, Mack was a bright spot, pushing away the shadows. It's always been like that. But without the shadows distracting me, certain needling mental voices grabbed more of my attention.

Hello there. What, exactly, are you doing?

I'm watching my kid sleep. What does it look like I'm doing?

Your kid. Hm. Are they, though?

Yep. There it was. That voice had basically been gone for years. At worst, it had been an occasional nagging whisper I could ignore, but as soon as Nate called and told me there'd been an accident, it stuck its head out of its damn hole and yelled at me. It went right back into hiding because it's a cowardly little shit, but it's an opportunistic little shit, too, and it rode like an echo on every triggering thought about everything in that house and in that room that wasn't mine. Hell, most of it was Mack's or Nate's. I'd kept on my long-sleeved shirt, but that was my brother's air mattress and his pillow and his blanket. I still thought of the house as Grandma and Grandpa Keagan's, but that was Nate's, too, wasn't it? It sure wasn't mine. And Mack's surprisingly functional bedroom in the attic, which Nate had put together when I'd failed to even show up. When I'd failed. Dammit.

And Mack. Even Mack. *Especially* Mack. My wife's kid — definitely. My brother's, too. But mine?

Are they, though?

Mack and I had been a part of each other's lives almost since they'd been born, and constant fixtures since they were about two. I truly couldn't imagine those years without them. I still can't. But there had always been times when I knew I was just a stepmother. A poseur. An impostor.

The only window in that attic room was on the south side. It lightened with the dawn, but it took a while longer for the sun to really get around the corner from the east. And when it did, I was still sitting on that borrowed air-mattress with a borrowed blanket in a borrowed room in a borrowed house. I knew I should have felt at least some contentment. Some peace. Me and Mack and Nate and maybe even James and Angie, those of us who were left, we were together, and we were safe, but it wasn't because of anything I'd done. None of it. Nothing. Not a damn thing.

"Shit. Mom. You're awake."

I swallowed, I blinked, and I rubbed my eyes, and I said, "Yeah. I've been awake."

"Are you OK?"

"Nope," I said. "I'm not even close."

"Yeah. Neither am I."

We traded sad smiles, and then I stood up. "I'm going to get dressed and get some breakfast, and then I want to ... I don't know. I want to go somewhere."

Mack rubbed their shoulder and did something with the straps of their sling. "Where?"

"I don't know. Out," I said. "I just need to be somewhere else. I need to breathe."

Mack lightly chewed their bottom lip, and then they said, "Can I come with you?"

"Please," I said.

***

Nate was already gone, probably to open up his shop for the first time in a couple of days. I felt bad about that, but I was glad I didn't have to face him that morning — mainly because I felt bad about that. Luckily, we weren't stranded. I'd driven my own car back down from Seattle with James following me in his own to make sure I made it in one piece and at a reasonable rate of speed. Three-and-a-half hours with his car in my rearview mirror, constantly reminding me of a curated collection of my failings. But hey. I was there, my car was right outside, and Mack and I could *go*. I didn't know where, but we could go, so we went.

I planned as far as Burwell, which means the ten-mile trip to a McDonald's drive-thru and then a stop at Wal-Mart, which was basically around the corner. I bought some cheap-ass clothes, just enough to get me through the next couple of days. I knew I could wash them if we wound up staying at Nate's longer than that, but I didn't want to *know* we'd be staying longer than that. Mack, of course, was wearing some of the clothes that had been brought over from our house. That day, they'd gone for plaid slacks and a baggy striped sweatshirt. They'd considered their Tom Peterson baseball-cap but had wound up leaving that at the house. Not our house. Nate's house. Nate's home.

Mack stood guard as I changed in my car in the Wal-Mart parking lot. They leaned against the fender and finished their McMuffin and coffee — black. That surprised me. They usually dropped a couple of creamer-cups into it.

After that, we drove across Burwell, turned right onto the highway, and headed in the general direction of Salem. If we kept going a little past Salem, we'd be heading in the direction of Batchley, too, but I think we both knew that wasn't happening. Maybe in a day or two. Maybe. But not yet.

Just before we entered Salem, Mack looked up from their cell phone and nodded at the 45th Parallel sign jutting up from the side of the road. It said:

45TH PARALLEL
HALF WAY BETWEEN
THE EQUATOR AND
NORTH POLE

That was one of *our* signs — a family landmark. Mack said, "That's one of the last things I really remember from the other day. The one from the other side of the road, 'cause we were coming that way, but ... yeah. Then I don't know if I fell asleep or just kind of zoned out, but basically, the next thing was the bridge." They nodded again and looked back down at their phone. "I don't know. Anyway."

"Tessa always had to say something about that," I said, and I felt myself smiling. No, not really. It felt like someone else smiling.

Mack shrugged and scrolled through something on their phone. "It's a cool sign."

I tugged at one of the long sleeves of my brand-spanking-new sweatshirt. The elastic was a little too snug there. It squeezed and pulled at the gauze, making my wrists throb. "Who are you textin'?" I asked.

"No one now," Mack said. "I'm actually just looking at random shit on Instagram."

"Oh. I thought you'd be talking with your friends."

"I'm not now," Mack said again. "I texted Sera a little earlier, but I think she had her phone taken."

"Someone took her phone?"

"Yeah, probably Mr. Lewis. That's who she has at that time."

Mr. Lewis. A teacher. "Oh. Because she's in school," I said.

I turned onto Lancaster. I don't know why. I avoid Lancaster whenever I can, and I didn't have anywhere particular in mind to go, so I don't know why I went there. At the first of what always feels like a hundred stoplights, I asked, "When do you think you'll go back to school?"

Mack set their phone in one of the cup-holders, looked out the window, and shrugged. "I don't know," they said.

"Well, I guess you don't have to decide it now."

"Yeah, but I've thought about it," Mack said. "I mean, I don't even really *have* to go back."

Green light. Go. "What?"

"I have all my required credits," Mack said. "I'm just taking electives now. They'd probably be able to give me partial credit and just end it here, but even if they didn't, it's not like I wouldn't graduate."

Red. "But wouldn't that mess up your GPA?"

Mack shrugged again and kept looking out the window. I tried to remember the last time they'd looked at me. "Yeah, a little. But if I started at MPCC or somewhere, it's not like it would matter. And when I transferred to a four-year, they'd just look at the community-college grades."

"Is that something you want to do?"

Shrug. "I don't know.

Green. "Mack," I said, "Is that something you want to do?"

Mack rubbed their good hand on a leg of their plaid pants, scratched the back of their neck where the strap of the sling was rubbing, and then looked at me. Finally looked at me. Tears shimmered in their hazel eyes. I hate myself for saying this, but I wished they'd look away. "I hate quitting. I hate quitting anything," they said. "I don't want any of those jocks or cowboys or just basic bitches and assholes to feel like they won. But I hate that place. I used to be able to hold onto little bright spots and just power through it. And it actually seemed like it was worth it."

Yellow light coming up. I was the fourth car from the stop line. *Shit.* But there was a strip-mall parking lot right next to me — one of its entrances was *right* there. I pulled in, parked, and looked right at Mack. They sniffed, wiped their eyes, and looked past me, at the Ross Dress for Less and the big vacant storefront that used to be a Borders. "It is worth it. It's still worth it," I said. My voice cracked, but I was thrilled — God, I was thrilled — by the confidence and the certainty I heard there. Talking to both of us, I said, "Hold onto the bright spots. Yes. That's right. I think I told you that, right? No matter how small they are or —"

"Oh, just fuck off," Mack said. "I know there are still bright spots, OK? There's still you and my dad and unicorns and rainbows and whatever other bullshit. But one of my biggest 'bright spots' is fucking gone, OK, so now it's dark as fucking shit!"

My heart broke again, and my hands, my face, everything went cold. I saw it all right there — all of my anger, my anxieties, my sadness, my darkness, *everything*. All of it was piled up *right* there in the passenger seat. I didn't have a single doubt: Mackenzie Keagan Hatcher was absolutely, positively, 100-percent my kid.

We talked, and we yelled, and we cried, and we hugged, and then we did all of that again but in a different order. And again. And that's all you're getting. Some things aren't meant for ink and paper.

At some point during the post-breakdown/breakthrough, still-sitting-in-the-parking-lot period, someone's phone buzzed. Mack and I both looked down at their phone in the cupholder, and I asked, "Oh, is that Sera? I wonder if she got her phone back."

"No, they usually keep them at the office until the end of the day," Mack said. Then there was another buzz, and their phone remained rattle-free. "Actually, that's yours," they said.

I unbuckled my seatbelt and pulled my purse up from the floor behind my seat. I fished my cell phone out of the depths not long before the call would have gone to voicemail, but then I saw who it was, and I almost let it go anyway. But I was a good girl, and I sighed, and I accepted the call, and I said, "Hi, Mom."

Evidently, my need to get out of the house that wasn't my house had ruined my mom's surprise. She'd driven all the way down from Washington to take me, Mack, and maybe even Nate out to lunch, but no one was home. I cracked pretty easily and told her where we were, and then we agreed to meet up in the food court of what I'll always think of as Lancaster Mall. I don't care how many times it changes its name.

Mack and I got there first, of course, and we waited a reasonable amount of time, but we're both wired the same way: we can only be surrounded by the delicious smells of shitty food for so long before we need to eat some shitty food. I bought each of us an Orange Julius and an Auntie Anne's pretzel, which was a tradition, but I don't know if they knew why. A pretzel and a Julius was always my dad's go-to treat. When he was killed in Desert Storm, I was barely ten, and it felt like every day, I had fewer memories of him. I held onto what I could. The little things were big.

"You just couldn't wait." Mom sat at our table with her purse on her lap. "I said I was going to buy you lunch."

"This isn't lunch," I said with a bite squirrelled into my cheek.

"Then what do you call that?"

"I call it a pretzel," I said. "That's what lots of people call it."

"I actually don't think I'm hungry for lunch, Nana," Mack said. "I'm still kinda full from breakfast."

"Then why are you eating that?" Mom asked.

"Because it's a pretzel," Mack said.

"Would you like a pretzel, Mom?" I asked.

"No, thank you," she said.

"Are you sure? I can pay for it," I said.

"I'm sure. I'm fine," she said.

"Have you ever had one of these things, Nana?" Mack asked. "I think it's called a 'pretzel.'"

Mom sighed and said, "Two peas in a pod." She said it quietly enough that she may have been talking to herself, but Mack and I both heard it, and it was the perfect time for us to hear something like that. We laughed, and Mom managed to smile. "Well, I guess there are worse things to be talking about," she said. Then, to Mack: "How's your arm, sweetheart?"

"Well, I mean, it's OK for what it is," Mack said. "I guess I'll be able to look at it in two weeks."

"Is that when they take the cast off?"

"Well, it's when they take *this* cast off, and I can say good-bye to this stupid sling, but then I'll get this, like, vinyl thing that I can take on and off. And I guess I'll start PT."

"How's the pain? Does it hurt?"

"More like an ache, but I'm handling it. I don't even think I took a pill this morning."

"Oh. It's only been three days."

Mack checked the time on their phone and said, "Yeah, actually. Almost exactly."

"Well, that's great, honey. You need to be careful. But you should take them if you need to. That's what they're for."

"That's what I told them, too," I said.

Mom lightly cleared her throat. She didn't openly comment on Mackenzie's pronouns anymore, at least not to us, but she still acted like they physically impacted her. Whatever. She'd suffered through a similar process in the '90s: first I came out, then her favorite comedian, Ellen DeGeneres did. Mom had been through a lot.

She turned to look at me — which meant she looked away from Mack, but maybe I'm reading too much into that — and she took a hand from her purse so she could put it on my arm. "And how are *you* holding up?" she asked.

I shrugged and stared down at the plastic lid of my Julius cup.

"How long do you think you'll stay here, at ... Nathan's house?"

"I don't know, Mom."

"You know my door is open, too," she said.

"Yep," I said, still gazing at the lid and now also slowly, slowly rotating the cup. "But that would take us even further from where we should be."

"Do you mean your house?"

"I mean our home."

"Hm," Mom said. "And what are you doing about school?"

I stopped turning the cup. Dammit. She'd sprung a trap.

Mack said, "Actually, I —"

"We're looking at online options," I said, looking at Mom because I was actually strong enough to do that. But I couldn't look at my kid. "Mack's really, really close and may just have to, uh … well, they might just have to write a couple of papers, and that would be all of it."

Mom raised her eyebrows and looked at Mack, but she still didn't take her damn hand off of my damn arm.

"Yeah," Mack said, and then, without a hint of irony: "My school's awesome."

"Well, I guess it's not something we need to decide today," Mom said, and she *finally* sat back and let me go. "We," though. That bugged the shit out of me.

"You sure you don't want a pretzel, Nana?" Mack asked.

I've always loved that kid, but dammit, at that moment, I *really* loved that kid.

"Yes, I'm sure, Mackenzie," my mom said. "Whenever you two are done, though, I have some things for you in my trunk. I spotted your car in the parking lot, and I parked as close as I could."

"Are you in a hurry?" I asked, and I tossed a quick glance to Mack that I hoped Mom didn't catch, too.

"Oh, I'm not in too much of a rush," Mom said, and then she shrugged. "I mean, I was planning on having lunch."

"Cool," Mack said. "We're almost done." And then they tore a piece off of their pretzel, chewed it slower than anyone has chewed anything in the history of chewing, and said, "Mm. This is really good."

Yep. Love.

***

The things in my mom's trunk — I refuse to call them "junk" even though the joke is right there — turned out to be a big ol' box of stuff left over from one of my and Tessa's moves. Or maybe more than one. We moved a lot in the early years, and the new places weren't always bigger places. There were also the three weeks or so the three of us had spent at Mom's during our last move, when we were waiting to get into our last house.

Last house, I thought. That meant a couple of things.

I moved the box into my own trunk, and then, with the trunk lid still open, I turned and hugged my mom good-bye. She said something about eating right, and then she said something else about open doors, and I just nodded and told her again that I knew. Mack hugged her, too — with one arm — and then we both waved like idiots as Mom drove out of the parking lot.

I went to shut the trunk, but Mack said, "No, wait. I kinda want to see what's in here."

I'd been too busy thinking about both everything and nothing at all to consider that, but I said "Oh. OK," and I let go of the trunk lid and pulled open the flaps of the box.

Honestly, I wasn't that impressed. I didn't see any secret or forgotten treasures. There were some graphic novels, some not-graphic novels, a scrapbook, several picture frames — two of them were even empty — a couple of old cameras, and what just looked like some miscellaneous ... oh, I don't know. Shit. Stuff. Things. Just things. "I have some things for you in my trunk" — that's what she said. Evidently, she'd been telling the truth.

"Well," I said, "what do you think?"

"I want to look at that scrapbook at home," Mack said. "I mean, uh ... at Dad's house."

126

I said, "I know what you mean," but I wondered if I did.

"Those cameras look pretty cool."

"Yeah," I said, picking the weirdest one up. For its size, it was heavy, and it was either made out of really shitty metal or kinda-decent plastic. Most of the body was black, but it had a silver top and a silver lens. That much was pretty typical, at least for an old film-camera. But the lens was odd. Knobby. Bulky. And there was this weird gear-thing at the front of the lens, and some kind of mechanism or something going from the lens to the body, and there were three little windows on the body — but only on the front. It looked like only two of them went all the way to the back, and they were tiny back there. "How could you even look through this thing?" I wondered, and then I turned it back to the front again. "Ooh, 'Anastigmat Special,'" I said, reading the words around the lens. "And 'Special' is *red!*"

"What does that mean?" Mack asked.

"Oh, I don't know what any of this means," I said, but then I tapped what I guessed was the make and model, stamped on the front of the camera's body. "OK. 'Kodak 35.' So it's a Kodak camera, and it's got to be a thirty-five millimeter. I can figure that much out." I put the camera back in the box and asked, "Are you done with this now?"

"Yeah, sure," Mack said.

I shut the trunk, and we walked around to our respective sides of the car. "You know the old SLR that I've used for my film-stuff," I said.

"Yeah, of course I do."

"Well, I can tell you all about those. But Tessa and Nate were the ones who were always into things that were weird and old."

"Well, like her typewriters," Mack said as they opened their car door.

"Yeah, and evidently, cameras." I got in, started the car, and said, "We should take it to Nate and see what he has to say."

"At the ... shop?"

"Well, that's where he'll be," I said, and I started backing the car out. But then I felt Mack's silence. I mean, our conversation was probably over, but it was something more than that. I pulled back into the space, shifted the car back into Park, and asked, "Mack? What is it?"

No tears this time, but there was something worse in their voice: "We were going there when we got in our wreck. That was going to be our next stop."

"Shit," I said.

Staring forward, Mack sort of flapped their good hand. "No, it's fine."

"Mack ..."

"It's good."

"We can just show it to him at the house." I couldn't call it "home." I wouldn't let myself.

Mack took a deep breath and faced me. "Please. Let's go. I want to."

"OK," I said, and I don't know if it was the sorrow or determination in their eyes, but I said, "OK" again.

We went.

***

I couldn't tell you the last time I'd been into Keagan's Collections, either. Part of that is because all the times sort of run into each other. That shop was part of the family before I was, and the nature of the merchandise means that nothing significantly changes, at least not at a glance.

Nate had two customers at the counter when Mack and I brought the box in. Another one came through the door just as we set the box on the counter. I didn't comment on the bottle of Gatorade on the counter, or on what I knew was Alka-Seltzer residue scumming up the bottle.

As my brother dealt with the customers, Mack wandered off to dig through the record crates, and I took the chance to keep standing right there and just sort of scope out the place.

128

It wasn't like it was night-and-day, but there were definitely differences.

First, near the area that had pulled Mack in, several cassette decks helped populate what I guess was the electronics section. There may have even been a CD player over there. When Grandpa ran the place, those things would either have been new or just not old enough to be called vintage. He picked up a lot of his stuff from garage sales, flea markets, and thrift stores, but he never wanted to look like he was running any one of those. He was an interesting guy. I'll say that.

Right on the counter, right by the box from my mom, there was a touchscreen credit-card thing. That definitely wasn't from Grandpa's era. That guy had been so baffled by universal remote-controls that he'd rubber-banded his VCR and TV remotes back-to-back and labeled them with Wite-Out: VHS and TOOB.

Finally, only we Keagans were left in the shop, and we all gathered around that glass counter. Mack stood by me, and Nate stood on the other side, drinking his augmented Gatorade and almost looking like a grown-up businessman. "OK. You said Mom gave you this?" he asked, opening the box.

"Yeah," I said. "A lot of it's just miscellaneous-whatever, but there's at least one —"

He pulled the weird Kodak camera out of the box by its leather strap.

"Yep. You found it," I said.

"I thought it looked cool," Mack said. "Do you know what it is?"

"I do," Nate said. He set the camera on the counter, and he took a step back, but he didn't take his eyes off of the thing. "It is a Kodak 35."

"Well, I figured that part out," I said.

"More accurately, it's a 35 RF."

"OK. I didn't know that."

"What's that weird thing on the side of the lens?" Mack asked.

"That is part of the rangefinder mechanism," Nate said. "That's what the 'RF' means: rangefinder. That's also why there are three of these windows in the front and only two in the back. Two of the front ones work with mirrors and this focusing wheel—" He tapped the weird gear-thing at the front of the lens, on the other side from what was evidently called the rangefinder mechanism. " — to focus. And then, another interesting thing —"

Ting ting.

I looked toward the door, and I was immediately glad I was standing that close to the counter. If I hadn't been leaning against it, I'm sure I would have fallen right down to that old hardwood floor. I tried to talk, but I couldn't, but what would I have said?

I looked at Mack for help, for something, but they looked like I felt, and that scared me more than anything. It also got me to focus.

Nate moved stuff around behind me. I was slightly curious but didn't turn to see what it was. Instead, I looked back at the door and at the man who'd just come through it. The tall man with the long coat and the big gold ring, which he turned as he strolled toward us. The man from the gallery and, impossibly, from the air museum years before. I remembered all that, but I couldn't remember his name, not at first. Then I said it, before I was fully aware I'd recalled it:

"Jacob."

Mack whipped around to face me. The whites showed all around their eyes. "You *know* him?"

Before I could even try to respond to that, Jacob was at the counter. Well, he was close enough. He stood between Mack and me, but he'd stopped a respectable distance from us. He smiled and said, "Well, the gang's all here. This could be efficient, awkward, or quite a bit of both. Could I, uh ..."

He gestured toward the counter. Mack and I both took a couple of steps back, moving away from him and further from each other. I hated that part. Still smiling, Jacob gently rapped his knuckles on the empty glass countertop.

So that's what Nate moved, I thought.

"Hey. I wondered if you'd come back," my brother said. He had a fantastic poker-face, but I knew his tells, and I realized that each one of us — Nate, Mack, and I — seemed to be exactly as thrown-off by Jacob's arrival as every other one of us. I did not like that. I didn't like that at all.

What the hell is happening? I thought, but even then, that didn't sound quite right. All three of us had evidently met this guy before, at least one of us more than once, so it was more like, *What the hell* has *happened?*

"Yeah, I was back in the area, and I figured I might have better luck today," Jacob said, looking at Nate but talking to all three of us. "Has one of those cameras come in?"

"Now, you were looking for an old rangefinder, right? A Kodak 35?"

"That's right," Jacob said.

Nate took a deep breath and then shrugged. "You know, I haven't. Haven't had a chance to go to any sales, and eBay's been pretty dry, too."

"Ah, that's too bad."

"Yeah," Nate said. "You know, if you gave me your name and, uh, some way to get in touch with you, it would save you from wasting another trip down here."

"His name's Jacob," I said. "At least, that's what he told me."

"What?" Nate said, losing a bit of his composure.

"I don't know what's happening," Mack said, their voice sounding small and far away.

I left my post, went around Jacob, and grabbed Mack's hand. I leaned toward them and asked quietly, "How do you know him? What's wrong?"

Mack just shook their head.

"So it's going to be awkward," Jacob said. "Well, there's always a good chance of that. Now, Tomlin, 'Jacob' was probably a little formal. Not too many people call me that. Most call me Jack." He offered Nate his hand. "Jack Beacham."

Reflexively, Nate took his hand, but then he blinked and said, "What?"

"It snowed the night Eleanor Kidd helped an angel and met Jack Beacham," I thought. Out loud, I said, "Yeah, this isn't funny. Who are you?"

"Jack Beacham," he said. "Sergeant. Serial number —"

Mack crowded past me and jabbed their finger two inches — *maybe* two inches — from the man's face. "Bullshit!" she said. "I *know* his serial number. We all know it because my mom, who fucking *died,* made it up! Sgt. Jack Beacham is a *character*!"

The man grinned and said, "Well, I like to think so. Call me whatever you want, but we do need to talk — about shoes and ships and sealing wax. Cabbages and kings."

He leaned against the counter, slid his hands into the pockets of his long coat, and added, "And music, and war, and Genesis 6:4."

From *A Woman Named Kidd* by Theresa Hatcher

It snowed the night Eleanor Kidd helped kill an angel and met Jack Beacham.

She tore down River Road South in her '68 Cougar, taking a 25 mph corner at 50 and kicking up a torrent of needles and leaves in her wake. In the passenger seat, Taija grabbed the armrest with her right hand and the Cougar's center console with her left. "Ellie, slow down!" Taija said.

Eleanor laughed and shifted. The tach needle dropped to indicate slightly more sensible RPM. "Oh, come on. You need to live a little!" she said.

"Yeah, uh, I'd kinda like to!"

Eleanor laughed again, but she lightened her foot. A little.

"*Thank* you!" Taija said. "Oh, look: a cross on the side of the road."

"Oh, stop it."

"No, I'm serious. Hey, there's another one. Ooh, look at the pretty flowers."

Eleanor sighed and raised her foot a bit more. "Here," she said. "Now we're going a perfectly reasonable 40 miles per hour."

They continued in that fashion for a mile or so, and then Taija said, "I wasn't asking you to drive like a grandma. You could go a *little* faster."

"Oh, seriously? Could I please?" And Eleanor laughed once more. That's how she'd remember it: ending with laughter. "You know, sometimes I wonder if you — "

Eleanor stomped the brake pedal just as the windshield shattered. The car spun. Glass swarmed into the car like glittering locusts. Eleanor's forehead cracked the steering wheel, but she didn't feel it. Because she'd seen Taija. Something was wrong with Taija's arm. Her hand still gripped the armrest, but she had a second elbow now, halfway down her forearm. Her mouth hung open. Her eyes were shut, and her head pressed against the glass of the passenger-side window. *She always looks so peaceful when she's sleeping,* Eleanor thought.

The car stopped, and Taija's head lolled, revealing the crimson spiderweb slapped onto the glass. Eleanor heard *plott ... plott* and tracked it to something dripping from Taija's long hair onto the seat. *Upholstery's blue,* she thought deliriously. *Purple spots. Ooh, look at the pretty flowers.*

Eleanor ran her fingers through Taija's sodden hair, smoothing it back from her face, tangling in a snag at the back. A burning river flowed down each of Eleanor's cheeks. She blinked rapidly, damming the tide, and extricated her fingers from Taija's hair. She looked over Taija's shoulder, through the passenger-side window of the spun-around car. She looked at the thing that had fallen onto their car. She looked at the thing that had murdered her friend, standing in the center of the road with its back to the car and wearing what looked like a long and shimmering coat.

There was a *pop.* The creature looked up to the sky and changed its stance, putting its arms out and bending its knees.

A *whup.* Another *pop.*

Whup.

Pop.

Like vapors, like a heat haze on the highway, the shimmering coat-that-wasn't-a-coat unfurled to each of the creature's sides, and the creature leaped into the air and took flight.

Whup.

Pop.

A yell.

A second being, and this one *was* wearing a coat — a long, light-brown one — fell, hit the Cougar's hood, and rolled onto the pavement.

Eleanor got out of the car.

The creature touched back down on the road and folded its twin shimmers — its wings, or nameless things that were closer to wings than anything else. The thing stepped toward the person who lay moaning on the ground —

No, it can't be a person, Eleanor though. *They both look like people, but neither of them can be a person. And at least one of them killed Taija.*

— but then it stopped, sniffed the air, and jerked its head to look at Eleanor. Lank dark hair obscured and shadowed much of the thing's face, but its wide and wild eyes burned with a terrifying clarity. "*Two,*" it said. "Hm. What luck."

"What are you?" Eleanor asked.

"Dedicated. Purposeful. Unhurried," the creature said.

The second figure, the one who actually was wearing a coat, stirred near Eleanor's feet. The creature looked toward him — but no. Not now. Not yet. Eleanor had questions, so many questions. She needed things to slow down.

She closed her eyes, and she heard that: *Slow.*

No. She didn't hear it. She felt it.

No. More than that.

With her eyes shut and her shock shutting her other familiar senses off to the world, a new one opened. A limitless meadow bloomed. Eleanor looked at the flowers.

Slow.

She saw, no, she felt, no — it was something more, something less — she *knew* the speed, the nature, the *heat* of every single thing. Taija — cold. So cold. The car. The trees, the leaves, the ground. The man in the long coat — warm. The creature — hot. Too hot.

Slow.

A roar. The creature cooled.

Slow down.

A growl. A grumble. Even colder now.

Stop.

Eleanor opened her eyes and found herself standing on a light powdering of snow. Flurries whirled around her. It all seemed ... odd. *Isn't it May?* She thought.

The man in the actual coat looked up at the snow and the newly gray sky and pushed a hand through his sandy hair. And he *was* a man. Somehow, Eleanor knew that, just as she'd known —

"Huh," the man said. "Well, look at that."

Eleanor blinked. The man wasn't looking up at the sky anymore. Instead, he looked at the creature, which was standing still, totally still, as if sculpted with a horrendous yet satisfying grimace contorting its face and one arm stretched out, hand up, fingers splayed. Grasping. The shimmer was gone, but there was ... what was that?

Eleanor stepped closer.

Ice.

The thing was completely ensconced in a form-fitting, inches-thick prison of ice.

"Well," the man said, "thank you for the assist."

"What ... what ..."

"I know."

"What ... " Eleanor's knees buckled. She stumbled back against the Cougar, slowing her fall but not stopping it. The man grabbed her arm and pulled her back up. "Taija," Eleanor said, looking desperately into the stranger's sea-green eyes. "We need to help my ... my friend."

The man looked over Eleanor's shoulder and into the car. He sighed.

Eleanor gulped and shook her head furiously. "No. No! No, no, no, no, no ..."

"Hey," the man said. "Hey. Listen. I need you to —"

Behind him, a creaking, cracking sound.

He sighed and stepped back from Eleanor, and then four especially impossible things happened in an afternoon of impossible things.

First, the stranger instantly, totally disappeared with a sharp *pop*.

Second, with a *whup,* he reappeared immediately behind the slowly but surely thawing creature and wrapped an arm around the thing's neck.

Third: *pop*. The stranger, and his crooked arm, and the creature's head disappeared.

Fourth: *whup*. There he was again, right there by Eleanor with a monstrous football held in the crook of his arm.

"Wh —" she swallowed. "Who .... what ..."

The man glanced down at the creature's head and then looked back at Eleanor. "Let's start with an easy one," he said. "I'm Sgt. Jack Beacham. Retired, I suppose."

Tomlin

I never read all of anything Tessa wrote until it was published. It was always like that. She'd ask what I thought about a line or maybe even a whole paragraph, but that was it. And that was fine. I would have read and read and reread whatever she asked me to, or I would have tried to, but I think she knew what would work best with my reading stamina. What that means is, I have almost no reading stamina. I own more art and reference books than I can count, and I've gone through each of them several times, but a picture's worth 1,000 words, right? And if I'm lucky, after every 1,000 words in one of those books, there's a picture. It's like a reward. I need that.

The first time, for the first book, it was a whole paragraph. Whoo-hoo. In fact, it was from the first chapter, and it was the part where the me-character dies horribly. "Oh, no, that's not you!" Yeah. Bullshit. But anyway, I was with her at her grandparents' house when she let her grandpa read more.

Tessa and Grandpa Henry sat at the big clubfoot table in the dining room. Well, that's where I'd left them. Tessa was probably pacing around the living room or pretending like she was paying attention to something on the TV, or maybe she'd gone outside. I know that I was in the kitchen with Grandma Edith. We sat at the little formica-topped table, drinking coffee from Corningware mugs and eating some of last night's popcorn out of wooden bowls. I could handle her coffee without cream, but that's because it looked like tea. She still had in her mind that she had to stretch her grocery budget to feed all her kids. Grandma Edith's coffee was made with a lot of love, but it wasn't made with very much coffee.

"So what did you girls get up to last night?" she asked.

I didn't blush, but I was still glad to have that mug in front of my face. I mean, we hadn't "gotten up to" anything, but we'd stayed up late, and we'd talked about a lot of stuff. About everything. Some things I'd never even really consciously thought about or put together, let alone said out loud. Tessa was my friend, and then she was my *best* friend, before she was anything else.

"Did you watch *ER?*"

Nope. "Mm-hm," I said.

Grandma Edith's eyes twinkled. She glanced toward the dining room, and then she leaned forward and dropped her voice. "Isn't George Clooney something?" she asked.

"Oh, yeah," I said. "He's a good-looking guy." That wasn't a lie. He was. He still is. Those are facts.

Grandma Edith giggled, took a sip of her coffee, and said, "He doesn't look like any of my doctors."

"Yeah, mine either."

She chuckled again, patted my hand, and took another sip of her weak coffee. And thank God, she stopped talking about *ER* before it got any weirder for either of the people at that kitchen table. I didn't want to hear any more of her thoughts about George Clooney playing doctor, and I sure as hell wasn't ready to share my thoughts about Julianna Margulies playing nurse.

We'd shifted the topic back a few hours to the tricky final puzzle on *Wheel of Fortune* when we heard some noises from the dining room. First, there was a long sigh — almost a moan — then a shuffling of papers, a familiar phlegmy cough, and the *flick* of Grandpa Henry's Zippo lighter.

Tessa must have gone outside at some point because right after we heard Grandpa Henry hack up that lung and light his cigarette, we heard his heavy footsteps carry him across the red-and-orange shag that covered the floors of the dining room and living room. He hit every creak along the way. Every creak of what was probably a gorgeous hardwood floor. Why did people put carpet over floors like that? Even then, at age fifteen, that confused me as much as my sexuality.

Grandpa Henry pulled open the old wooden front door and then the metal screen door and said, "Theresa. I'm finished."

Grandma Edith and I left our coffees at the kitchen table. By the time we got to the pocket door separating the kitchen from the dining room, Tessa and her grandpa were in the front room, hugging. Grandma Edith put her hand on my shoulder and said "Oh" with a lot of extra Hs.

A couple of beautifully awkward minutes later, all four of us sat at that dining-room table. Grandma Edith and I had fresh cups of weak-ass coffee in front of us, and we'd filled cups for Tessa and Grandpa Henry, too. He'd lit another cigarette. He must've burned through two or three packs a day, but I don't know how many of those he actually smoked. More often, I think, he'd just take a few puffs and then hold it in his fingers while he just sort of stared off and thought about whatever. The cherry would get longer and longer before inevitability made it fall just about anywhere but an ashtray. Seriously, you could've eaten off of most of those ashtrays. The linoleum floors in the bathroom and kitchen, though, and the dark, thickly varnished surface of that table were never so lucky. They'd been pocked all over by meteors from countless half-forgotten cigarettes.

Everyone said some things, but no one said much. Then Grandpa Henry asked, "Can I say somethin' about it?"

"Yeah, of course," Tessa said. I heard the tremor in her voice and saw the apprehension in her eyes.

Her grandpa picked up on it, too. Of course he did. He brought his hand down on top of hers. His huge, calloused mitt and those sausages he called fingers totally enveloped his granddaughter's hand. "Hey. You did something no one else could. No one," he said, and then he clenched his jaw and said through his teeth, "You hear that?"

Tessa nodded, and then she raised her free hand to pat her Grandpa's.

Grandpa Henry nodded, stood, and went over to the unofficial border between the dining room and living rooms. He faced the wall there and looked at the framed black-and-white photo that, as far as I knew, had always hung right there, right above the telephone on its little glass-and-chrome stand. Staring at the photo and at all the memories swirling within that frame, Grandpa Henry sucked on his cigarette and said, "It's magic, though. Your story. It's magic."

"Well, it's sci-fi," Tessa said.

Grandpa Henry took another drag and squinted at Tessa through the cloud of exhaled smoke. "Hm?" he grumbled.

"It's science fiction," Tessa said, still with that adorable tremor, but there was an enthusiasm there now, too. Not quite confidence — that wasn't there yet, but it would be. I would wind up loving that enthusiasm almost as much as I'd wind up loving her. "It's only part of the first chapter, so you don't know this yet, but Jack has learned that everybody — everything — way down in their cells, their atoms, has these strings. And these strings are what makes a rock a rock and a person a person. Whatever. And Jack has learned, and now Ellie has started to learn, how to play those strings and ... change things. Reality."

Grandpa Henry raised his eyebrows. "Change reality."

"Yeah. Well, part of it. Yeah."

"Hm." Grandpa Henry took another drag, and then he ground out his cigarette in the ashtray next to the phone. He actually used it. That's how I knew the story had gotten to him.

He looked back at the photo, put his fists in his pockets, and rocked on his feet. "Well, it was somethin' that took Tommy Keagan away from in front of me, from *right* in front of me, while it just about left me alone. You got geometry, you got physics ..." He shrugged. "Guess that's science, but there wasn't any fiction to it. But I do think it would take magic to bring him back."

He didn't say it unkindly, but it threw Tessa off for a moment. She blinked a couple of times, and she cleared her throat, and she said, "You know, Arthur C. Clarke said that a sufficiently advanced technology would be indistinguishable from magic."

"Hm. You say Arthur Clarke?"

"Yeah."

"Well. Good for him." He lit another cigarette. "Good for Arthur Clarke."

Grandpa Henry sighed and turned away from the photo of the ruined plane. He came back to the table, gripped Tessa's shoulder, and rapped his thick knuckles against the short stack of pages that formed that part of that draft of *A Woman Called Kidd*. He said, "Your heart's in it. And I'd love to be wrong."

"Thank you, Grandpa."

Henry nodded, patted Tessa's shoulder, and picked his lighter and half-empty pack up off the table. He left the coffee. "I'm takin' a minute," he said. "I'll be back in for dinner."

He went out to the front porch and closed both doors behind him.

Grandma Edith gathered up the mugs and took them back into the kitchen.

That left Tessa and me alone at the table. We listened to her grandma rinse our mugs and load them into the dishwasher. Tessa looked at me. I shrugged.

Then Grandma Edith came back into the dining room, put her arms around Tessa's shoulders and gave them a squeeze. I was both grateful and a little envious.

Tessa watched as her grandma sat back down at the table, sighed, and contemplated her hands.

"Do you think I should write something else?" Tessa asked.

"Don't you dare," Grandma Edith said. "Uh-uh. No. You know, that museum ..." She shook her head. "I think working at that museum — and I know they call him a volunteer, but it's work for him — I think working at that museum has been the best and worst thing he could've done. Shoot, even I've learned more about that war and that damned plane in the last few years than I ever did before. But sometimes ..." The words failed her, or maybe she held them back.

She rose, rested a hand on Tessa's shoulder, and said, "You let him and me worry about all that. About Tom Keagan, and that war, and about whether he wants to read any more of your story. But you keep writing it."

Tessa looked down at the table and nodded.

"He's a survivor, but sometimes he forgets he's not alone. And that's for him. You turned Tom Keagan into a ... into a traveler, and that's nice. That's better than what happened to him." She stooped and kissed the top of Tessa's head. "Write that story. You do whatever you need to do to get that done."

Nathan

Jack Beacham. Jesus Christ, I thought, and then I laughed and wondered, *Jesus Christ and Jack Beacham walk into my shop. Which is harder to believe?* The possible answers to that, the solutions to the riddle, moved from rational to spiritual to agnostic, two of which I was pretty familiar with, and snapped back again. And snapped back and forth between all them. It was too much. It was just too much.

I lifted my glass and was very, very sad to learn that it was empty. I brought down the footrest and got up out of my chair. I hadn't dozed off or passed out — I don't think I had — but I'd been dog-paddling through my thoughts for a while. Jimmy Kimmel giggled gleefully about something on the TV, though it wasn't my Jesus/Jack Beacham joke. I don't think he was on that wavelength.

I figured Tomlin was upstairs, either in the attic space or the just-about-ready-for-her box room.

Mackenzie was still downstairs, though, sprawled out and snoring on the couch. I envied them. Whatever they dreamed about couldn't have been any weirder than our day. Their sling was on the floor, their cast-encased arm lying across their chest. I snatched the sling off the carpet, carefully draped it across their injured arm, and called it good.

I turned away from the couch and spotted Mackenzie's half-empty glass on the coffee table. I waited for another couple of snores, decided they wouldn't miss it, and drank what remained of their whiskey and Coke. Tomlin and I had let them join us. It had turned into exactly that sort of day. And they'd left their pills in the medicine cabinet upstairs, so it almost seemed sensible.

Hell, it *was* sensible. Logical. Necessary. After our afternoon, none of us could have been expected to finish the day sober.

I took all our glasses and the empty whiskey bottle into the kitchen, and I saw the lights on in the workshop outside. I hadn't done that. I drank a couple glasses of water because I was a responsible adult, dammit, and then I grabbed another bottle off the top of the fridge. The bottle, my glass, and I went outside.

I found Tomlin sitting at the desk inside the workshop. The box she'd got from our mom was on the concrete floor, but it was empty. All its contents, including that old Kodak rangefinder, were laid out on the surface of the desk. Tomlin sipped from a can of seltzer as she perused the scrapbook. Plain seltzer. Just seltzer.

"Hey. That all you're drinkin'?" I asked. "After what —"

"Nuh-uh," she said. "We don't talk about the antique shop."

"Got it," I said.

"We can deal with whatever that was tomorrow. Maybe. I just know I can't right now, and drinking won't help me. I thought I should hydrate, and water's boring."

"That's really just water, though."

"Yeah, but there's bubbles."

I plunked the bottle on the desk and gestured at it.

Tomlin didn't even glance at the thing. She just turned the page. "I said I'm fine. Please be careful, Nate."

"Eventually. These are desperate times, though." I pulled over a metal stool so I could sit at one of the short sides of the desk. I spun the cap off and poured a few inches of liquor into my glass. "I think I'm allowed."

"Of course you're allowed, but that doesn't mean you should," Tomlin said. "Mack needs both of us, and they don't need us ... numb."

"This is my house," I said, and I realized immediately that I sounded more than a little like the previous owner of said house.

Tomlin certainly caught it, too. "Right," she said. "Well. Maybe I'm not the only fragile one."

"Oh. That's nice."

"I'm just saying, if Angie can help us tomorrow or let us use her truck, we'll get out of here as soon as we —"

"Oh, dammit, that's not what I meant!"

"'Booze doesn't make the beasts. It unlocks the cages that were already there.' Remember Dad saying that?"

"Yeah," I said.

"I see a lot of him in you," Tomlin said. "There's a lot of Grandpa in you, too."

"You think you dodged it?" I grumbled something else, put my full glass on the desk, and smacked it with the back of my hand, shoving it into one of Tessa's forgotten cameras. The whiskey sloshed. Some of it hit the camera, and some hit the scrapbook. Tomlin blotted it from both places with the cuffs of her sweatshirt, but she didn't say anything.

Not about that. What eventually did say was something that, to my recollection — then and now — she'd never brought up before. "Is that why you picked them?" she asked. "Is that why you stayed here?"

"No," I said, and I felt OK with that answer, but I couldn't have articulated anything deeper. I didn't know what she was doing. Why was she digging all that shit up?

"All Mom ever said was you were a little older, you were in middle school, it would have been even harder for you to leave your friends. Even though it sucked for me to leave mine."

"No, that's bullshit," I said. "I mean, she might have told herself that, and maybe that was part of it, but we lived in Burwell. Still had to change schools to come here."

"Yeah, but was that the original plan, or did Grandpa just decide he —"

"I don't know. That was a long-ass time ago, Tomlin." I sighed and rubbed my face. "All I can think is, that move to Seattle was ... it would've been too far from Dad for me. But none of it ever made sense. I don't know what went in that coffin, but —"

Tomlin pressed her fingers to her temples and looked up at the ceiling. "Oh my God. I'm going to have to do that for Tessa!"

"Or not," I said. "Don't feel like you have to. I'm telling you, we went through the funeral and put all of us through all that for a goddamn box." I pointed at my glass. "May I?"

"I'm not going to stop you."

I heard the words under the words, but I took a sip. Just a little one. "Maybe I thought I could find some of Dad here." I shrugged. "I don't know. It was either Westley or Iraq."

"Do you regret it?"

"Christ, we're digging deep tonight."

Tomlin acted like she was interested in the scrapbook again. "No, I'm sorry. Forget it. I shouldn't have asked that. Like you said, it was a long time ago."

I noticed I'd left the whiskey bottle open. I screwed the cap back on, and then I said, "Not every day. I didn't regret it every day. I mean, it was weird not being around you, and I missed Mom, but ... I don't know. Not all of it was bad. It wasn't ever paradise, but it wasn't all bad."

"I get that," Tomlin said.

"That's good," I said. "I don't think I have anything else."

"Still, though. Grandpa."

"Yep. Still." I pointed at the scrapbook. "Can I get in on that?"

Tomlin nudged the book toward me and flipped back to the beginning.

***

I drummed my fingers on the deadbolt lever, then I dropped my hand, turned the knob instead, and stepped out onto the sidewalk.

147

"Nate!"

"Yeah. Just a minute," I said. I pulled the door shut but didn't go much further. Basically, I just stood there, hands in my pockets, breathing in and out and in and out. That rye-whiskey binge had made the day rough enough, and now this shit. Thanks to Alka-Seltzer and lime Gatorade, an old family remedy, the hangover had finally faded, but a brand-new headache was cruising up right behind it. This new misery was fed almost entirely by the six feet of ring-wearing what-the-fuck currently browsing the record bins in my shop. Sgt. Jack Beacham, a fictional character based on my dead great-uncle, Thomas Lynne Keagan. It was impossible — I mean, it was utterly fucking impossible — but why would he claim some absolute bullshit like that if it wasn't true?

Well, so what if he thinks it's true? wondered a surprisingly sensible mental voice, and that got me thinking. Tessa had been a reasonably well-known author for just about twenty years. She had to have gained some goofy fans in that time. Maybe not Annie Wilkes crazy, but cosplaying ring-and-coat crazy? Sure. And it figured they'd come out of the woodwork after she died.

Except he hadn't. No, the still-probably-nuts mystery-dude had popped into my shop before the wreck. Wasn't it Thursday? Friday? Hell, I didn't know. Saturday and every day after that had felt like a month-long each, and much of the right-before time just felt like ... mud.

I took another breath. It was easy enough. It was something I could do.

Mud.

One more breath. I looked across the street at the feed store and the auto-parts store to the left of it, and then I looked down my side of the street at Doc Geary's veterinary office and at the real-estate office next to it. That one had always seemed weird to me. Westley had about as much resident turnover as the Hotel California.

A little past that, on the corner of the next block, was the Broken Spur. *Hell yes. That sounds delicious,* I thought. And it wasn't like I'd forgotten my recent misery. The possibility that I could trade what currently banged against my temples for a mundane debilitating hangover sounded fantastic. At that time, in that place, for the first instance in my life, I craved it.

My phone buzzed. A text from Tomlin. Then another one, and another one:

Uh hi. Left us alone with Land of Make Believe guy.

Wanna come back?

Or take us with you?

My next breath turned into a sigh, and I went back into the shop. I flipped the bolt and wondered when the last time was that I'd stayed open until the time painted on the window. Maybe Friday? Saturday, I'd stepped out a little early to check out Mrs. Carey's Adler typewriter — which, until that moment, I'd completely forgotten about.

Jack Beacham, the Amazing Impossible Man, still searched the bins. He'd made it about halfway down the "Not Rock" section. That's how I labeled them: "Rock" and "Not Rock." Made things easy. Both Mackenzie and Tomlin stood behind the counter, flipping through the scrapbook they'd gotten from my mom. Tomlin caught my gaze, glanced at Mystery Dude, and pointed down at the counter with her chin. Actually, she pointed through the counter — at the box, and the camera in the box, that I'd stashed under there. Thanks to that little bit of sibling shorthand, I knew Mystery Dude still hadn't learned it was there.

"Alright, Sarge," I said.

"Jack is fine," he said without looking up from the bin.

"Well, we probably shouldn't get hung up on that," I said. "I'm just speaking for myself here, but I'm *just* willing to hear you out before I kick you out."

"Yeah, that sounds good," my sister said, and Mackenzie added, "Mm-hm."

"Well, what more can I ask?" Mr. Jack-is-Fine said. He pulled a Mingus album from the bin and held it up for my approval. "I could use some music, though."

"You want to buy that?"

"I want to play it. Is that OK?"

"No, but fine," I said. I pointed to a squat late-1960s cabinet not far from him. "That Zenith over there actually sounds pretty good, but you'll have to plug it in. And that'll cut into your time."

He went to set that up, and Tomlin waved me over. I joined Mackenzie and her behind the counter. "What?" I said.

"What? What are you doing?" she hissed. "What, we're just chilling with this guy now?"

"Show me someone who knows what to do in this situation," I said.

Tomlin rolled her eyes but put up her hands. Mackenzie shook their head and laughed.

Jack turned the record, dropped the needle, and moseyed on over to us. "Slop" — the first song from the first side of *Mingus Dynasty* — served as his backing music. He'd taken his long coat off and draped it over his arm. He absently turned his ring and nodded slowly, almost imperceptibly, seeming to just be listening to the music.

"Oh, come on," Tomlin said.

"Yeah, I'm right there with you. Why are we here?" I asked him. "Why are *you* here? Come on. And none of that name-rank-serial number shit."

"If you really thought it was 'shit,'" Jack said, "you wouldn't —"

"I don't *know* anything," one of us said. It might have been me.

"It's something you feel, then. It has to be, or you would have kicked me out of here by now. Like you said."

Tomlin laughed bitterly and said, "Oh, man. Please don't tell me what I would do or what I feel. My feelings are *full*. Shit, Nate. I can't do this. This is —"

"I have questions." That was Mackenzie, who took a small photograph from the scrapbook, handed it to me, and nodded toward Jack. "Give that to him."

I walked the picture down the counter and set it at the end. Jack and I basically looked at it together. It was an old square photo with a once-white border, a black-and-white shot from something other than a 35-millimeter camera but too sharp to have come from something like a Brownie. My gut said it had been produced by a pseudo-TLR like a Kodak Duaflex or maybe even by an actual TLR like an Argoflex. Of course I thought that. Of course I went there — assessing the photo instead of actually looking at it and registering what it was a photo of.

Two boys — one of them could maybe have been called a "young man" — sat on a lawn with their arms around each other's shoulders. A brick house rose behind them. I knew that house. It still stood about a mile-and-a-half, certainly no more than two miles away, just one block east of Main. My great-grandparents' house. My grandpa's childhood house. He was the younger of the grinning guys in the photo. I recognized him despite the fact that the boy's smile held no cynicism, no snark. It was so wholesome. So pure. Unadulterated, in every sense of that word. I put him at eleven or twelve in the photo, so no wonder. That was decades before his son died, saddling him with me. Years, even, before the birth of that son. Before Korea. Before his marriage. Before his favorite brother didn't come back from Europe.

Tom Keagan — that was the other person in the photo. Four years older than the kid who would become my grandpa but with a similar grin and the same light-brown hair. The eyes, though. They definitely had different eyes. In that nearly eighty-year-old picture, Boy-Grandpa's dark-brown eyes were almost rendered as black. But the older boy's eyes ...

If I hadn't seen those eyes in my real and increasingly puzzling life, I wouldn't have known what color they were supposed to be. But if you took the Tom Keagan frozen in that picture and aged him another ten or so years, you'd have the man who called himself Jack Beacham, who was standing right beside me, which meant Grandpa's brother's eyes had been that same strange shade of green.

I hadn't noticed the resemblance, but why would I have? I'd only chatted with the guy once, and briefly, and about a camera I didn't have. Plus, Grandpa had been gone for years, and I couldn't remember the last time I'd run into one of his close relatives, or if any of them were still around. Even if there were pics of Tom around the house, none of them would have been in color, and they all would have been part of the house. Background static. This Customer = Thomas Keagan's Doppelganger is just not an equation I would have built.

Yet here he was. But he couldn't be. I flashed to Grandpa Keagan hunched over the bathroom sink, scrubbing a corpse's ring with my toothbrush, chanting, *"Don't make sense ... don't make sense ..."* For once, he and I were in total agreement.

Something about that ring tickled at the back of my mind. Identical to Jack's — the impossibly recurring one-of-a-kind ring worn by the Impossible Man. I was sure I'd told Tessa about finding the ring, the *actual* ring, but I didn't remember it showing up in her books. I was absolutely sure she hadn't put it on Sgt. Beacham's hand. "Where did you get the —" I started to say.

"I used to have one just like this," Jack said. "Almost." He flipped the picture over. On the back, in faded pencil, it said:

Tommy 16   Jimmy 12 (bday)

Aug. 1941

Jack smiled and told us, "Mine said Jack and Charlie. Haven't seen either version in ... well, years."

I took the photo back to the scrapbook. I tucked its corners back under those little anchors. My questions would keep for a while longer, especially because I didn't think I knew all of what I wanted to ask. Tessa hadn't given Jack Beacham the tourmaline ring, no, but dammit, there was something else. "Jack and Charlie — right," I said. "Jack Beacham is the name Tessa gave the Tom Keagan character, and Charlie Beacham is the stand-in for my grandpa."

"From your point-of-view, yes," Jack said.

I looked at the guy, who was either Jack Beacham, who didn't and couldn't exist, or Tom Keagan, who had existed but didn't now, or some random asshole. "OK, here it is," I said. "Here is what I — what *we* — will do for you. Tell us a story. Tell us a *good* story. Tell us how any of this ... is. And you'd better make it as fully developed and well-organized and heart-wrenching as anything Theresa Hatcher or Eleanor Kidd ever wrote, or I will personally run you out of this shop and out of our lives on a fucking rail."

"And so it goes," Jack said with maddening calm.

"That's right," I said, missing the Vonnegut reference but running with it anyway. "And so it fucking goes."

"Well, that's one way to do it," Jack said. He laid his overcoat on my shop counter, and then he brought his hands together in a single, soft clap before he spread them apart. "What do you want to hear? Charlie's birthday party? Four months later, when we learned about Pearl Harbor? Or about when I enlisted and wound up breaking his heart?"

"Actually, that one," I said, because I knew something about it, not just from Tessa's books but also from Grandpa's stories. I remembered one time in particular when he'd been remarkably sober and surprisingly forthcoming. I thought it would be a good test for "Jack," to see if he could reveal deeper knowledge than he could have gained from a series of novels or Google searches.

"Fine," Jack said. "I can do that." He rapped his knuckles on the end of the counter, and then he said, "You saw your grandpa's and uncle's ages on that photograph. It was the same for Charlie and me. I was still in high school when they bombed the harbor and when Roosevelt got us into it. God, I wanted to join up. A few of my friends did right away, and a lot more of them did not too long after that. But Pop, he wouldn't have it, and I get why. You look at your Westley High School yearbooks from those years. I'll bet they look just like the ones from Chapel Cross, from my town. Lots of girls. I mean, more than usual. More girls finished school than boys in those days anyway, but it was something else during those years. The draft would take enough of 'em, but you could sign up at seventeen with a parent's signature. Even younger if you lied about it and didn't make it hard for them to believe you."

It was all Wikipedia shit. Dammit, though, there was something there, shading his eyes and running through his voice. "Something," though, is as far as I could define it. Of course, knowing what we do now, it's easy to justify the time we gave him and our tolerance of him. But what had he given us then? I think we were all so shattered by the happenings of the past several days that it was easy to turn our backs on what we knew was real. We clutched at something different, even when it was something that had to be impossible.

I closed the scrapbook, pushed it aside, and rested my arms on the counter. He may have been full of shit — he had to be — but dammit, he had my attention.

"Anyhow," Jack said, "Pop, he made me finish up with school. I think he knew I'd be going but figured that if he pushed it out, he might be able to talk me out of it or find a way to keep me back." He shrugged. "I don't know. I don't think he had much pull out of this town — Chapel Cross, I mean. *My* town. But, see, he'd been just a little too young for the Great War, and he'd seen what happened to the boys who were just old enough. But I wasn't going to wait for my number. I graduated in '43, and not too much later, that's when I signed up."

Jack looked up and past us, through the shop walls. *He's seeing the old brick house,* I thought.

"I've seen and done a lot. Been a lot of places," Jack said. "That day, though — saying our good-byes." He shook his head. "That was something else. Mom inside the house 'cause she didn't want me to see her crying. And a handshake from Pop that he wouldn't let go of. He probably thought he wouldn't be crying, too, but I saw it." Jack gestured vaguely at his own eyes. "I mean I saw it starting. He did a pretty good job holding it back. Just shaking my hand — he wouldn't let go. Now, I don't know how *I* managed to hold it together. I think I was just focused on soaking it all up. All those details. And God, I'm glad I did. Standing there on the front walk right in front of our house, Pop shaking my hand, Charlie waiting his turn, and Mom in the parlor, thinking she had a good hiding space there behind the curtains." He chuckled. "So Pop finally let go of my hand, and he clapped my back, and he said, 'Get one for me, son! Get one for me!' He put all of himself into that. I was only standing a couple of feet away, but if I'd been over in Europe already, I think I would have heard him."

Jack laughed. It wasn't a chuckle that time — it was a full-on laugh. Then he shook his head and rubbed his eyes and looked back at the record player. The record had stopped at some point, and the tone arm had automatically returned to its cradle. "How am I doing for time?" he asked us.

Shit, I thought. *How'd he know about the curtain?* That could have been a natural embellishment, a storyteller's detail that just happened to sync up with the story Grandpa had told me. But had I ever told that to Tessa? Was that something from one of her books? I couldn't remember. I wasn't entirely certain what was and what wasn't at that point.

I looked at Tomlin and Mackenzie. Tomlin shrugged, and Mackenzie nodded. I told Jack, "You got a few more minutes."

Jack smiled and went back to the stereo cabinet. He lifted the Mingus record off the turntable, slid it back into its sleeve, and returned the album to its proper place. He took another record from another bin and got that playing. It was a Moody Blues album — *In Search of the Lost Chord*. I thought that was an odd choice, but if he was who he said he was, Mingus would have post-dated him, too.

If he's who he says? A baffled voice raised an alarm in my head. *You're really buying this shit. If he's who he says ...*

"Anyhow, then it was Charlie's turn," Jack said. "Pop went back up on the porch and sat in his chair. He didn't know I saw this, but he reached behind him and touched the window glass. Mom, her hand came through the curtain, and she pressed on the other side."

Jesus. Well, that's a strong detail, but it doesn't mean a damn thing, I told myself.

"Well, Charlie came up to me, and he shook my hand, too," Jack said. "And he said, 'Thank you for walking me to school all those times.' And I said, 'You're fourteen now, Charlie. You'll be fifteen in the summer. You walk yourself now.' And he said — "

Jack's voice caught. He cleared his throat, put up a hand, and cleared his throat again. Then, hoarsely and with a weak smile, he said, "And Charlie told me — that little shit — he said, 'Well, you always been a good brother, and I guess you started that then.' I guess you started that then ..."

I swallowed. My grandpa had never told me that part. I'd never heard it or read it. So why did I buy it?

Because when it doesn't echo, it rhymes, I thought.

"So," Jack said, "there was me leaving. October of '43. That was almost exactly a year before —"

"The *Tawny Terror*," Mackenzie said.

"*Screaming Lucy*," Jack said, "but you're close enough."

After that, and for a considerable stretch, Jack's story covered ground that was very, very familiar to me. All that meant — and I kept telling myself this — was that he'd read all of Tessa's books and read the same articles and shit I had. But I traded glances with Mackenzie and Tomlin at points throughout Jack's story, and I saw they were having the same thoughts and struggles I was. All that proved, though — all that *really* proved at that point — was that we were all the same kind of broken.

After he left Chapel Cross, Jack Beacham eventually made his way into the 398th Bombardment Group, stationed in Nuthampstead, England. And one year and two days after swapping farewells with his mom, his dad, and his brother, Sgt. Beacham boarded the *Screaming Lucy* and took up his position as bombardier.

And after he left Westley, Tom Keagan eventually made his way into the 398th Bombardment Group, stationed in Nuthampstead, England. And one year and two days after swapping farewells with his mom, his dad, and his brother, Sgt. Keagan boarded the *Tawny Terror* and took up his position as bombardier.

Lucy and the *Terror* were B-17s, heavily armed but also heavily loaded and a hell of a lot less speedy and agile than the Luftwaffe fighter-planes they had to defend themselves from during each bomb run. B-17s depended on every member of their ground and flight crews as well as those of the Allied fighter planes escorting them, not to mention prayer and luck, to get where they needed to go and back again.

On 15 October 1944, *Screaming Lucy* and the *Tawny Terror* each ascended from their version of the Nuthampstead airfield to bomb their version of the railyard in Cologne, Germany.

Each of the Flying Fortresses got to their relative theres OK, but as soon as they did, their pilots and crews knew getting back would be tricky. As usual, flak fired from anti-aircraft guns on the ground. In both my world and Jack's, a surviving member of one of the other crews said the flak around the railyard was "unusually precise." The exploding shells always made a sort of aerial minefield. That day, it was closer to a blanket.

The pilots decreased altitude to put more of a cushion between them and the "blanket," and miraculously, not one piece of German flak hit any of the thirty-six American bombers or their escorts on their approach.

Tom Keagan and Jack Beacham spotted their twin targets through their matching Norden bombsights. Each held his breath, each waited for the perfect moment, and then each released "4,000 pounds of hell." That was how Jack described it.

But here's the thing. That sudden loss of four thousand pounds — two tons — made every one of the bombers in the formation that much lighter and threatened to lift them toward the flak, toward that exploding blanket. Every one of the pilots anticipated this. Every one of them felt that split-second lift, and every one of them compensated for it instantly and beautifully.

In each world, though, one of the planes had the unvarnished, unbiased shit luck to rise right into an exploding anti-aircraft shell during that fraction of a second.

And in each world, that same survivor provided the same horrible description — that the shell "exploded right in the lap of that crew's bombardier."

That's where Jack Beacham's story diverged from Great-Uncle Tommy's.

"Things got funny the closer we got to the bomb run, but that wasn't anything unusual," he said. "Adrenaline, pressure, I don't know what did it, but it was like it was like things moved way too fast and way too slow all at the same time. I don't know if any of you've experienced anything like that."

"Yes," Mackenzie said, simple and firm. They scratched at their shoulder and loosened the strap of their sling.

"Well, so that's where I was," Jack said. "In that headspace. You know, that's not a word I'd ever heard then, but it's the best one I've found."

Nice cover, a part of me thought, but it was a small part, and it was getting smaller.

"Anyhow," Jack said, fiddling with his ring, "That's where I was when I heard it. I know it's hard to believe it when I say I saw that shell coming — hell, I've struggled to believe it for more years than I want to count. But I'm telling you, I promise you, I saw it. And that's because I was looking for it, because I was tracking a sort of, uh ... a sort of sound. And that's something I know I can't describe. Just like that headspace, there's no ... there's nothing in our language that does it."

Mackenzie made a small but definitely odd sound and began sort of pacing behind the counter. I didn't think much of it. I sure didn't hold anything against them. There didn't seem to be any bottom to the weird. How were we supposed to handle it?

Jack said, "That's what I call it, though. I call it a sound. And I found it, but then I heard all the other sounds. And I mean that. *All* the sounds. The sound of the plane, of the glass in front of me, of the bombsight, of my ... of my damn hands, of Ed Fenton — he was the navigator working behind me."

So Henry Clairvaux. Tessa's grandpa, I thought, and I'm sure Tomlin was thinking the same thing.

"Everything had a sound," Jack said. "Everything *has* a sound, and that was the first time I heard it. The song of everything. All the notes. All the instruments. And as time made its first move back toward something natural — a small move, but it was there — I heard that, too. The song changed. And I was scared, I knew what was coming for me, but somehow, I knew I could change it. I could tune the song to something I wanted to hear. So I did that."

"How?" Tomlin asked.

"I don't know," Jack said. "I suppose it was like kicking out after a doctor strikes my leg with that little hammer, only I had to let the song kind of hit me first." He frowned and shook his head. "No, that's terrible. Something like a reflex, I guess. Like I said, no words. After a while, though, it became more like this." He raised his hands and waggled his fingers. "Now, that's something we can all do, right? A baby can do that and gets better at it with practice. But can any of you tell me how we make our fingers move?"

"I need a pill. Or an edible," Mackenzie said. "I don't know, but I need something."

Tomlin put out her arm, brought Mackenzie in close, and held them there.

I said, "OK, so you keep saying you don't have the words, but what are you saying? October 1944, you're in the *Tawny Terror*."

"*Screaming Lucy*," Jack said.

"Whatever. And then you heard the fucking music of the spheres, and then what? What happened after that?"

"The music was different, and I opened my eyes." Jack shrugged. "And I was someplace else."

"Where?"

Jack scratched his ear, then rubbed his chin, and then he said, "I don't think it matters. That'll just be another detour — like this was."

"Oh, come on," I said.

"Like a baby, I learned to stop clawing my face. It took a while. And eventually, I made my way here. Like flipping through records in your bins."

"Oh, so that's the deal with the music," Tomlin said. "Thought it was just for atmosphere. Nice."

"More like a palate cleanser. It helps me to filter things, to hear what I want to hear, what I need to hear after I've traveled." Jack put on his coat. "But it's all music."

"OK, that's enough bullshit," I said.

"You didn't ask me to convince you," Jack said. "You told me to tell you a story."

"Oh, and it was a hell of one," I said. "No, really. It was. But how the hell could you prove to us that any of it was true? Any of it. I'm not greedy. Any of it. Even a little bit. Just a skosh."

Jack nodded. And then Jack disappeared. A *whup* of air rushed into the space he'd so recently filled. A *whup* that Tessa had perfectly transcribed in her books.

Mackenzie yelled. And yelled.

My sister cried.

My knees wobbled, and somehow, I managed to sit instead of fall on the cold floor. And I laughed, because why not? I mean that. Really. Why the hell not?

***

We did just fine flipping through that scrapbook and not mentioning a single word about our afternoon. Over time, I did finish my drink — I mean, it was there — but I didn't pour another.

After we got to the end of the book, I stood and stretched and asked Tomlin, "How'd Tessa get these? I never knew about this."

"Well, I think we got the scrapbook at Goodwill," Tomlin said. "The pictures came from here."

"What?'

Tomlin stood, and with a smirk and a little sparkle in her eyes — familiar signs of mischief but ones I hadn't seen much of in the last few days — she nodded toward the tarps in the corner. She asked, "Is my 'sculpture' still under there?"

"Yeah. I never knew what to do with it."

"Neither did I," Tomlin said. "I'm not a sculptor. I just needed to have some reason to be rooting around in that corner."

I didn't get it. I was extremely confused, and I didn't think it was all because of the booze. "That corner?" I said. "There was never anything in that corner except for old magazines — National Geographics and shit."

"Well, yeah, but there was a box of old photo albums over there, too. And I knew Grandpa wouldn't give me or Tessa a whole album, so ..."

"Wait," I said. "This was a damn *heist*?"

Tomlin grinned. "Yeah. Isn't that awesome? I asked Grandpa to let me store all that stuff here as a longshot. I didn't think he'd say yes. But then he did, and whenever I moved something around, looked like I was building something, I'd swipe a cool-looking picture or two. I mean, nowadays, she could've just Googled everything. But that was the late-'90s, man."

"Yeah, times were tough," I said. "Why didn't you tell me? Why didn't either of you let me know what you were up to?"

Tomlin's smile stayed, but it tightened. I noticed that but didn't understand it. And I should've. Hell, I should've seen it coming. "Yeah," she said. "Why didn't we tell you what we were doing, or why didn't we just ... not do it."

And dammit, it still didn't click. I was physically, mentally, and emotionally exhausted, and I was also moderately buzzed. I'm not sure if any of those are valid excuses, but I know none of them helped. In any case, I blundered onward. "I'm just saying, Tomlin, if he'd found them missing, it would have been my ass for that."

"Your ass."

"Yeah."

"While you were getting a piece of ass," Tomlin said, and her smile truly, fully fell that time. "I'm just gonna say, Nate, I don't think I was too worried about that back then."

My eyes got wide, and my throat went dry. Stress- and fear-sweat squirted into my armpits. Such a ridiculous and outdated response. But just like my staying in Westley, when had we ever addressed this? "Come on, Tomlin, you gotta be kidding me," I said. "What are we talking about here — nineteen, twenty years ago? More than that?"

"Oh, that's a good question," she said, coming around the desk. Coming for me. "You know, I've never been totally clear when it started. I remember when Tessa told me you'd knocked her up. I remember that day pretty fuckin' clearly."

"Tomlin, come on," I said, putting up my hands, stepping back. "Who cares when it started? Huh? We both know it ended a long-ass time ago, and now Tessa's gone, and Mackenzie's here."

"Right, so the ends justify the means."

"Oh, Jesus. Just stop."

"I love Mack," Tomlin said. "I love Mack more than anything. But why Tessa? Why her?"

"Seriously? We're doing this now. Today. This decade."

"I loved her!"

"So did I!" I said, and that's when she slapped me. I reeled, then steadied myself against the big red Craftsman toolbox. "OK," I said. "That's fine. Fine. Fucking whatever. You been saving that up since high school?"

"Kind of, yeah," she said, wincing and rubbing her palm and fingers.

"Oh, gee," I said. "I'm really sorry you hurt your hand."

"Nate, you had to know what you were messing with. No one understood me like you did. Not until Tessa. You had to know what ... what was building there."

"I ... I don't know what I knew and what I *knew*," I said.

"That's bullshit."

Yes, it was, but I couldn't say it. It's hard enough to write it. I probably couldn't even say it out loud now. I nodded, though. I summed up enough strength for that.

Tomlin went back to the desk, opened the whiskey bottle, splashed some into my glass, then poured some into her seltzer can. She took a drink from her can and nudged my glass toward the edge of the desk. The side nearest me and furthest from her. The safer side. I went that far, glad that we had a solid, sturdy object between us, and raised my glass. "Well," I said, "here we are."

"Yep. Fighting and drinking," Tomlin said.

"We should mark the calendar," I told her. "Today is the day we officially became Keagans."

"Yeah." She chuckled. "Seriously, though, you should be careful with that."

"What?"

"Drinking."

"You just poured me this drink."

"This one is medicine. For your cheek. But be careful with the rest."

I laughed, and then I said, "Move. You take the stool. I want my chair back. We'll call it even."

"Not sure that's even," Tomlin said, but she moved around the desk, and we took our seats.

We drank silently and wandered through the scrapbook again. At that point, it was just something to do. There were a couple of newspaper articles and even a school report card, but most of it was photos. Our great-uncle and our grandpa and their other siblings as kids, then as slightly older kids. Landscapes. Random shit. Whatever Tomlin could get her hands on at the time.

"I can't believe you stole all of these," I said.

"Yeah, I'm pretty badass."

A full half of my face told me not to argue with that. I kept quiet and just flipped through the scrapbook. Flip ... flip ... flip ...

Wait.

I flipped back a page and hunched over to get a closer look.

"What's wrong?" Tessa asked.

"Nothing's wr —" I cut myself off my pulling my cellphone out of my pocket. I opened the Kindle App, found *A Woman Named Kidd* in my library, and ran a search, looking for one word.

"Nate?"

"Yeah, hold on. Give me a minute." No hits. I tried again with *Fenton's Runaways, Turning Paige,* every one of Tessa's books. Searched the same word. No hits, no hits, no hits.

Tomlin pulled the scrapbook toward her and looked at the photo that had hit me like that, that had smacked me across the face harder than she had. That had clarified that weird mental tingle, that *something* I'd wanted to know that afternoon about Jack Beacham's ring.

It was the only photo on that page, mounted right there in the center. Thomas Lynne Keagan, sitting on a beach towel and looking pretty damn spiffy in his 1940s swimming trunks. A side shot, and he was looking over his shoulder at the camera, the wind blowing his hair. And because it was a side view, his right arm and hand were clearly visible. Thank God he had those big Keagan hands, those long fingers, because they'd helped me spot the ring he was wearing on his third. That heavy gold ring, set with a unique tourmaline stone.

"I see it," Tomlin said. "But ... help me out. What am I seeing?

"He told me it was one-of-a-kind."

"Who?"

"Jack."

"OK, so he lied," she said.

Just then I remembered some else Jack had said: *"Well, as one-of-a-kind as anything is, anyway."* I licked my lips and took a deep breath. I wanted a drink. I wanted to get smashed. Shit, I wanted to be there already. But I also knew it would be better if I was at least somewhat alert and cognizant during the step I was about to take. Something needed to be said — or asked. "Tell me, sis. What part do you think he was lying about?"

Tomlin drummed her fingers on the scrapbook. She glanced up at the bottle, and then she looked back down at the page. "I said I didn't want to talk about it," she said.

"Yeah, but here we are."

She nodded, and she put her head in her hands. She groaned, and then she asked me, "What were you searching for on your phone?"

I said, "Tourmaline. It doesn't show up in any of Tessa's books. None of 'em."

Tomlin lowered her hands and looked at me. She'd aged five years in the last five seconds. "Nate," she said, "what's a tourmaline?"

"A gemstone," I told her, and I thumped the scrapbook photo with the first two fingers of my right hand. "It's what you're looking at right there. And it's what's set in Jack Beacham's ring."

Grandpa, scouring the ring. "Don't make sense ... don't make sense ..."

My scalp prickled. "Holy shit. And Grandpa knew it."

I shoved my hand through my hair and said, "OK, if Tessa based a character on Grandpa's brother, then yeah, they'd look alike and have similar stories, but if she never wrote about the ring, then where the hell did his ring come from?" I thumped the photo again. "Grandpa Keagan recognized this ring when we found it. "

"You said that."

"But that's just the ring. They never ID'd the —"

Tomlin gasped and clapped a hand to her mouth.

"There, you see?" I said to her. "Tom Keagan and Jack Beacham both either had or have this one-of-a-kind ring. And someone wearing it wound up drowned in Echo Creek."

Mack

After Jack Beacham's sudden departure, and after a suitable recovery period, we left Keagan's Collections and regrouped at my dad's house.

"OK, so why do you think he wanted this?" I asked. That weird old Kodak camera sat on the coffee table. Its cracked leather strap pooled around it. We'd left the scrapbook and all the other stuff in the car.

"I don't know, but he definitely did," my dad said. He came into the shop and asked me about it — ah, hell. Last Thursday? Friday? I can't even keep my days straight anymore."

"Either way, that was before Tessa, um, *died,*" Mom said, putting some extra oomph on that horrible word to force it out of her mouth. "It's like he knew it would be there. I don't like that."

We were putting a lot of work into talking about the camera and into not talking about the really weird shit. "Hey, remember when he disappeared?" I asked. "I mean, that was fucking crazy, right?"

"Stop that," Mom said.

"What, cussing? And what was that thing he said about Genesis?"

"No, I can't do this." Mom got up, went into the kitchen, and yanked open the refrigerator door. "I need to eat. We all should. Because I'm pretty sure we'll be drinking."

Dad rubbed his lips and chin. "Yeah, I'm getting thirsty," he said.

"Sweet," I said.

Mom, as she pulled some leftovers out of Dad's fridge: "No. You're eighteen."

"Yeah, but these last few days have aged me beyond my years," I told her. I mean, it's like I'd never had a drink before. That said, it's not like I even really wanted to drink then, but I did kind of want to drink with them. My regular life had gone to trash. I wanted something new.

"No. I don't know," Mom said. "Nate, is this still good? It looks OK."

"Yeah, probably," Dad said.

"Cool." Mom banged the fridge door shut with her hip and took the containers to the counter.

"'I don't know' means 'yes,' right?" I asked my dad.

"Oh, don't put me in that," he said. "I don't have the energy right now to fight either of you."

"Nice," I said. "Yeah, I can work with that."

Dad smiled and picked the camera up by its body. I don't think he trusted the strap. He sort of hoisted it like he was testing its weight, then he held it out and gazed at it like Yorick's skull. He brought it back toward him and fiddled with the knobs on the top. "Hm," he said. "Don't know if that's an answer or if it just gave me more questions."

I moved over to sit on the hearth, closer to him. "What's wrong?" I asked him. "What were you doing up there on the top of it?"

"I was checking to see if there was some old film in it," he said. "There's some old film in it."

"What?" That was my mom, from the archway to the kitchen.

Dad set the camera back on the table. He let out a deep breath, pulled the lever, and kicked back in his chair. He closed his eyes and pressed the back of his hand to his forehead. "I said there's film in the camera," he said back to his sister, talking a little louder than he needed to. "Which means there's probably something absolutely wonderful on the film in the camera."

"Yeah, I told you, I can't do this." Mom went back into the kitchen and called out, "I'm putting something together for us to eat."

Dad's chuckle turned into a sigh, and he brought the footrest down. "Oh, she's probably right. Food would be good. Definitely wouldn't hurt."

He got up and joined my mom in the kitchen, which meant he left me all alone in the living room. Just little lonesome me and my damn sling and that spooky-as-hell camera with a roll of film stuck inside.

Undeveloped, I thought, thinking of someone who might be able to help. Someone I'd inadvertently been ghosting for days. I got my phone out of my pocket and texted my friend Sera.

> *Hey. You still shoot film?*

I didn't have to wait too long for her reply:

> **Seriously? That's what we talk about? Where are you?**
>> *Ha. Sorry. Still at my Dad's. W/ Mom.*
> **That's weird.**
>> *Yeah a little. We're fine.*
>> *Kinda.*
> **When you coming home? Or can I see you there? Miss you. Worried about you.**
>> *Don't know. And sure. And thanks.*
>> *Sorry. Been crazy. And crazier. But I think we're OK*
> **Good. Can't imagine it.**
> **Anyway**
> **What about film?**
>> *Do you?*
> **Do I film?**
>> *Do you still shoot film?*
> **Oh. No**
>> *I guess I mean do you have stuff to develop it?*
> **Yeah still no**
>> *Shit.*
>> *Found film*

OK. Can help you develop but don't know where to get chem or order anytime soon.

Amazon?

Maybe. Maybe homegrown

Yeah, we still talking about film?

Ha. Actually I meant homebrew. Like household chems. Hold on.

Googling something

A few minutes passed. Drawers opened in the kitchen, forks and plates clattered and clanged, and the microwave dinged a few times. "Mack, do you want to eat out there or in here?" Mom hollered at me.

"In here," I yelled back. "Or the dining room. That kitchen table's too small."

My phone went *brrb*.

Washing Soda 54 grams/liter, Vitamin-C Powder 16 g/l, Instant Coffee 40 g/l

Seriously? That develops film?

Yep. Called Caffenol. That'll develop it. Think I know how to fix

Fix what?

Last part of developing.

Don't worry. I got it.

When and where are we doing this?

Those were excellent questions. I took a deep breath and looked over the recipe again. I thought I knew what washing soda was. I got a huge lump in my throat when I read "Instant Coffee" and thought about that last full day at home, at my *real* home, and my mom comforting me in the kitchen as we waited for our water to heat up.

I cleared my throat and wiped my eyes, and I sent another text to Sera.

Yeah, I have some of this. Inst Coffee and Vit C powder I think.

Def coffee.

Sweet. When do you want me to go up there?

No it's in Batchley. At home.

Maybe tomorrow though? Right after school?

Can you?

Yeah.

Can you?

Yeah.

I'll work on Mom but yeah.

We're eating now.

Talk after dinner.

K.

Just in time. Right as I got my phone back in my pocket, my mom and my dad brought all the plates into the dining room. I worked up a smile and joined my weird little family at that big old table.

***

There was another window just outside the Attic panes, and little Mackenzie looked through that one as two of their parents argued on their dad's ginormous front yard.

Tomlin had barely turned onto the gravel driveway before she'd parked the car and run out to talk to her brother, who she'd spotted mowing the grass. "Just wait there," she'd called back. And that's what Mackenzie did, though they also shut off the radio so they could hear better.

Up in the Attic, the single bulb swayed slightly above my head, just like always. It was almost comforting. And also like before, my cast and my sling were gone. I liked that, too.

A particularly small box had started this particular picture-show. Just a little guy with some especially odd stuff inside, like a handful of freshly cut grass and a broken shoelace. I didn't know this one. Judging from the viewing angle and glimpses of Mackenzie's little shoes and little hands, I figured she was something like five years old. That helped place the memory on the timeline, but it didn't do much more for me beyond that.

Maybe-five-year-old Mackenzie still couldn't hear shit in the car, so they tapped the window button and cracked the window down just a little bit. They didn't want to get into trouble

At some point, I'd taken the shoelace from the box. I worked it through my fingers.

Nathan and Tomlin stood there on the other side of the slightly open window, between Tomlin's parked car and Nathan's parked riding lawn-mower. Nathan's hands were on his hips, and he talked through his clenched teeth. Tomlin's arms flew free, and her hands waved like crazy. This is what Mackenzie picked out of the conversation and boxed up for me:

"Tessa."

"Book-signing."

"Babysitter." "No notice." "Not my fault."

"Don't have a bed," "Your kid," and "Be a FATHER."

"Oh, now it's 'my' kid?" That was Nathan. That was our dad. "'My' kid has two parents. Yeah, you and your partner made that pretty damn clear."

And our mom: "Well, after what you said to her?"

And from both of them, some words Mackenzie hadn't heard before. But I sure as shit had.

The car window swung out as five-ish Mackenzie opened the car door, and I thought, *There you go. Get 'em, kid. Go kick some ass.*

"Hey, Mackenzie. Mack," Tomlin said.

Mackenzie shook their head and just kept on walking. Walked right on past them.

"I told you to stay in the car."

"Oh, the kid's fine," Nathan said. "Don't take it out on —"

"OK. Yeah. Now you're a white knight."

"What the hell are you ..." A groan that turned into a wordless yell. "I never said no, OK? I just said I don't have a place for —"

"You literally have *rooms* you're not even using. This house has been yours for, what, six months now, and you still don't have a bed for —"

"Right, because six months is plenty of time for this."

"For someone who should be your biggest priority, yeah, I think it is."

Mackenzie reached the big elm tree, which was the single thing besides grass growing in that big front yard. They rubbed their palms on their jeans and then climbed the tree, filling the Attic windows first with bark and then with the glorious view from the first big branch. That was usually as far as they went. But they could still hear Nathan and Tomlin fighting below them.

"Oh, fuck off. Fine. I'll put an air mattress in the living room, OK? It'll be great. It'll be like a fucking sleepover."

"Oh, thank you so much. That's nice, Nate. Yeah, that's really nice."

Bark slid past the window as Mackenzie went higher, and it felt better in the Attic with every inch she climbed. Warmer but not as stuffy. Not as oppressive. At least for the moment.

"Mackenzie, be careful, honey!"

In the Attic, I pulled the shoelace tight between my hands.

"You and I both climbed that same tree."

"Yeah, and Mom worried *every* time, and now I understand why!"

I knew it felt better for Mackenzie, too. They crept out onto that second big bough, sat down, and let one leg dangle. Then they moved the other.

They tried to.

The shoelace snapped between my hands.

The view through the window flipped, lunged, surged, quaked. The whole Attic shook. The resonance of the shelves and the unseen walls synced with the screaming and yelling from Tomlin and Nathan, who finally agreed on something.

Behind me, a box rattled off its shelf. I got out of the chair even though I thought the Attic would eventually put the box back on its own. I needed to turn my back to the windows. I couldn't get away from the sounds or the general chaos, but I didn't have to see another of Mackenzie's broken bones through those windows.

"No, wait," I said out loud, and I turned back to face the windows. The car wreck. My arm. That was my first broken bone.

Of course it was. I knew that.

Right?

The view tilted from the blue sky to the car parked way over there on the driveway as Tomlin and Nathan sat Mackenzie up.

"Oh my God ... oh my God ..."

"Hey there, Mackenzie. Just breathe, OK? Let's just take a look at you. Let's just breathe."

"Oh honey, look at your poor leg ..."

"Tomlin."

"I know, I know, but —"

"Tomlin."

"Right. Right. Where's your phone?"

"No, I don't have it on me. I left it in the house."

"Mine's in the car."

"OK. I'll get it."

"OK. Thank you. Thank you."

So much fretting, so much worrying, and it came from both of them. Again, here was something they could get together on. The view wobbled and tilted a bit as Tomlin adjusted her hold on Mackenzie so Nathan could stand up and go get the phone.

"OK, honey," Tomlin said. "OK."

The view sharpened and all the sounds clarified as Mackenzie came out of their daze. Some traffic, a couple of pickup trucks passing by on the road. Tomlin's car door opening.

"No, it's … sorry. It's in my purse, Nate. It's in the truck."

"Ah."

The car door, shutting.

Looking out at the road and the strawberry field on the other side of it. Green leaves, workers, irrigation wheel-lines.

The view tilted. Lowered.

No. Mackenzie was standing.

"Mack, honey, no. You need —"

"No, I'm fine, Mom. Mom, I'm fine."

"No, you need to sit down, honey. You're in shock. I can see —"

"What? I'm fine, Mom. It hurt at first, but now I'm fine."

Two shifts. First, looking down, past Mackenzie's T-shirt and down down the length of their jeans. Down their two definitely skinny but, evidently, perfectly fine legs.

Then over to Tomlin, looking at Mackenzie's legs. She looked up, then she looked back at the legs, and then she looked back up at Mackenzie. She had a strange expression. Relieved, she was definitely relieved, but she also appeared shocked and sort of fearful.

"That's … amazing," Tomlin said. "Oh, you're so lucky. I thought your leg was broken. Oh, I could have sworn it was."

I hadn't seen the broken shoelace creep back into the box, hadn't even felt it leave my hands, but the box flaps shut, the blinds closed, and the only light, again, was from that swaying hanging bulb. It always seemed like plenty of light and not enough, all at the same time.

I carried the box over to the shelves. I'd never figured out the Attic's filing system, so I had no idea where it went, but I thought holding onto it would anchor me to the place for a little longer. I didn't want to leave yet.

Then I remembered the other box, the one that had fallen during the tree-quake. I put down the broken-leg-that-somehow-wasn't box and picked up the other one. I thought about opening it, knowing that would keep me there, but I wasn't up for more revelations. No more trips down Memory Lane. So I put that fallen box back in its pretty obvious empty spot and pushed it all the way in so it wouldn't just fall off again.

And I still heard it sliding back — even after I took my hands off.

I grabbed the box, held onto it, and I heard that sound again. So it wasn't the box. The longer I listened to it, the more I knew it couldn't be. The sound wasn't right, it was too quiet, and it didn't sound like a box on a shelf anyway.

And I recognized it. Remembered it. That scuffing sound, interspersed through my fragmented memories from the car wreck and after. Like a trunk, or like something heavier than a trunk, being dragged across a floor. Yes — dragged across *a* floor. Not across my Attic floor. It was too far away from that. It wasn't right.

No, that's not right. It can't be. That's not right, it's not right, it's not right, I thought when I located the sound.

When I looked up.

***

"Uh, Mack?"

"Hm. Yeah."

"Mack."

I looked at my arm, which was encased in its cast-splint thing, which in its own turn was wrapped in that stupid blue sling. Then I looked up and blinked at the sunlight glaring off the dusty windshield, and then I looked over and blinked at my mom. "Yeah, what?" I said.

She shut off the car, and I took that to mean we were parked. I looked out my window and saw Sera's house. "Oh. Hey," I said. "We're here."

Mom laughed, but there wasn't a whole lot of humor there. "You know, we don't have to do this. Not if you're not up to it. It doesn't have to be today."

"I'm up to it," I said. "I was just thinking about something else. I'm good. Don't worry about it." And just to show her how OK with it I was, I unbuckled my seatbelt and opened my door. Like a boss.

"What were you thinking about?" she asked me.

I stopped with one foot on the curb and one still on the floor mat. "I said you don't have to worry about it," I told her. "Seriously, I'm fine. Are *you* fine? Are you up to this?"

She nodded.

"Yeah?" I said. "Really?"

"Yeah," she said. "I think so. Yeah. Really." She shrugged. "We have to get back into that house sometime, and it'll be nice to have some help. Go get Sera."

"Yeah. Cool. That was my plan."

I got the rest of myself out of the car and shut the door. I felt sort of bad for snapping at Mom, but I got past it, not because I'm an asshole but because I didn't have the room to wonder about or worry about anything else. Like she said, I was distracted. My brain was full of bony thoughts, of bones that had been broken and then weren't, and bones that had been broken so recently I still had to carry my gimpy arm strapped to my chest.

I shook myself out of it and knocked on Sera's door.

The door opened, and I saw Sera standing there, I saw my *best friend* standing there, and I almost cried. She just looked so damn beautiful. It seemed like forever since I'd seen her.

Sera grinned and said, "Hey, asshole!" and before I could ask, "What's up, shithead?" she was out of the door and had her arms wrapped around me. And then I really was crying. We both were. "Oh, I'm so glad you're standing there!" she said. "I mean, I'm glad you're standing at all, and I'm glad you're alive, and ... wow, did you put on makeup just for me?"

"Kinda. Just mascara and some liner. It's probably getting all fucked up now, though."

I raised my good hand to wipe my eyes, but Sera smacked it down. Gently. "No, you should leave it," she said. "It almost looks like you're going for that look."

"Oh, almost."

"Yeah, but it's close. No, you look good." She slung her backpack over her shoulder, and then she stepped forward and let the screen door slam shut behind her. "Come on. Your mom's waiting for us."

"Missed you, shithead," I told her.

Sera didn't stop or even look over her shoulder as she kept walking toward the car. She did, though, raise her right hand and pop her middle finger, and dammit, I just about cried again.

***

Just like Westley, nothing in Batchley is too far from anything else, and our house was especially not-far from Sera's. It felt like I'd hardly buckled my seatbelt when we pulled into our driveway, and I unbuckled it again.

Sera lingered around the trunk as my mom and I trudged toward the door. "Hey, uh, don't we need to get the boxes or something?" she asked.

"No, not yet," Mom said as she fumbled for the right key. She took a deep breath, and it didn't shake too much. "I just want to get inside and, uh ... see. It might be a real quick trip."

Sera joined us at the door just as I bailed Mom out by sliding my own key into the lock. Sera asked, "Should I even be here for this? I kinda feel like I should just chill out here."

"We want you here."

Sera looked at me and raised her eyebrows. I smiled and nodded. "Well, OK," she said. "Let's, like, go inside then. I'm getting tired of carrying this backpack."

The question *"Did you find my backpack?"* rolled around in my mind. I shook my head to clear it and opened the door.

I'm not sure what I expected, but it was our house. It was just our house. There were still some breakfast dishes in the sink, including my and Mom's — as in Tessa's — coffee mugs and cereal bowls from that last Saturday. That last morning. And that hit me. But then Sera touched my arm, and I gave her a nod, and it didn't feel like a lie. It was fine. It wasn't anything more, but it was fine.

"I'm going to get some clothes," Mom said, and she walked on down the hall.

"You good?" Sera asked as she set her backpack on the dining-room table.

"Yeah. I said I was good, right?"

"Yeah, you said it a few times. But are you good?"

"I'm fine." I looked down the hall, and I asked, "I should probably be in there with her. But I should also probably leave her alone. If she's getting clothes, that means we're not coming back — like, back-back — right away."

"Did she really move your bed there?"

"My dad did, yeah."

"That's weird, right?"

I shrugged. "I don't know. What isn't?" Bits of my last Attic trip tried replaying in my head. "Yeah, come on," I said. "I'm just gonna poke my nose in there and see how she's doing, and then I'll probably just grab a few of my books to take with me."

Sera closed a kitchen cupboard. She'd already found the instant coffee. "Cool. You said you have the Vitamin C?"

"Ooh, that's in the master bathroom," I said. "That's a good excuse to go in there."

We went down the hallway together, but then Sera pointed at the door to my room and asked if she could chill in there. We agreed that was probably best. I didn't know what I'd be walking into in my moms' bedroom, like whether it would be just a bunch of clothes tossed from the closet to the floor or Tomlin collapsed on top of them, too.

I knocked.

"Yeah. Go ahead. Come in."

"Yeah?"

"I'm not lying to you," Mom said. She also didn't say she was sure, but I opened the door.

I found her sorting an already-ridiculous assortment of clothes into stacks on the bed. Her half of the closet was wide open. Other Mom's was shut tight.

"Hey," I said. "Can I help?"

Mom shrugged, smiled slightly, and set a folded shirt on one o the stacks on the bed. "No, I ... I don't think so. I feel like I shouldn't be asking you that."

"You're not. I asked you."

"Well, I know I'm not ready to sleep in this bed again, I'll tell you that. It's hard even being this close to it, but covering it helps. It just ... I don't remember it being so *big*." She tossed a half-folded sweatshirt onto the bed. It landed in a heap on a pile of jeans. "But we could probably come back here tonight. To the house."

"But you just said —"

"I could sleep on the couch or maybe maybe even on the floor. In your room, like we, uh ... like we have been. Of course, we'll have to see if Angie or someone with a truck could bring your bed back."

I felt pulled in two directions, wanting to move on and recognizing that she'd given me the perfect opening. I dove into the breach. "Why doesn't Dad have a bed or a room for me?" I asked.

"He does. He did a good job with that."

"He didn't. He never has. And I'm eighteen."

"Well, you didn't spend the night over there too much."

"Because I didn't have a room. Or a bed."

Mom picked up that sweatshirt and gave folding it another shot.

"Right, so there's an answer, isn't there?" she said.

Mom looked at me, and then she swallowed and stared at the far wall, which was covered with photos of her and Tessa. That meant it hurt her less to look over there than to look at me. She said, "A lot of things got stirred up when Nate and

Tessa got together. Well, when I heard about it. And even more got stirred up later."

"You mean when I was born."

She looked at me. Pleaded with me. "I can't do this now," she said.

"Sure," I told her, but she had to know I wasn't totally letting her off. Just for a while. I didn't mind puzzles, but I wasn't going to go another eighteen years without all the pieces.

"I'm sorry, honey. I know it —"

"Hey, do we have any Vitamin C?"

She sighed and nodded toward the bathroom. "Yeah, if we don't have the powder, we have the tablets. The chewables."

"OK. Thanks."

She nodded again and started working with another shirt.

It turned out we had both the powder and the chewables, but the powder was old and basically cement. It must have collected some moisture. Sera thought the tablets would work, but the additives and shit that made them tablets might get in the way. We decided to go for it, and no one suggested calling my Dad first. We did want it to work, but I also think we kinda hoped we'd blow our one-time shot and ruin the film.

I'd taken pictures with a film camera before, but there had still been places in Salem and Albany that would develop it. I'd never messed with that. It was cool to watch Sera work through the process, though that was probably at least partly because it gave me something to focus on.

First, she opened up her backpack, and she pulled out an old bottle opener, a pair of scissors, a plastic developing-tank, and something called a "dark bag." She put the bottle opener, scissors, tank, and the camera into the dark bag, zipped it up, and slid her arms through elastic-banded holes at the side. Her hands worked inside the bag, which looked funny as hell from outside the bag. After about five minutes, though, maybe even less, she pulled her arms out of the bag, unzipped it, and pulled out the sealed developing tank. "Ta-da," she said.

"What, it's in there?" I asked.

"Yeah, it's a light-tight tank," Mom said. "This is fun. I haven't done this in a while. And now we just pour the developer in, let it soak, pour it out, and go from there."

"Basically, yeah," Sera said. "Oh, wait." She rummaged around in the dark bag and came out with the now-empty film cartridge, which she'd unsealed with the bottle opener. The label was lime-green and lemon-yellow and said:

TX-135 20

20 EXPOSURES

KODAK TRI-X PAN

Sera nodded. "Yeah, cool. I thought it would be Tri-X or Plus-X. I just need to look up the developing time, but yeah. We can do this."

"How old do you think that is?" Mom asked.

"Oh, I don't know." Sera rolled the empty cartridge around in her hand. "Maybe the 1950s? Sixties? That's when the film was made, and that's *probably* when it was shot, but who knows? Someone could've got some old film on eBay."

I looked at Mom and said, "That doesn't really help much, does it?"

"No," Mom said. "But maybe when we see what's on the film."

Sera was already scrolling through search results on her phone. "OK, yeah. Looks like eleven minutes or so. About what I thought. Then the stop bath, fix, and rinse, and we'll have it hanging to dry right after that."

"You said something about fixing it," I remembered.

"Yeah, but hey, I got you covered." Sera grinned, plunged a hand into her backpack, and pulled out a Rubbermaid leftover container filled with little white crystals, like extremely coarse salt. "Sodium thiosulfate. We use it to bring down the chlorine in our pool."

"Huh," Mom said.

182

Sera nodded. "Yep. Now, come on. Let's do this."

Something like fifteen minutes later, she clipped the strip of black-and-white film to the shower rod in the bathroom, letting it hang straight down so it could drip-dry onto the towel we'd draped over the side of the tub. We left it there and took a coffee-and-donut break.

Batchley had a couple of decent drive-thru coffee places, but we went for a sit-down coffee shop that was kind of OK. We each had a coffee drink and a donut, and then Mom offered to buy each of us another pastry. As we stuffed our faces with those, I wondered if she was stalling our return to the house and to our makeshift darkroom. When she said we should go over to the school and talk about options for an online wrap-up, that did it. I was certain. It was good to get some of that shit out of the way, though, and eventually, we made it back.

Sera snipped the film into five-frame strips, and we took turns holding each strip up to the light before she slid them into a plastic sleeve. Then we held the sleeve up so we could see them all at once.

Little black-and-white rectangles, something like an inch by an inch-and-a-half, and reversed, too. I mean the tones: we were looking at negative film, so light was dark and dark was light. I didn't have any experience with that. I couldn't make out shit. Mom and Sera did a little better, though. Mom thought she recognized some buildings from Westley. And, pointing at the third strip, Sera said, "Look. These are a few shots of the same couple of people."

"Let me look at that," Mom said, and she practically snatched the sleeve out of Sera's hands.

My friend looked at me, startled but amused.

I just shrugged and said, "Don't tell me you can recognize someone in that."

"No," Mom said, peering at the film strip, holding the sleeve up close to the bathroom's marbled window. "No, but I think she's right. Two people ... two guys, I think ... and the hair's the same ..." Her eyes widened, and she got closer, almost pressing her nose to the sleeve. "Oh, you've got to be kidding me."

"What?" I said.

Mom didn't say anything, but she handed the sleeve to me. "Fourth one on the third strip."

"What do you want me to do? I looked at all these. I can't —"

"Look."

I did, and I kept looking, and then I shrugged. "OK, so there's only one person in this one."

"Look closer. What else do you see?"

"Only slightly more than jack shit," I told her. "I don't know. Looks like a dude, and I see dark hair and dark eyes. That's it. So what?"

"It's a negative," Mom said.

"OK, so it's lighter hair and — " The words stopped in my throat. "No. Come on. It could be a lot of things. There's no way to know this."

"You're right," Mom said. "We'll have to print it or scan it to make sure."

"I have an old film scanner I can let you borrow," Sera told us.

"Cool," Mom and I said together, neither of us looking at her.

"I hope they're blue," Mom said, "but I think you and I both know they'll be green. Seafoam green."

I handed the sleeve to Sera — poor, totally baffled Sera — but talked to Mom. "Film's from the '50s or '60s, so it pretty much can't be Tom."

"Yeah, but is it really any more possible it's the other one?" Mom asked.

I closed my eyes and rubbed my forehead. "We've seen impossible," I reminded her.

Sera said, "Um ..."

"Do you want to walk away?" I asked, and I thought, *Oh, I wish I could that.* "I mean, at this point, you could still walk away."

"Um ..." Sera looked at me, then at my mom, then back at me. "No? I don't think so?"

"Mack," Mom said, already reaching for her phone, "maybe we should —"

"No. Hey," I said, and there must have been something in my tone I didn't mean to put there, because Mom's empty hand popped right out of her pocket. It wasn't a conscious thought. I wasn't thinking. I couldn't think. I was done with thinking. I just plowed forward and hoped I wouldn't crash into a wall. "We're here, and she's helped us. If she wants us to, we should tell her."

"She's going to think we're nuts," Mom said.

Sera: "I'm cool with that."

There was something else. Another feeling. Another impossibility. I forced a smile and said, "OK, see? Why don't you and Shithead go to the kitchen or something. You can tell her, or you can wait for me. I need to do something in here."

"I'm sure that's the best way you could have said that," Mom said.

I shrugged. "It ain't the worst."

Mom and Sera left the bathroom. The door opened a second later, Sera's hand snaked in, and she flicked the fan on before shutting the door again. I laughed and made sure the door was locked, but no shit did I take. Instead, I searched through the drawers and the medicine cabinet, trying to keep the volume of my rummaging beneath the level of the background noise provided by the fan.

I found the scissors under the sink, of all places, but I found them. I loosened my sling and yanked that damn thing off. I worked the scissors under the shit wrapping my arm. It took some time, and I wasn't delicate — and it didn't hurt, which told me something — but I cut it all away. The scissors clattered in the sink and then settled on top of the shredded mummy-wrap.

"Mack?" That came from outside the bathroom door.

I didn't say anything. I was much too busy looking at my arm, which I'd broken so badly four days before that the possibility of surgery had been discussed. We'd been urged to make a decision soon. I was ready to make it then.

"Mack?" *Knock knock knock.* "Mack, are you OK?"

"Yep," I said, bending my elbow and wrist and flexing my fingers. "Yeah, I am perfectly fine."

From *Beachams Bridge* by Theresa Hatcher

The marker squeaked, and the whiteboard screamed SO IT GOES. Like a tardy keystone, the phrase brought together the other proclamations scattered on the board, including PILGRIM and UNSTUCK and PORCELAIN TEAPOT and POO TWEE TWEET. "Now, the book basically starts twice, which is a little weird," Eleanor said. She capped the marker and tapped its butt-end against the word UNSTUCK. "And you're bound to get a few headaches after that, but that's sort of the point. It's part of it, anyway."

She placed the marker beside its siblings on the tray beneath the board and turned to face the class. Twenty-four students looked back at her with varying levels of engagement and interest. The whole spectrum seemed to be represented there, from near-catatonia to groaning boredom to ridiculously comprehensive note-taking. Eleanor put her hands in her pockets, leaned against the board, and briefly wondered if she'd just transferred the terms to the back of her light-colored shirt. "Anyway. Read Chapters 1 and 2 by tomorrow. It'll give you a good feel for the book, and you'll run into everything I've written on the board. And, you know, we might actually start with some warm-up questions to make sure you've done the reading."

A *lot* of groaning, spanning the spectrum. Ms. Kidd had really brought her students together.

"OK, so we'll definitely have some warm-up questions," Eleanor said, the word "questions" drowned out by the bell. As twenty-four students jammed binders and notebooks and school-issued copies of *Slaughterhouse-Five* into their backpacks, Eleanor raised her voice and said, "I promise you, the book's not that bad. Try to have a happy Thursday. I'll see you tomorrow."

Someone flung her classroom door open, and the din of exiting students melded with the cacophony from the hallway. Eleanor followed the last of her students to the door, and then she shut it and dared to enjoy a moment, maybe even two, of relative quiet.

Then music blared behind her, from the speakers hooked up to the computer on her desk.

Eleanor whirled to face it, ultimately more surprised by the suddenness of the sound than by the sight of the man now sitting behind her desk. Because of course it was him. This was what he did, though he hadn't done it, hadn't intruded upon her life, for years.

"Do you still have third-period prep?" Jack asked her.

"I have it again," Eleanor said. She made sure her door was locked and then strolled across the vinyl-tile floor. "For the last three years, it was fourth."

"Three years?" Jack said.

Eleanor smiled. "I haven't seen you for five, Jack."

Jack Beacham nodded slowly and drummed his fingers on Eleanor's desk. "It's getting harder to keep track." He pointed at the computer screen. "Is this a new version of Windows?"

"Kind of," Eleanor said. "I think it's more like, the school finally upgraded to the last one."

Jack nodded again, or maybe he just kept nodding.

"Is something wrong?" she asked. "You seem a little ... lost. Did you have trouble finding the right notes?"

Jack paused the music, pushed the chair back, and got to his feet. "Do you want your chair back?"

"I'm fine."

"It's not about finding the notes. It's more like ..." He shook his head, looked toward the classroom windows, and muttered under his breath. "I don't know how to put it," he finally said, "or if it's even something that can be 'put.' It's science, and it's an art, but I also wonder how much of it's luck. Or if I'm the only one plucking the strings."

Eleanor smirked, and the temperature in the room dropped suddenly and severely. Frost spread over the windows, crackling slightly.

"That's not what I mean," Jack said, "though that was nice. It's a nice trick. I wonder how many more of us are out there. I don't think there's ever been a lot, but they're out there."

"'The heroes of old, men of renown,'" Eleanor recited, and then she played a different "note" herself. That was how Jack thought of it, at least — how he felt it. As she had that first, terrible night on River Road South, Eleanor Kidd perceived it not as music but as a sort of velocity lurking in everything. She agreed with Jack: it wasn't something that could be "put," but that seemed reasonably close. She turned the dial, speeding things up again. The room warmed, and the frost thawed, water pooling on the windowsills.

Jack clapped briefly. Politely.

Eleanor got the marker-stained white towel from the whiteboard tray and mopped the sills.

"I wonder how long I've been doing this," Jack said. "I'm not even sure how old I am. That would probably help."

"You don't —" Eleanor started to say.

"I was nineteen when the shell hit *Lucy*." He gestured at himself from his light-brown hair to his fancy shoes. "But this ... you'll see. And this is what I mean. Maybe it's just a natural part of —" He chuckled and shook his head at that phrasing. "Maybe it's a *part* of what we're able to do, like a positive side-effect, or maybe someone's doing it to us — I don't know. But the strings or the *things* or whatever is in us, either they tune themselves up or someone's doing the tuning. When was the last time you took a sick day?"

"I take them all the time."

"OK, but when was the last time you *had* to?"

Eleanor thought about that, and then she thought some more. And then she said, "Huh."

"You see? I'd wager it was before you and I first met." He rapped his knuckles on the top of her PC tower. "Before you booted up."

Before that monster killed Taija, Eleanor thought. *Crap, what if I'd "booted up" a couple days sooner? Or a couple of minutes? I could have —*

Jack blessedly cut into her woolgathering before she could fully think *I could have saved her.* "I suppose I should be grateful," he said, "I could have been killed in that plane when I was nineteen. Maybe I should have been. Starting to feel like that was my time."

"Don't say that," Eleanor said quietly, speaking to both of them.

Jack took a deep breath and then roamed throughout the classroom. He kept one of his hands in one of the pockets of his long, heavy coat, but he kept the other free, occasionally using it to absently touch a book, a pencil, a loose piece of paper left on a desk. Whatever was there. "I've seen great things, and I've seen terrible things, but … it doesn't matter," he said. "I see these incredible things, and then I leave, and I see something else. I don't travel; traveling suggests a destination. It requires one. I wander." He shrugged and held that shrug, basically freezing in that position. "Why? Where am I going?"

Eleanor was disturbed but not because she didn't understand him. Her apparent successes — such as her teaching career and the poems and short stories she'd had published — composed a thin veneer that lay over her existence, of her sense of that existence. Jack was one of the few people who had ever truly understood that, or had ever truly understood her, and that had especially been true since Taija's death. But she realized now what that meant: Jack Beacham understood her because Jack Beacham was precisely as brokenhearted and fucked-up as she was.

She checked her watch, and then she checked the clock on the wall, and then she frowned. The school was on an assembly schedule, so she had even less time to navigate to the end of this conversation than she would normally have had. "I'm your friend, Jack," she said, knowing it sounded weak but hoping it would be enough.

"You are, and I love you for that," he told her. "You've been one of the few, close or otherwise, for a very long time. And you're probably the only one I won't outlive by … I don't know. Decades. Centuries."

"Jack, what happened?"

He sighed and rubbed his temples. "I went somewhere."

"I figured that." Eleanor smiled feebly. "Like you said, it's what you do."

"I went … further. I knew I'd gotten the pitch wrong, and I was going to change it, but I could already hear the song." His eyes glistened. His head shook slowly. "It was … I don't know what it was. 'Beautiful' isn't the right word. Everything I hear now, everything I've heard, is like a copy of a copy."

Eleanor glanced at her watch again. "Jack, look, that bell's about to ring, and —"

He put up his hands. "Yeah, I know, I know," he said.

"Maybe you should just 'pop' on over to my place." She smiled weakly at her sad little pun. "I can be home by 4:00."

He nodded. "Yeah, that's probably good."

"Will you be there?"

"I will. I promise. I'm not ready to go anywhere else yet. Hell, I don't know where I'd go."

"Jack, where *did* you go?"

He smirked, and Eleanor saw a bit — just a bit — of what she wanted to see there: a hint of the familiar. "You're going to want to wait until 4:00," he said.

"I don't think I do."

"You have a little bit of time between your last class and the official end of your day, right?"

"Yeah, school lets out at 2:55, but we're supposed to stay until 3:30."

"I'm going to ask you to wait until 2:55 to open this," he said, reaching into his coat.

"OK."

"I mean that. You won't be able to get through the rest of your day otherwise."

"OK," Eleanor said again, her curiosity piquing already.

Jack pulled a well-read paperback book from an inside pocket of his coat and handed it to Eleanor. The title was *A Woman Called Kidd,* and it was written by someone named Theresa Hatcher. Eleanor turned the book over, and she gasped when her own face looked back at her from the author's photo. The caption said:

> Theresa Hatcher is a mother, teacher, and writer living in Oregon. She is a graduate of Western Oregon University. *A Woman Called Kidd* is her first novel.

"I'm telling you, don't open it yet," Jack said again.

Whup.

Eleanor looked up. She was alone.

Nathan

A teenage girl with long, jet-black hair, a chain wallet, and forest-green Doc Martens stood in my kitchen, blowing lightly across the surface of a fresh cup of coffee. She didn't seem nearly as disconcerted as I was that she was in my kitchen.

"Hey," I said as I pulled the sliding door shut behind me.

"Yeah, hey," she said.

"Is that good coffee?"

"Yeah, it smells good. It's still too hot to take a drink yet. Do you want some? I mean, it's yours."

Well, we agreed on that point. "Yeah, sure," I said. "Yeah, I'll have a cup of my coffee."

As she filled a cup for me, she asked, "You're Mack's dad, Nate, right?"

"Yeah," I said. "Yeah, I am. Have I, uh, met you before?"

"Yeah, I think at a birthday party or something," the girl said as she handed me the cup. "Pizza was involved. And some video games. So, yeah, it was probably a birthday party."

I took a sip of the coffee much earlier than I should have, but I bounced it around my mouth and swallowed it down without suffering too much permanent damage.

The girl laughed. "Remember when it was hot?" she said.

"Yeah. Wow. It's very clear now." I put the mug on the counter and asked, "Serena, right? I think I remember you kicking my ass on an old *Street Fighter* game."

"Actually, it was *Mortal Kombat,* but your defeat is recalled correctly," the intruder in my kitchen said. "But yeah, that's me. And you can just call me Sera. The only ones who call me Serena anymore are my family when they're pissed at me."

"Got it," I said. "I'm guessing Tomlin and Mackenzie are back here, then?"

"Mack."

"Yeah, Tomlin and —"

"I mean, they prefer to be called Mack. Like Sera. Or Nate."

My face warmed up, and I couldn't blame that on the coffee. "Is that right?" I said.

Sera narrowed her eyes. "Yeah, that's been right for a while now. You never noticed that?"

"I knew people called them that."

"Yeah, because they asked them to. I don't know. Maybe they never asked you." Sera sipped her coffee and shrugged. "You're getting their pronouns right. That's something." She turned and walked toward the dining-room. "Mack and her mom are hooking up my film scanner in your office. Come on."

As I followed her, I thought, *Hooking something up in* my *office?* I felt a primal sort of offense to that, but I shouldn't have. At that point in our increasingly upside-down lives, it probably wasn't something to get all worked-up about. But still. "Yeah, I know where that is," I said. "I don't need you to show me through my house."

"Hey, I'm just heading there, too, man," Sera said. "Thanks for the coffee, though."

By the time she and I got to my home-office space, our coffees in-hand, Tomlin and Mackenzie — *No, it's Mack,* I reminded myself — had moved an alarming number of things out of their proper place but had given up on setting up the scanner. "Hey. Dad. What's your password?" Mack asked.

"Oh, sure, let me just give that to you," I said.

"Well, if we even make it that far," Tomlin said. "Right now, we're just trying to find a place to even plug this cord in, but you already have all of your USB holes taken."

"Ports," I said.

"Whatever," Tomlin said. "They're full."

"Yeah, how does this even happen?" Mack asked me. "Usually, there's more ports than you'd ever use."

"Well, it's an old computer."

"Yeah, I'm seeing that."

"It's done fine for me." I put my mug at the desk and looked at what all they were messing with. What all they'd *done*. My computer pulled out from the wall and left a little cock-eyed, the dust bunnies distrubed from the top of the surge strip, the film scanner on top of one of my filing cabinets. "What are you scanning?" I asked. "Or what are you *trying* to scan? I mean, my printer's an all-in-one."

"Yeah, but we're trying to scan these," Mack said, and they handed me a transparent sleeve that held a roll of 35-millimeter film cut into five-frame strips.

I held the sleeve up to the light coming in through the office window. Through what used to be Grandma and Grandpa Keagan's bedroom window. "What are —" I started to say, but then I realized what I was looking at, and something electric popped at the back of my skull, trickled down my neck, and sizzled along my shoulder. "Oh. You developed the film from the rangefinder."

"Look about three strips down," Tomlin said.

Then Mack: "We think it's our friend."

I saw it. I saw him. "Oh. Well, shit," I said, and then I checked the markings between the sprocket-holes and put that together with what else I knew. "OK. So the camera's from the '40s, plus Tri-X in 35-millimeter, which puts us at probably mid-1950s, at least ..." I caught myself and looked at Sera, and then I looked at Mack and Tomlin.

"Oh, they caught me up," Sera said casually between sips of her coffee. "Actually, and that was, like, an hour or two after I ate the edible I found in the desk, which may have been a bad idea, but I'm enjoying it so far."

I offered the sleeve of film back to Mack, and they took it. With their left hand. I blinked. It was too much. It had been too much, and it still was too much, and I was starting to think there'd always be more. "OK, what the hell?" I asked.

Tomlin hardly glanced at Mack's arm before saying, " There have been some ... developments. And maybe an explanation. Do you remember when Mack was five and —"

I put up my hands and said, "No. No. Stop. Not yet." I thought of an old *Far Side* cartoon. A student raises his hand and asks his teacher, "May I be excused? My brain is full." That was me. I was there.

I stepped up to the computer and typed in my password. "There. That's Step One. If you get kicked out or something, it's 'GinBlossoms.' One word. Capital G and B."

"Gin Blossoms? Why is it Gin Blossoms?" Tomlin asked.

"Don't worry about it," I said, and I hoped I wasn't blushing, because I'd remembered why. "I'll probably be changing it tonight. But you're in. Use the all-in-one."

"It's a negative," Mack said.

"And really, really small," Tomlin said.

"Yeah, I know this," I said, and I looked at Sera. "You know how to use GIMP?"

"Yeah, kind of," she told me. "I mean, it's basically a poor-man's Photoshop."

"Well, then I guess I'm a poor man," I said. "I think I still have it installed. If you have an Adobe account, you could install Photoshop, but that would take longer, and I don't know if the old girl could handle it."

"OK, yeah. Cool," Sera said.

"I'm just thinking, you could probably scan the negatives at a high resolution, then blow 'em up and invert." I shrugged. "It's not ideal, but that'll at least make 'em look right. It'll show you what's there."

Tomlin said, "I thought you'd want to stay here for this."

"Angie called me," I said. "I'm meeting her at the police station when she takes her break. She found the file from that ..." I glanced at Sera. I'd met her, but I didn't really know her, and I still wanted some things to be mine. "From that thing with me and Grandpa," I said, "The chief's OK with me taking a look, but I guess he doesn't want me taking it out of the station. I don't know."

"You have to leave now?"

"No," I admitted, "but I'm going to." I gestured loosely at the computer, at the film, at Mack's miraculous arm. "I'm going to drive. I need to breathe. I'll have my phone with me."

"Be careful," Mack said.

"I will," I said, and I made my way to the office door. I paused there, though, and rapped my knuckles on the frame. "Hey. Sera."

Mack, Tomlin, and Sera all looked toward me. Sera asked, "Yeah?"

"That coffee's not gonna do it in the end. You need to hydrate."

"Will do," she said, raising her mug. "Godspeed, Mack's dad."

"We can hope," I said.

***

The Westley Police Department building looked exactly like it had to. Most of the up-front area was a big open area with regularly spaced desks. A few glass-walled offices sat at the back. To each side of the offices, there was a door. One of those led to the cells, and the other one led to the break room, conference and interview rooms, things like that. They probably joined at the back. It would have made sense if they did.

I walked across that tough, tight, dark-brown carpet, which was the same color as the coffee stains I could almost smell. I nodded to all the cops and added a wave for the ones I knew. I mean, we're talking Westley, so no one there was entirely unknown to me, but some of them, like Angie, had been classmates of mine. Drinking buddies. Partners in [redacted].

Angie stood in Chief Murdock's doorway, holding a stack of folders. As I got closer, I saw she was talking to the man himself. He sat behind his desk, leaning back in his chair with his hands folded behind his head. Murdock was about ten years older than me, and it's not like I'd ever disliked the guy, but I often wondered if he ever dialed down his swagger.

We all said our hellos, and then I stepped back so Angie and the chief could wrap up their conversations. It didn't take long. Angie waved for me to follow her toward one of those doors at the side — the one that didn't lead to jail cells.

"Mr. Keagan. Could I have a word, please," Murdock said. I didn't put a question mark there because he didn't, either.

I looked to Angie for a hint. She tapped the top of the stack of files she was carrying, but then she shrugged.

"Sure thing," I said, and I doubled back and went just inside Murdock's office.

Still leaning back, still with his hands like that, he said, "Listen. I'm real sorry about what happened to your, uh, to your sister's wife. And I'm even sorrier we haven't been able to do more."

I nodded.

"Now, uh ... I'm trying to think of a way to say this next part that won't make me sound like an asshole."

"I can hack it," I said, wondering where he'd dare to tread.

Murdock cleared his throat, leaned forward, and rested his arms on his desk. He capped and uncapped a Bic pen as he talked. "She was a writer," Murdock said, "Now, I've read one or two of those books."

Bet you couldn't name 'em, I thought.

"And they're, you know, they're OK. But it's not too hard to recognize some people and, uh, some places and things from around here in those books."

He capped the pen and set it down. He looked up at me, moving only his eyes.

I shrugged. Where was he going with this? What the hell did he want?

"Do you write?" he asked me, making it sound like a particular odious question.

"No more than I have to," I said.

"What about that ... kid of yours?"

"I've never had a problem with you, Chief," I told him. "Let's both be careful here."

"That's all I'm saying," Murdock assured me. "I'm not saying a thing against your family. I just want it understood that those files are for your personal edification only."

"Scout's honor," I said, raising my fingers in what I thought was the correct formation.

"You were a Boy Scout?" he asked.

"Cub," I clarified. "I got out after I made Bear. My troop never went camping, and I wasn't comfortable being called a 'We-Blow.'"

That got him to smile, or something. He showed his teeth. "Alright. That's fair enough. I still don't want those originals leaving here, but Officer Lara can make you copies of whatever you want. And we'll be keeping track of that.'

"Sounds fair," I said, though I wondered if he'd shown me some graciousness or threatened Angie's job. At the time, it felt like both.

"OK. Get on with it, then. Good to see you."

I nodded again but didn't say anything. It seemed right, and it seemed safe. Then I resumed my journey with Angie through that side door and down the hall.

We sat right next to each other at one side of a large meeting-table in what, according to the sign on the door, had been cleverly named Room 1. Angie spread the folders out on the table. Two rows of them, side-by-side, thirteen in total. The bottom row was longer. She handed me one of the folders and said, "OK. You're going to want to start here. This is the file from when you and your grandpa found the remains."

I nodded and leafed through it.

"I didn't see a statement from you in there," she said. "Just one from your grandpa."

"Yeah, that's probably right," I said. "He would have done all the talking."

"It just seems strange they wouldn't have talked to you, too."

"Not really. I don't know what I would have said that he didn't," I said, though I thought, *I could've let something slip about a piece of jewelry.* I wondered what that would have changed. Probably not much of anything. "Plus," I added, "Grandpa and the chief at the time were old hunting buddies. Probably just helped each other wrap it up quickly."

"That's not how it would be handled now," Angie said.

"Really?" I asked.

"Really," Angie said. "Greg's not a bad guy. You actually got a pretty good taste of what he's like on-average."

"Ooh. I'm lucky."

"OK, he's a dick when he feels like he has to be, but he usually switches gears at the right time, too." She reached for the folder I was holding and flipped through the pages, clearly looking for something specific. She tapped a sheet. "There. I wanted you to see that. That's the cover page from the lab that tested the remains. That packet there is the results."

"Really?" I said.

I must have sounded a little too excited. Angie said, "This was the late-'90s, so there's probably something there, but I wouldn't get my hopes up too high. It did have some ideas about the person, like age and height, so it helped me find some other things that might help you." She took the folder from me, shut it, and put it back on the table. She gestured at the others. "These are all unsolved missing-person reports from what I thought was a reasonable timeframe before you found the remains. All the ones that fit the little bit I could get from that lab report."

"Whoa. Twelve of them?" I said. "How far back do they go?"

"The oldest I pulled is 1951," Angie said. "If there's nothing here, we can keep going, but the records get *really* spotty before that, and I figured we needed, like, a manageable group to start with."

"Yeah, I like that," I said. "Thank you. Yeah, this is plenty."

Angie nodded, looking at the folders and not saying anything. Not saying something.

"What's wrong?" I asked.

"I hope it's here," she said. "I actually have a good feeling it is. But there's also a chance that it wasn't reported."

I laughed, then frowned. "What, were things that wild around here back then?"

"Hey, you were the one talking about hunting buddies."

"True."

"There's still problems with that now, with under-reporting," Angie said. "I can't think of anything big from here, but I know of at least three bodies found in Burwell recently that weren't tied to any reports. One of them was a homeless man found next to the train tracks. Not on them, thank God, but right next to them. One was a body found in a dumpster. The other one was a Latina, I think in her twenties. They found her when they were digging a new trench for irrigation."

"Jesus," I said, and then a bell rang dimly. Just one. "I might remember that one."

"Well, that one made news again recently because they actually identified her. Sort of by luck and after fourteen years." She knocked on one of the case files. "All these had people who were looking for them. But then you have hitchhikers, or that homeless man, or just a woman who was a state or two away from where her little bit of family thought she'd be."

"That is really fucking awful," I said.

"There are shadows and alleys everywhere," Angie said, "even when you think you're standing in the sunlight." She gave my arm a little pat. "Chief Murdock told me that."

"Alright," I said, "he's not an asshole."

"Not a total asshole," she said. "Not constantly."

I nodded, gazing at the case files arrayed before me.

"You want me to copy all of this, don't you?" she asked.

"I do," I said. "Sorry, but ... yeah. All of it."

"Every page."

"Every page."

Angie expertly slid the folders back into stacks. "See, I know you, so I actually started that when I got here. I can probably bring it all after I get off tonight. Will you be up?"

"I'll be there," I said.

Tomlin

The scanning did not go swimmingly. First off, it wasn't my house, which also meant it wasn't my workspace or equipment. My brother's aging PC might have been fine for whatever he used it for, but it didn't have the programs or any of the oomph any of us were used to working with. As it happened, Nate didn't have GIMP installed, so we had to wait to download that. Then we learned that even though GIMP had the same basic idea as Photoshop, it kept things in different menus, different places. That's not even saying anything about the scale of our project. We developed the workflow as the program installed: scan the strips of film, select each frame and save them individually, then, one-by-one, enlarge, invert, and look for stuff. Sera swore she didn't have to be home anytime soon, and she loved the challenge. Good for her. It drove Mack and me nuts.

As Sera started actually, really scanning the strips of film, Mack and I went into the living room. I took one of the recliners, and Mack sat on the couch. "How's your arm?" I asked them.

They chuckled hoarsely. " Yeah, you know, it's pretty hunky dory. I should probably be happy. I mean, I basically have this healing factor like Wolverine. It's not teleportation or anything, but I guess it's pretty cool. And it's not confusing or terrifying or anything."

"Must run in the family," I said, the words just sort of spilling out.

"What?" Mack asked me. She looked somewhere between startled and horrified.

I took a moment to put all my thoughts together, including the ones I hadn't been aware I was thinking. "I don't know. I don't know why I said that, but ... Tessa based Jack Beacham on your great-great uncle. Your arm's totally healed-up after five days. Your leg might've —"

"No, it did," Mack insisted. "I saw it."

"From your Attic," I said, and Mack flinched like I'd slapped them. "No. Wait. It's just ... they're memories, and anyone's memories can—"

"Both of you helped me make the Attic," Mack said.

"I know, Mack. I know what you were going through, but —"

Mack stood so quickly they sort of stumbled forward and bonked a shin against the coffee table. It hurt me to see it, to hear that, but Mack didn't even react to it. Instead, they narrowed their eyes and stared at something past me. They looked like they were staring right through the dining-room wall. "To organize my thoughts, but we assumed all of them were mine."

"Mack."

No response.

"Mack."

Nothing. I brought the footrest down and got to my feet, and then I approached Mack slowly, afraid their talk about the old days had pushed them into one of their own episodes. They hadn't withdrawn like that for so many nears, at least not without controlling it. I tried to remember: was this how it had always looked? Was this what I looked like from the outside during my own dark times? I swallowed drily and tried to think through the pain of my breaking heart. It was me. I was contagious. Infectious. I'd given this to them. I'd given this to my kid.

My kid, I thought. *Yeah, that's damn right. My kid. This is my kid.*

"Mack," I said, grabbing their arms. "Just focus on me, Mack. Listen to my voice. What are you —"

Their eyes suddenly locked onto mine. I'd asked them to focus, but now I wanted to take that back. "There's an upstairs," Mack said with a calm that terrified me. "Someone is upstairs."

They stepped out of my grip and ran up the stairs.

"Mack!" I said. "Honey!"

"I'm fine, it's cool," they called back. "I'm going to look for the box that Nana gave us."

I looked down. The box from my mom's trunk — without the scrapbook, which was still in the workshop, and the Kodak 35 Rangefinder, which was still in my car — sat on the floor to the side of the couch. But I knew that while Mack meant that box, they didn't mean *that* box.

I shut my eyes and pressed my hands to the sides of my head.

"Both of you helped me make the Attic."

I pressed harder, realizing that while we'd told Sera a crazy story, only Nate, Mack, and I had actually seen anything, had even experienced any of this.

"Must run in the family."

Was that that this was? Just a common delusion, born from … what? Shared grief? Shared genes?

"Uh, Tomlin?" Sera called from the office.

I took a long, ragged breath. "No, Sera. Not now. Just … give me a minute."

"OK, but when you see this, you're gonna be pissed you took that minute."

***

First, Sera and I just looked at it. We just stared at the computer screen, neither of us saying a thing. Then she did some more work to the pic, dodged and burned, cleaned it up, and we stared at it some more.

"Print that," I said.

We were standing shoulder-to-shoulder, looking down at the printed photograph, when I heard the sliding door open and shut and as I listened to Nate's footsteps carry him through the kitchen and dining-room. Sera and I were still like that, still looking at that photo, trying to make sense of it, thinking it might change, when Nate stopped in the office doorway and said, "Hey. I think we might be onto something."

"Yeah," I said, or I tried to say that. I couldn't hear my voice, so I figured he couldn't, either. I cleared my throat, tried it again, and had a little more luck that time. "Yeah? You too?"

I handed the picture to him slowly, so slowly, feeling like my arm was moving through syrup.

Nate took it and looked at it, and his eyes got wide, his mouth dropped open, and every bit of color drained from his face. There was something reassuring in that. It seemed right. Not normal — just right. One little thing that almost made sense.

"Jee-zus tits," my brother said, dusting off one of our dad's go-to curses. He handed the picture back to me with a shaking hand, and then he grabbed the back of the desk chair, spun it around, and managed to sit right before he would have fallen down.

I looked at the photo again. I hoped it had changed. I could have lived with being ridiculously wrong about what I thought I'd seen, but dammit, there it was. There it kept being.

Two men stood side-by-side in the black-and-white photo, all buddied-up and grinning. One of them was Jack Beacham, and he didn't look any younger or older than he had at the air museum, at the art gallery, or in my brother's shop. But I'd gotten numb to that. To the fact that he evidently didn't age. Hell, to the fact that he evidently existed. To just about every evident aspect of him.

As for the other guy in the picture, he didn't look too different from the person sitting in that chair about three feet from me, and he certainly didn't look different enough. It was him. I didn't know how, but it was him. The two men in that photo were my brother and Jack Beacham, and I recognized the setting, too. I knew those corrals and the big structure next to them, though all the Western hats and horse trailers didn't hurt, either. Westley doesn't have much, but it does have its rodeo.

A banner stretched high over Jack and Nate's smiling faces, spanning the road that ran between corrals. It said:

Grand Centennial Rodeo

Happy Birthday Oregon!

July 1-2-3-4 1959

"Where's Mack?" Nate asked. "I thought they'd be down here with you.."

***

We knocked. We yelled. Mack didn't answer. Nate took a step back and gestured for me to open the door.

"It's your house," I said.

"It's Mack's room."

"You're their parent, too."

"I'm trying," he said, "but that's you."

I swallowed and tried to blink away the wet fire suddenly burning my eyes. I could process that later. I'd have to. "Thank you," I said, and I opened the door. And for a second, for just a second, I felt very relieved and very foolish. Mack was right there. On their bed. Sleeping.

"I'm going to look for the box that Nana gave us."

"Mack?" I said, charging into the room. "Mack! Mack!" I crashed into the bed, kneeled down there, grabbed Mack, shook them. "Mack! Mack! Honey, Mack! Honey! Honey!"

Nate pulled me away. Pried my hands off of Mack's shoulders. He might have said something. He and Sera both probably did.

He kept pulling me back until I hit the wall, and both of us sat on the floor there. He didn't let go. That was nice, and that was smart. I would have run right back.

Sera — amazing Sera — put her hand up by Mack's nose and touched her fingers to Mack's wrist. "They have a pulse, and they're breathing," she told us, "and they both seem right. I mean, as far as I know. They're just ... they're not responding."

"They're stuck," I said. "They said they were going up to their Attic, and they got stuck."

207

"I know it looks that way, but that's not what this is."

I whipped my head around so fast to look toward the new voice that my neck popped. Jack Beacham stood in the bedroom doorway, looking in, looking at Mack, looking at my kid, with an infuriating expression of satisfaction on his face. "Mack isn't stuck," he said. "They're not stuck anywhere. In fact, they're probably moving further and more freely than they ever ha —."

Nate surged toward Jack Beacham. They tumbled in a tangle and punched and kicked each other on the hallway floor.

No. Nate punched. Nate kicked. Jack blocked, and he blocked so easily, so smoothly, that I knew he could have killed my brother if he decided to. If he wanted to.

I ran toward them. Sera stayed by the bed, keeping an eye on Mack, protecting them.

"Stop it!" I shouted from the doorway. "Nathan, stop it!"

"What about him?" my brother yelled.

"He's not doing anything! How can we learn anything this way? Stop it! Just stop!"

Nate stopped striking, but he didn't break away. He straddled Jack's torso, drew his right fist back, and twisted his face into a darker sneer of hate than I had ever seen.

"*Talk!*" Nate screamed. "Who are you?"

Jack smiled. "Jack Beacham. Sergeant. Serial —"

Nate punched him. Honestly, that time, I couldn't blame him.

Jack turned his head to the side, spit out some blood, and laughed. "Oh, we are going to laugh about this one day. Did you see the pictures?"

Nate pulled his fist back again. "What do you want from us?"

"I'd like a smooth road," Jack said. "I know I won't get that, but there are things I need to do."

"Five," Nate said. "Four. Three."

"I close loops and open doors," Jack said. "That's all."

Nate punched Jack again, this time instantly and obviously breaking his nose. I gasped and covered my face with my hands. Their voices came through the cracks between my fingers..

Nate said, "No jokes. No fucking riddles."

"I understand. Christ, you can be a quick-tempered son of a bitch." He spat again. I heard that. "Dammit, Nate. I hope it's different this time."

Whup.

Silence. Darkness and silence.

Footsteps behind me.

I slid my hands down my face as I turned my head. Sera stood beside me. "Tomlin, what happened?" she asked. "What was that sound ?"

I didn't say anything, but together, we looked out into the empty hallway.

Letter from Thelma Keagan to Theresa Hatcher

Dear Tessa,

You sure surprised me with your letter the other day. The envelope you used made it look like junk mail, but I guess you know that. Jim leaves the junk and the bills for Nathan and me to go through.

I don't know if there's much you'll gain by asking me about Jim's brother Tom, but you're right that you wouldn't get anything by going to Jim. He's never liked talking about that brother, and I didn't know Jim until after the war and after Tom died. He first started courting me in 1949, and we were married in 1950, not long before Jim went off to Korea. He's wearing his uniform in our wedding photo because it was the only suit he had.

Anyway, you asked what I thought about your ideas for your story. I used to think I might become a writer, but life had other ideas. Some of it's been happy, but it's good you're taking the chance. You should be sure to use your time while it's yours.

It's nice to think of those boys having special powers to get themselves through the war. It would have helped them after, too. I don't know how anyone could expect them to go through that and still be the same person afterward. A lot of those boys struggled to feel like a person at all.

I call them "boys" because they were, or they should have been. Are you around Nathan's or Tomlin's age? Nathan's around the same age now that Jim was when he left for Korea. Jim's brother Tom was younger than that in WWII and when he died.

That's not what you asked me about, is it? You wanted to know about Tom, and I'm sorry I can't help you there. You asked about your idea of "Nephilim," too, and I had to look that up. In my Catholic Bible, you're right, that's what it says. In my old King James though — I had to become Catholic to marry Jim — they're called "giants." I think I like that better. They'd have to be giants, maybe not in height but in their heart and soul, to get through what they did.

I don't know if I helped you, but I don't know what else I can say. I think Nathan's taking me to my doctor's appointment on Wednesday, so that's when I'll try to mail this. I'll tuck it away until then. This is kind of fun, but it would be just as easy for you to call here. I'm usually the one who answers the phone.

Nathan has a little more of his grandpa in him than I thought, but they should both soften up a bit when that baby comes. If you're not good at waiting, you will be. We women learn to be patient in this family. I know I'll make sure to see that great-grandchild of mine. I know how to save up for the right fight.

You take care, and remember a phone call is probably better.

Sincerely,
Thelma Keagan

Mack

My mom and I went into the living room when Sera started scanning the film. I felt bad for just dumping that on her, but only a little. She'd just dipped her toes into the shallow end of all the crazy shit, while we'd been swimming in it for days.

Anyway, I sprawled out on the couch, and mom sat in one of dad's recliners and asked me how my arm was. I know she had to say something, but I had to laugh. "Oh, it's fine," I said. "Yeah, it's hunky-dory. I'm like Wolverine over here with this healing factor, and that doesn't, like, freak me out or anything."

"Runs in the family," Mom said.

My eyes snapped wide and something opened behind them. I sat up, lunged forward, and my hands slapped the coffee table. "Wait, what does that mean?" I asked her. "What do you mean?"

Mom blinked like she didn't even know. She sort of stammered and stuttered for a bit, and then she said, "I don't know."

"Oh, come on. Don't do that to me."

"Well, Tessa based Jack Beacham on your great-great uncle, and look: your arm's healed-up after five days. And your leg might've even —"

"No, my leg didn't 'might have' anything," I insisted. "It broke, and then it was fine. I saw it, Mom. I fucking *felt* it."

"You were in your Attic," she said, like that dismissed everything, and I was heartbroken. That was a fucking betrayal. "No, no, wait," Mom said. "I just mean they're memories, and anyone's memories can—"

"You helped me make the Attic," my voice said, sounding far away. "You said it would —"

"I know, Mack. I know. I know what you were going through, but —"

"No, you said it would help me!" I told her, and I stood up so fast I banged my shin against the coffee table. I heard it, but I didn't feel it. "To organize my thoughts. To — "

To pack away the voices, I thought. I blinked against the glare of a mental floodlight that only illuminated a thousand more questions.

Distantly, I heard Mom drop her footrest, and then she grabbed onto my arms. "Focus on me, Mack," she said. "What are you —"

I locked my eyes with hers and swatted away her hands. "You told me they were all mine. You put it all on me," I said, feeling the burning start in my eyes and the sob building in my throat. No. Forget that. It wasn't the time. I closed my eyes, and I gulped, and I heard that dragging sound again from above.

I thought, *Above.*

"There's an upstairs," I said with a level of calm that impressed me. It grounded me. "Someone is upstairs."

I was already jogging up the stairs when Mom yelled out, "Mack! Honey!"

"I'm fine. It's cool," I called back as I opened the door to my room. "I'm going to look for the box that Nana Ronnie gave us."

I lay right on top of the covers of my unmade bed in the attic and went straight up to my Attic. The box from Nana was already open on the floor, its contents arranged around it and somehow making me think of the rays of the sun. Or of that funky, spiky starburst clock that used to hang on Nana's dining-room wall.

The shades were up. The show was on. I stood behind the chair and rested my hand on its scratchy, ratty back. I didn't know how long I'd be up there, but I didn't want to waste my time sitting.

Nana's garage, facing out. Both the doors open. That was her car parked out at the curb. Both Tessa's and Tomlin's cars were backed up to the garage, one to each door, with their trunks opened. My view through the windows bobbed and wavered a bit as Mack lugged a box through the garage and dropped it into the trunk of Tomlin's car. It took some maneuvering to get it in with the other boxes that were already there, and it took even more finesse to shut the trunk lid, but they got it done. "OK, can't get any more back here," they said.

Tomlin nodded as she staggered toward the car, struggling to maintain her hold on a heavy box of her own.

"Mom, the trunk's full," Mack said.

"Yeah, I heard ya," Tomlin said, and she sketchily balanced the box between her leg and the back bumper. "Open the back door. I can put this on the seat."

The image narrowed as Mack squinted to peer through the back window of the car. "No, that's full, too."

"Then I'll put it on the passenger seat. Come on, I think there are plates in here."

She picked the box up again, and Mack went around her to open the front passenger-side door. Tomlin lunged and basically dropped the box onto the seat. Whatever was inside clattered a lot more noisily than it should have. They did sound like plates, but they were probably fine; that move wasn't too long before, and I didn't remember any significant breakage.

"Whew. OK," Tomlin said.

"So where am I gonna sit?" Mack asked her.

"Probably in the other car," Tomlin said, and she shut the door. "It doesn't matter, does it? We're all going to the same place."

"Yeah, it's fine. Other Mother has a better stereo, anyway."

"Stop it, or you might hurt my feelings," Tomlin said.

"Really? Will I?"

"You could," Tomlin said, "but probably not like that. I'll see you both at home."

"Cool, yeah," Mack said, and they gave each other a hug, and Tomlin got into her car.

In the Attic, I plucked at a frayed thread on the back of the chair and wondered where this was going. I remembered the move, of course, but I remembered it as being exactly as mundane as it still looked.

Mack waved as Tomlin pulled out of the driveway. Behind them, a door opened. They turned and reframed the view, which situated the cluttered shelves and the chest freezer in the left window and the door into the house, the water heater, and the utility sink in the right one. Tessa and Nana Ronnie stepped out from the house into the garage. Each one of them was carrying a box. They looked similar — I mean, boxes gonna box — but I recognized the printing on the side of the one Tessa was holding.

"Guess you're riding with me?" she said.

"Yeah, guess so."

Nana Ronnie worked the box she was holding into the trunk and said, "We should be able to get both of these in there."

Tessa nodded, but it was at her own thoughts, not at what her mother-in-law had said. She said, "Here," passed her box to Nana Ronnie, and shut the trunk.

"What — " Nana said, but she cut herself off when she looked at the box in her hands. Which is to say, when she looked at *the* box, which she held in her hands. "Oh. Geez. Honey, this just doesn't make any sense."

Tessa said, "It will. I think. Or maybe it won't." She glanced briefly at Mack. They thought nothing of it if they even noticed it at all. I only picked up on it in the Attic because of my hyper-awareness to All Things Box. "You can handle one box, right? I just want to leave this one here for a while."

Nana Ronnie nodded and took the box over to the freezer. She set it on top of the chest but didn't turn back around.

Still facing the wall of the garage, she asked, "OK, and how long is a 'while'?"

It wasn't anything unusual for an Attic picture-show to carry more weight than the original experience had. I mean, even for a normie, that's how memories work, right? But this was different. For one thing, I had no idea why Mack — why I — would have just stood there, watching, not saying anything, but I hadn't heard them say a thing for a while, and the perspective hadn't changed at all. Then I realized that wasn't true. By then, Mack had to be in the car. The view had changed because the box had moved. It had tracked the box, which wasn't how it ever was. This wasn't a regular trip down the lane.

Then, because of course it happened then, there was that sound. That dragging, scuffing sound. I jerked my head up and tried to look through the ceiling. No. I didn't even look *at* the ceiling, because there wasn't one. There'd never been one. *You're not even in an Attic,* I reminded myself. *You call it one because it makes it easier.* But did it? For my moms, maybe. It had made it easier for them to help me. To understand me. Tomlin especially.

"I don't know why I do it. I think I just want it to have a shape," Tomlin said. I spun around to face the windows again and saw her there, her bashful face half-transparent, overlaid on the concluding scene in Nana Ronnie's garage. A second, smaller box had joined the peanut gallery. It was open, too. A battered spiral notebook had wormed its way into the starburst formation on the floor and squatted at the 11:00 position. The words DREAM JOURNAL were written on the front in black Sharpie, standing out but not alone. Doodles, scribbles, and sketches surrounded them.

"What do you mean, you want it to have a shape?" Mackenzie asked.

"I don't know. Dreams, I guess. My daydreams. So I'll know what to make."

"Like, your paintings and drawings?"

"I sound crazy. Can I have my notebook back?" Even at that reduced resolution, where I could see Tessa and my grandma and my grandma's garage through her, I could tell she was blushing.

"No, I think I ..." Mackenzie started to say, but they trailed off as they handed the notebook back to their mom. "Like, can you control your dreams?"

Tomlin held the notebook against her chest and smiled. "Kind of," she said. "I'm not sure if I want to do it completely. There's no adventure in that. I just like to have an idea of where I'm going."

The windows shattered. I looked down at my hands, held out toward them. Then I lowered my hands to the back of the ratty recliner, and they landed right on that frayed thread again. I pulled it, and I pulled it some more, and the chair sort of ruptured into something less than dust. Even the thread was gone.

I faced the shelves and saw what they really were. Not metal or wood but bones. Tissue. Cysts. Following instinct or something even more basic than that, I pressed my palms together, pushed my arms out in front of me, and spread my hands apart, and then ....

I mean, oh my God ...

No more shelves, no more boxes, but not Nothing because now Everything rushed toward me, engulfed me, caressed me, filled me. Everything. Everything I'd ever smelled and seen and heard and felt and tasted. Everything. Everything.

I can't say how long that lasted because that doesn't mean anything. There'd never been such a thing as time in the Attic. There'd never been an Attic. It was. It is.

Dammit. I knew I'd hit this wall. There isn't a word. Then what is there? It. All. Memory. Knowledge. I wasn't high then, and I promise I'm not now, though I kind of wish I was. It would help at least one of us.

I opened what I'll call my eyes, my ears, I opened everything, and I'd never found the ends of the "Attic," but what I'd imagined of it wasn't even a speck compared to the swirling, pulsing, eddying Everything that ...

Dammit! Words! There are no words!

But there was a current. Currents. Pushing and pulling me and nudging and ...

That dragging sound. That scraping sound. I felt it. Heard it. I *knew* it. And I found it: a glimmering current strengthening from my attention. From our connection. Just a single, simple current, flowing in the Everystream.

Shit, there's something. Maybe that's the word. I'm going to use that.

"There's an upstairs."

I shifted. Dove.

"Someone is upstairs."

I swam. Shades and shapes I knew surged past me. And some I didn't, though I can see them now when I close my eyes; I know I'd feel them, I'd remember them again if I let myself as I drifted off tonight. They triggered images and tastes and sounds and smells and feelings as they brushed against my shoulders (which weren't there) and chest (which wasn't there) and my legs (which weren't there, either). I knew each one of them until I forgot them again. They loved me. They'd missed me. They'd been so lonely in the deep, deep parts of me.

Then it quieted, I guess, or slowed. Maybe both of those. The impossible array of colors congealed and reduced to a still-dazzling crayon box of colors, most of which you might actually find in a rainbow. And got solid around the edges. Shit, now there were edges. Funky tessellations at first, then simpler, smaller, and both more and less familiar. I made out a bed, a closet door, and a carpeted floor. So mundane. It made me sad. I'd never felt such a loss. But then I reminded myself I'd pass through the stream on my way back. I'd get to. I had to.

You're gonna have to find your way back home, I thought, and I felt a fifty-fifty mix of excitement and sheer fucking terror.

Then it got weird.

The closet doors lurched toward me, and a hand pushed out toward them. I recognized the POV from every one of my trips to my Attic, but there were no windows here, and that had never been my hand. That hand, though, was the hand that was *there,* and it pulled open the closet door. Then another hand joined it, another one that wasn't mine, and the view tilted down to center on an old metal footlocker on the closet floor.

The hands dragged the banged-up trunk out of the closet, and that *sound* — there was that *sound,* and it was both closer and quieter than it had ever been before. The hands popped the latches and lifted the lid. Whoever's windows these were — whoever owned these eyes — was totally transfixed by what lay inside the trunk, so everything sort of froze there. I appreciated that. It gave me a chance to catch my bearings and to reduce the general level of What-the-Fuck.

The footlocker was full, mainly with clothes. Old, olive-green army fatigues. A uniform shirt was all crumpled on the top, either like it had been folded in a less-than-half-assed fashion or like it had been pulled out and put back so many times folding it would have been a futile task. I made out the sergeant insignia on one arm but only two letters of the name patch that arm was draped across: EA.

The hands moved suddenly, startling me, and burrowed through the clothes and papers and little black cases. *Presentation case,* I thought. Somehow, I knew that. Presentation cases. Army medals.

The hands came up with a framed black-and-white photo of a skinny, grinning dude wearing the same fatigues that had been covering the picture and sitting on the same footlocker that had, until recently, contained both of those things. The locker sat on the floor at the foot of a cot. I couldn't make out much more than that. It looked like he was in a big tent, and those might have been toiletries on a little shelf behind him.

The view tilted up, making me queasy. Somehow, I knew I wasn't the only one. The eyes, the hands, and everything in-between sort of wobbled up and away from the chest and moved toward a dresser that looked only a little less banged-up than it did in my attic bedroom at my dad's house. But this wasn't the same room. I thought about the closet door and the short trek to this piece of furniture and figured I was in what I knew as my dad's office. But he was the one who'd started using it as that. It used to be his grandparents' bedroom, and that was his grandpa's face I saw in the mirror coming up from the back of the dresser. *That's a cool mirror,* I thought as Jim Keagan contemplated his reflection. *Wonder why I don't have it.*

Jim looked at the photo, then he looked at his sixty-year-old face, and then he grumbled something and tossed the picture aside and slapped his hands onto the top of the dresser. That gave him more than a little help in staying standing up. "Why, why the hell?" he slurred. "Oh, what the fuck an' why?"

His right hand shot out, and the mirror shattered. Something kind of like pain and kind of like lightning creaked and crackled past me. Through me. Then hands that shouldn't have been there grabbed onto my shoulders, which I didn't really have, and pulled me away from the windows —

They're windows now.

— and threw me down to what felt very much like a hardwood floor. I narrowed my eyes to cut the glare from the bare bulb swinging from the unseeable ceiling.

A figure stepped into the light and loomed over me, his hands balled into fists at his sides. In a normal, corporeal setting, his face would have been in total eclipse thanks to the bulb blaring behind him. But there was nothing corporeal about this, and little of it would have seemed normal to anyone but me. I'm saying I saw him perfectly. I identified him perfectly. I identified him as Jim Keagan, age sixty, maybe a little more.

"And who the fuck are you?" he growled, flexing his hands and clenching them again. Clench and flex, clench and flex. Bits of glass glittered on his bloody knuckles.

"Hey. You only have two hands," I told him. And then I laughed. I don't think he liked that.

***

Up until then, as far as I knew, I had only a single memory of Great-Grandpa Keagan. I'd just turned five when he died, and I didn't spend much time in Westley before then, so it's kind of ironic that one of my first memories is of that place. At least, it's one of the earliest memories I can access in the regular fashion, without climbing up to the Attic or taking a dip in the Everystream.

Yeah, I like that. I'm going to stick with that.

I must have been four. My dad and I got back to the Keagan house after seeing *Robots*, which was my first time in a theater. I still love that movie. He pulled open the sliding door for me as I finished the last of our popcorn. I stepped into the kitchen and tried to give the empty bucket to him. "Here, I'm done," I said.

"Cool," he told me, and he pointed at the wastebasket. "Take care of it."

I stepped on the pedal to open the lid and tossed the bucket in. I took my foot off the pedal, and the *whump* of the lid when it closed coincided with an incredible string of profanities emanating from the living room. I didn't move any further than the can, but I did crane my neck so I could know what was going on. I saw my dad's grandpa out there in the living room, clutching some of my toys in his hands and kicking some of the others across the floor. I'm picturing that now, and he seems huge and horrifying. I see him taller,

221

bigger than he was because he was usually louder than he needed to be.

"Well, guess it's 5:00 somewhere," my dad said, and then he patted me on the shoulder. "Hey. Stay here for a minute, OK? Get some juice or something from the fridge if you're thirsty."

"OK," I said. "I don't want him to hurt my toys."

"No, I won't let him," Dad said, and then he repeated: "Stay here."

"OK."

I gave him a head start, but then I started following him. He looked back over his shoulder and raised his eyebrows, and I stopped in the open doorway between the kitchen and dining room. He nodded and kept going, so I guessed that was good enough.

"Hey. Can I help you with something?" he asked his grandpa.

"Yeah, you can clean your shit up before you go jerkin' around," Jim Keagan said. "Just about broke my goddamn neck trippin' on that thing. Got these goddamn toys and shit all over the damn place."

"I see two toy trucks," my dad said, "and you've got a couple of action figures in your hands."

"'Action figures'? That what you call these things?" my great-grandpa asked, looking closer at the toys in his hands.

"Well, OK, so I take it back," my dad said. "That one's a Barbie, and that one's the Thing."

"The Thing?"

"Yeah, from the Fantastic Four."

"The Thing," Jim Keagan said again, and then he snorted. "Well, doesn't that sound about right."

"What does that mean?"

"Oh, I don't know. Means at least these dolls and 'action figures' know how to dress."

He shoved the Barbie and the Thing into my dad's chest. Dad sort of grunted, and then he took the toys and said to his grandpa, "Really. I mean, really. Oh, you never cease to fucking amaze, me, you know that? You're talking about a child."

My great-grandpa plopped into his recliner, and now, as I'm sitting here typing this, I realize it was *the* recliner. God, it's crystal-clear now. It's like it embedded itself in my head. In me. "Yeah, I know what I'm talking about, and I know it's the parents' job to set the kid right," he said, and then he shrugged and sucked his teeth. "But I probably should expect you or your sister's girlfriend to know nothin' about that."

He grabbed his beast of a remote control off the coffee table. Actually, it was two remotes rubber-banded together. My dad snatched that brick from his hand and hurled it blindly. The remotes had a short flight, but they flew straight and crashed through the glass of the triangular display case on the mantel.

My dad and his grandpa looked at that, and then they looked at each other. Neither of them said a word. Nothing. I don't even know if they blinked.

I got the jug of apple juice out of the fridge, took it to the counter, and poured myself some juice.

After a while, my dad passed behind me and went out the sliding door. Then he came back in. Back and forth, back and forth, carrying my shit out to his car and then coming back for some more: my vehicles, my action figures and dolls, my backpack. He kept making those trips, and I kept pouring and drinking juice. It was something I could do. I drank a lot of juice.

After just about forever, Dad tapped me on my shoulder and said, "Come on, put that away. Let's go."

I put my glass in the sink and the jug back in the fridge, and then here's something else I'd forgotten until now. I mean, hot damn. "I thought I was spending another night here," I said.

"I'm stuck here," he said. "You don't have to be."

I got up to my feet and looked over the digs. Some cardboard boxes were there, but mainly, they were trunks and lockers and toolboxes and even some equipment sheds. And those two windows and the chair. "Huh," I said.

"I'm gonna ask you again," he said. "Who are you?"

"Mack."

"Mack."

"Short for Mackenzie."

"Mackenzie."

"Mackenzie Keagan Hatcher." I frowned. "At least part of that should ring a bell." I stood by the chair, keeping it between us, and looked back at the windows and at the drunk man sobbing in front of his reflection. I'd just about thought I had it figured out, but once again, here was a whole set of things that didn't add up. "This is when your son died, right? When you learned he was KIA."

His eyes bugged, and he clenched his jaw. Through his teeth, he said, "And what the hell do you know about that?"

"I thought you were upstairs because I descended from you," I said, much, much more to myself than to him. "But this day, this was after my dad was born, and it was after his dad was born, so it's not like ... no, that doesn't make any sense."

"Oh, you're saying some of it does? You tell me then. Tell me a little more. Who are you, and how in the hell did you get into my place?"

My eyes widened, and my whole scalp prickled. "You don't know me," I said.

"No, and I think I told you. No, I don't know you."

"You don't even recognize my name. Not any part of my name."

"Mackenzie Keagan Hatcher. That's what you told me, right? Mackenzie Keagan Hatcher." He raised his eyebrows and put up his hands. "Nope. Don't hear no fuckin' bells."

The prickle spread: across my shoulders, down my arms, down my spine. "Well, that's who I am," I said. "I guess it's your turn. Who are you?"

"Name's Charlie Beacham," he said. "That help?"

Nathan

I scrambled to my feet in what looked an awful lot like my upstairs hallway. But it was only me. No Jack Beacham, no spectators in the doorway. In fact, that door was shut. All the doors were shut. I caught my breath and opened the door to what really, really should have been Mack's bedroom, but I only saw darkness. By the time I groped my way to the light switch and flipped it, I think I was expecting to see what I wound up seeing — an attic. Filled with stacks of boxes of shit and some random unboxed shit. And furniture. An attic. Just an attic.

I opened the other upstairs doors, I guess so I could spend a little more time with futility. The box room had boxes but fewer of them. The bathroom was the bathroom, which was oddly reassuring. I took a little break there. I took a leak, and then I soaked a hand-towel with cold water and pressed it to the places where Jack had landed especially solid hits. Then I sighed, tossed the towel into the sink, and opened the Jack-and-Jill door that opened onto my bedroom.

The room was right, I guess, but the posters and the pictures on the wall weren't quite there. As a man of just-past-forty, I didn't have much in the way of posters on my bedroom wall, but now, hanging over the unmade bed that looked like mine, there was a poster for the movie *Almost Famous*. And across the room from that, flanking the dresser, there were two more movie posters, for *Clerks* and *Pulp Fiction*. I'd had every one of those, and I'd hung them up right where they were hanging, but I remembered pulling them down something like fifteen years before.

"What, time travel?" I said out loud to the empty room. "Did he send me back?" And where was he?

I jogged down the stairs, calling for Tomlin and Mack and even Mack's friend, Sera. No answer. Then I tried calling for my grandpa and grandpa, but I was just answered by silence there, too. I didn't stop or even slow down on my way through the living room and dining room, so I didn't check to see if that was my office or my grandparents' room or something else to my left. Maybe I should have. Maybe it would have lessened my shock when I got to town.

I didn't stop until I got out on the deck, when I saw there weren't any cars parked out back. I patted all my pockets but couldn't find my cell phone. I glanced back toward the sliding door, wondering if I should go back inside and look. Somehow, I knew I wouldn't find it in there, either.

I did find my keys in my pocket, though. My house keys, keys to the car that wasn't there, and keys to the shop. I had my coat on, and it felt like the temperature had pushed past fifty. It was a nice day for a walk, and I figured that maybe something would make sense by the time I got to the shop. I don't know. It was all I had.

Overall, it was an easy walk as far as walks go. Just a straight shot down the shoulder of the highway with fields to each side for most of it. I think I passed four houses, maybe six in total. Then there was that final hill, though, just where it should have been. For once, I was glad to see that hill and to feel the pain of walking up it, first in my calves, then my thighs, then all the way up to my ass. Like I said, I was past forty, and I felt it. That was OK, though. I didn't mind. Pain meant real.

Until it didn't. I stopped at the top of the hill and not just because it was the top of that damn hill. I stood there with my hands on my hips, trying to catch my breath as I tried to make sense of this sign in front of me:

Welcome to

Chapel Cross

Population 1,295

You're only a stranger once!

I started walking again without really knowing why or where I was going. Like being pulled on a string. Outside the feed store, Polly crouched down by the A-frame board, swapping around the letters and numbers, changing the specials. That reassured me for about a second. It made me feel good. But that wasn't Polly. Chapel Cross, the changes at the house ...

"Morning, Leah," I said.

The woman who looked like Polly but wasn't Polly flinched and looked behind her. "Oh, you scared me!"

"Sorry about that."

She set her letter tiles on the sidewalk, stood, and dusted her hands off on her jeans. "Oh, don't worry about it. Don't worry," she said. "Good morning. We'll go with that."

"Morning," I said again.

"I didn't expect to see you today. I thought you were on vacation."

"Maybe I am," I said, and I spread my hands. "I mean, where else would I be?"

Leah chuckled and said, "Well, I can think of a few places I'd rather go, but whatever works for you. Hope you get a chance to get out and enjoy some of this day. Compared to what we've been having, it looks like it'll be a nice one."

"Yeah, maybe. You have a good one."

"Yeah. You, too," Leah said, and she got back to her sign.

She hadn't called me Nate, but she wouldn't have, not if she was Leah Leonard. I knew who I was or at least who Jack Beacham expected me to play. Directly across the street was an antique store, and I read "We BUY We SELL We TRADE" on the right-hand window, just as I expected. Then again, at that point, I couldn't exactly be surprised by the lettering on the window to the left:

BEACHAM'S BYGONES

Est. 1947

I crossed the street and tried my key in the lock. It worked.

***

Sitting here now, writing and thinking about the first time I opened the door to Beacham's Bygones, I'm trying to remember the first time I walked into Keagan's Collections. I don't think I can. Trips to Westley were always part of our weekly routine — Sundays, right after church. Sometimes, Mom and Tomlin would go off and do something else, but I was always there with Dad.

Here's one that's jumping out at me. I'm seeing myself as nine, on my way to ten. My dad's there, and I'm picturing him pretty much like I last saw him, so he still had some time on his clock but not much. I'd probably never heard of Kuwait or Iraq.

Dad was over at the record bins, flipping through them, every once in a while pulling an LP about half-out and sort of smiling at it before sliding it back. Grandpa sat on his stool behind the counter, flipping through a big hardback book. A coffee-table book. And I came up out of the back room, pushing the big shop-broom.

Grandpa chuckled. Dad didn't. "What the hell are you doing?" he asked.

"I'm sweepin'," I said.

"Not you. What, you can't afford real help?"

"Oh, it's good for him," Grandpa said, not looking up from his book. "A little work don't hurt."

"Is he paying you?" Dad asked.

No one else answered, so I said, "Is that for me now?"

"Yes, I'm talking to you."

"I don't know. He didn't say if he was paying me."

"No, I ain't paying him," Grandpa said. "What's wrong? What's the matter with you?"

Ignoring his own dad, my dad told me to put the broom back.

"But Grandpa told me to sweep the floor," I said. "And I kinda —"

"Your Dad's telling you to put the broom back."

"OK," I said, recognizing that particular configuration on my dad's face and knowing there was precisely zero point in pressing my view further. I leaned the broom against the counter and glanced around for something to change the subject. To take my mind off the weirdness.

"You should put that broom back where it goes," Grandpa said. "You gonna let him do that, Benji?"

"Am I supposed to put the broom back?" I asked.

"Yeah, put the broom back," Dad said.

I did that and lingered in the back room for a bit before venturing out again. When I did, my dad was up at the counter, arguing with my grandpa about a couple of the record albums. "I have the money, but that's not the point," Dad said.

"Oh, really? You were making it sound like it is," Grandpa told him. "Don't you have these on tape by now, anyways?"

"Yeah, I do."

"What are you bitchin' at me for, then?"

"These are my records."

"You don't know that."

"They got my initials written up here on the back of the sleeve."

"Oh, you ain't the only one with them initials."

"I left these records — I left a *lot* of records — at the house when I went into the bush in '69. Got back from my tour, and they were gone."

"Well, how long did you want me to store 'em? I figured either way, you weren't moving back."

"Oh, for fuck's sake."

"Look, you want to buy those, I'll give you a deal on 'em."

"I'm not going to buy them twice!" my dad shouted.

"Then what are we yelling for?" Grandpa hollered back.

Dad put up his hands, muttered a chain of somethings that I didn't recognize as words, and stormed out of the shop, slamming the door shut behind him.

"Hm. Looks like he forgot you," Grandpa said with a smirk that I'd get to know much too well. "Guess you can finish sweeping."

"What are you reading?" I asked, not because I was going against Grandpa but because I didn't feel like doing anything connected to the last few minutes.

"Not really reading it," Grandpa said. "Mostly just looking at the pictures."

"Then what are you looking at?"

"You sure ask a lot of questions."

"You're not answering even one of them."

Grandpa looked at me, raised his eyebrows, and I took a step back. He nodded, turned a page in his book, and said, "You're smarter than you look." He turned another page, and then he turned another one. "It's a book about World War II airplanes," he said. "Came in with an estate sale." He turned the book toward me and tapped one of the pictures. "There. That was my brother's plane."

I knew the picture, of course, but I'd never thought about it showing up in a book. It was part of our family's story, but it was weird to realize it might be part of someone else's story, too. "Oh, that was the one that he ..." I swallowed. "Was that when he died?"

Grandpa nodded and rotated the book back toward him. "Yeah, that's the one. And he was the only one who did. Doesn't seem fair, does it?" He shrugged. "But fair has never been the guarantee. Don't let anyone tell you it is." He sighed and turned the page. "Don't think none of us were the same after that. My folks especially."

"Why?" I stupidly asked, and Grandpa looked at me like I was just that stupid.

"Why? Because they buried their son, that's why. Can't think o' anything worse than that."

Outside, my dad honked the horn of his big Dodge truck.

"Well, usually," Grandpa said. "Go on. You need to go. A boy needs to listen to his father."

***

The bell at the top of the door went *ting ting,* or at least it tried to. I cupped it to silence it, just out of habit. Then I locked the door again and left the sign saying CLOSED. I wanted to have a few words with Jack Beacham, who was standing there with his hands in the pockets of his long coat, leaning back against the main counter. I didn't want any interruptions. I wanted to keep my eyes and all my attention on him, for all the good that would do.

"We're closed," I said. "Evidently, I'm taking some time off."

"No, that's Dan Beacham," Jack said. "I didn't want two of you running around the same place. That tends to confuse the locals."

"Right. Naturally. And I guess this is your 'locality.'"

"Oh, more or less. More 'more' than 'less.'"

"Stop it," I said. "I mean, please. How many more places do you need to take me before you cut the shit?"

"OK. Consider the shit cut," Jack said.

I nodded, appreciating that concession but not knowing where the hell to go from there. I wandered through the shop, pulled a random record from a bin without even slowing down, and got it playing on one of the systems that "Daniel Beacham" had for sale. The album turned out to be one of Springsteen's earlier ones. Actually, I think it was *Greetings from Asbury Park,* which was his first. In my world, anyway.

"You said music's a palate cleanser, right?" I asked.

"It can be."

"At first, I thought you'd sent me back in time."

"I've never actually time-traveled," he said. "I don't know that anyone can."

Says the unaged World War II vet, I thought, but I pinned the questions accompanying that to the end of the list. "So I'm in a book, right?" I recalled the posters on the bedroom wall and the cars I'd seen in-town. "What is this, *Fenton's Runaways?*"

"Not exactly."

"What, then *Turning Paige?* The third one?"

"Let's say it's adjacent to that, like any of those records in those bins."

"I think you made that reference the last time we talked."

"I think I did. Did it work?"

"Not a lot."

"Well, let me try this again. Every choice, every potential, is another record filed in there. Sometimes, it's almost an identical copy. Sometimes, the songs are different, but they're obviously made by the same artist. Earlier, later. And sometimes, the hop takes me into a whole different category. Like going from rock-and-roll to jazz. The one constant is that all those records, every one of those worlds, keeps on spinning. By the time I found the song for *my* Chapel Cross, there wasn't anything left for me. So I kept going." He looked up, sort of pursed his lips, and seemed to mull over what he'd said. "You know, that's pretty good. Next time, I'll open with that."

"Next time?"

"You're not the first Nathan I've pulled through," Jack said. "I learn a little, tweak a little each time. For the most part, it's getting smoother."

"Smoother," I said.

"Oh, there are so many variables," Jack said. "Especially the people. The traveling, that's just music and math. The real challenges come from the people."

"Great," I said. "Cool. So what are we doing? What's the point of all this?"

"All of it? I don't know. But this?" Jack pulled the tourmaline ring off his finger and set it spinning on the glass countertop. "It's impossible to pick a beginning, but let's just say that I, or someone like me, helps you, or someone like you, and then you, or someone likes you, helps me, or someone like me, and on and on and on it goes. Rings and chains."

The ring slowed, and then it wobbled to a noisy stop. Jack plucked it off the counter and slid it back onto his finger.

"Where'd you get the ring?" I asked him.

Jack grinned and said, "You. Well, *a* you."

Dry mouth. Bloodless face. Bugging eyes. Crawling scalp. "Bullshit," I said.

Jack spread his hands. "Is that really unbelievable at this point?"

"OK, so where'd I get it?"

"You haven't. Not yet," Jack said. "That particular you got it one way, but that's done. He may even be gone. There's no telling yet how you'll get it, or if you even will."

The music had stopped. I didn't know when. I started to lift the record to flip it, but then I let it fall back to the turntable, and I shut the lid. "Was that a me or a you who wound up in the mud?" I asked.

Jack turned the ring on his finger. And turned it. And turned it. "A lot has happened, but it doesn't have to happen like that again," he said. "You may not want to go comparing dental records or things like that. It could get a little spooky."

I nodded, ground my teeth, and sighed, and I drummed my fingers on the tinted plastic lid covering the turntable.

"Are you going to play Side B?" Jack asked.

"I don't think so," I told him. "Yeah, no. Not yet."

"This is what I chose," Jack said. "Break some chains, make some new links. Make them stronger." He shrugged. "It's something to do. But there's no requirement here. Not for you. I could take you back home right now and never bother you again."

"Good to know," I said, and it was. I could go right on back to my life. "And how often does a Nathan Keagan take a Jack Beacham up on that?"

Jack grinned.

"Yeah, that's what I thought," I said. "How can I help you, Sarge?"

***

234

I just sort of slid into Daniel Beacham's life, and it's not like it was too hard for me to "be" him. I mean, I'd read all of Tessa's books, and she'd largely based the character on me. In most ways, it was the same shit with a different name. As for my life back on Earth-Prime or whatever you want to call it, it wasn't too much of a stretch to look at it like Angie and I were just extending our break. We'd been off as much as we'd been on, even if it had felt like things were moving in the right direction again. Missing Mack and Tomlin, plus not having any sort of a substitute for them, that made me want to pull the eject lever if anything did. As far as I remembered, Tessa hadn't given Daniel a sibling, and he'd never had a kid. But I knew I'd make it back. I did. Jack promised, and he kept promising, that he knew the way back to my exact, actual, particular home. More often than not, I trusted him.

It all came to a beginning and an end just short of a year after I arrived in Chapel Cross. I knew the day. I knew to expect it. That night, I was like Billy Pilgrim in *Slaughterhouse-Five,* waiting for the Tralfamadorans to show up because, to him, they already had. I closed-up shop at the regular time, got something to eat down at the diner, and then I came right on back to Beacham's Bygones. I locked the door again but played some music, and then I played some more. And some more.

I heard the gunshots around 11:30. A little earlier than expected, but two of them, back-to-back, just like Jack had said. They didn't sound like they were too far away, but nothing in Chapel Cross — or Westley, or Batchley — ever is. I put them two blocks up and one block over, right where the Beam family lived. In Westley, it would have been the Remingers. In either case, they were two owners down the line from the family that had owned that house about seventy-five years before and had managed to turn a vacant building, most recently a failed bank, into a dry-goods store.

Sirens screamed down from the north and faded east, toward that house. I stepped out onto the sidewalk long enough to see flocks of lookie-loos come out of the tavern and the all-night market at the gas station to try and see what was going on. But just long enough for that. I went back into the shop, closed the door, and turned off the music. Like Jack had said, and like he'd kept saying, there was nothing I absolutely had to do, but I figured it would be easier for everyone if I stuck to the script.

Just before 11:45, the door handle jiggled, the door flung open, and a man stumbled inside before collapsing on the floor. I shut the door again, locked it, and hit the lights. I crouched, hiding in the gloom just as someone tested the door from the outside. "No, it's closed. He closes early," a voice said, and the owner of that voice and the small mob accompanying him moved on.

Still, I waited a little longer. I waited for the voices out on the sidewalk and street to diminish and for the traffic to get back to a usual late-night level, which is to say, not much at all. Then I crept over to the human-shaped heap on the floor. I tapped what look like a shoulder, and the figure, startled, scurried across the floor until he banged into the camera shelf. An Ansco box-camera and a light meter toppled to the ground. Several other cameras just tipped over on their shelves. "OK, take it easy," I said. "Hey. They're gone. You're good. You're safe here."

"Said it wasn't my house," a voice said from the shadows. Light from a streetlamp cut in through the window and showed leather boots and what looked like canvas pants and not much else. "That's what they told me before they ... they shot me. But it's my house. I should know my own house."

I spotted a a very small metal thing on the floor between him and me. "Looks like you spit out at least one of the bullets already," I said. "You heal pretty fast, don't you?"

"You don't sound surprised," the shadow said.

"No. Not anymore."

"I don't ... I don't know what happened. I started to think I did, but ... but ..."

"Well, for one thing," I said, "you got the place right, but you're about seven or eight decades too late. It's 2019. No, wait — here, it's 2010."

Silence. Then the shadow said, "What?"

I shook my head. "Don't worry about that. Not right now. That's not how I wanted to start this."

"If it'll help things make sense, then you can start over," the shadow said, with a hint of that particular humor that I'd get to know so well.

"Yeah, that's a good idea," I said. "OK. Here we go. Jack, my name's Nathan Keagan, and I can tell you exactly what has happened to you. How's that?"

Tomlin

I just stood like an idiot in that stupid poppy field because I was damned if I was going to prance again. I mean, what had that got me the last time? And it was nice. Poppies are nice. And it was a decent day. But what the hell was I going to do now?

I ventured in the direction of what I'm going to call "North," and it started to thin. I knew what that meant. Too much farther, and I'd either wake up or just keep on sleeping with no dream, and what's the fun in that? "Well, shit," I said, and I went back until things felt, I don't know, a little firmer. And I took a sec to regroup. To make sure I was anchored. I looked at my hands, front and back. My feet, too. I rubbed my arms, the back of my neck. I even pulled my hair. I just yanked right at that ponytail. It made sense then, in the dream. Like it would help me stay there.

But that's all it did. I just stayed there in the damn field of poppies. "Hey, think someone can help me out here?" I belted out, just shouting in my dream, which I knew was a dream. "Hello, Morpheus? Mamu, Manit, fucking Piltzintecuhtli? Think one of you could throw me a damn bone here? Huh? Anyone? I mean, come *on* now!"

I don't know which one of them I conjured or if it was just an answering service, but the poppy field rolled back like a rug, the sun and blue sky moved out of the way for fluorescent lights and a tiled ceiling, and bam, I was in a hospital room. I'd fallen asleep in a hospital room, I knew that, but this was a different one. That wasn't a flatscreen monitor but a CRT TV sitting on the little shelf-thingie screwed to the wall, and that wasn't my child but my grandma lying in the bed.

Shit, I thought. *Here?*

"Hello? Is somebody here?"

I cringed helplessly as Tomlin Keagan, age twenty-two, took one, two, three steps from her uncomfortable chair and took an even more-uncomfortable position by her grandma's death bed. "I don't want to be here, Grandma," Tomlin said, then: "I'm sorry. Oh, shit. I don't know why I said that."

Our grandma laughed. Kind of. Someone else might have called it a cough, but we knew it was a laugh. "I'll tell you something," Grandma said. "I don't want to be here, either." She reached out, patted Tomlin's hand, and said, "I'm glad you're here, honey. And I'm — " That time, she really did cough. Dammit, I'd forgotten about that. Panicking, Tomlin looked toward the door and tried to move toward it, but her grandma got her shit together and tightened her grip. "No. Stay here," she said. "I want you here. I'm glad you're here, and I'm ... I'm glad you're you."

Our aunt and my uncle, and our brother, and our grandpa, they all came in then from the cafeteria then, at least in the dream. I tried to remember if that was how it had actually happened.

Anyway.

Poppies rained from the ceiling as Grandma Keagan flatlined.

***

I snorted and jolted awake, and two things fell from my lap onto the floor: my grandma's Bible and her nearly twenty-year-old letter to my wife, which I'd found tucked inside of it. Stamped but unsent. One more mystery in a world of them.

"Hey, Mom. You're awake."

I jumped to my feet, and I clapped my hands to my mouth, but I probably screamed before then. I don't remember doing that, but Mack says I did, and they'd probably remember better than I would.

My kid sat up in their hospital bed, looking pale and with dark circles under their eyes, and with an IV going to their arm and monitor wires coming out from their chest, but grinning. And awake. I would've been happy enough just with that.

"Hey, remember when I woke up at Dad's house, and I saw you just looking at me like a creeper?"

"Honey, that was a week ago. Actually, it might have been more than that," I said.

"Whatever," Mack said. "We're even."

"OK. I'm OK with that." I stumbled toward them, already sobbing and with my arms already out. I hugged them, and I had no plans to stop.

"We need to talk about some things," Mack said.

"Oh, I'm sure," I told them. "But that's later. Hug me now."

And they did.

***

Two days later, at home, at our actual home, I made sure Mack was all snug in their actual bed in their actual room, and I stood in their doorway until they fell asleep. Maybe like a creeper, but you know what? I don't really care.

We'd talked a little but not about the "some things" they mentioned in the hospital. That was OK. I wasn't going to rush them, and I had a feeling they were things I wouldn't really want to know anyway.

I walked past my bedroom door and went right into the kitchen. I tried to think about nothing as I rinsed the dishes and loaded the dishwasher, and I almost pulled that off.

I found Angie on the living-room couch, drinking convenience-store coffee from her travel mug and trying to find hidden messages in the case files she'd spread over the coffee table in front of her. She looked up at me when I came in and gave me something that was almost a smile, but then she went right back to those files. I sat on the smaller loveseat, letting her keep the big sofa to herself.

"I didn't know how long you'd be," she said. "I can just pack all this up and take off if you want."

240

"No, I don't mind," I said. "It's good to have people in this house. And thanks for helping us move back in."

"No problem."

"You want a drink or something?"

She sighed. "Yeah, but I also want to stay sharp. And I want to keep the option open of driving home. Sorry."

I said, "I'm not offended."

"Good. I don't know. You can drink, though. I mean, of course you can, it's your house."

"Yeah, I could, but I think I'll try to be good, too. Probably should. I mean, I *think* Mack is doing OK, but they're also the first person I know who's recovering from a coma."

"If that's what it was," Angie said, and then she shook her head, closed one of the folders, pushed it aside, and opened another one.

"You're taking this all in pretty well," I told her.

Angie dropped the folder onto the table, slouched back, and drank her coffee. "There's no other way to take it. No other way that would help. I mean, people literally disappearing and ..." The sound that came out of her was a mix of a sigh and a groan but was also somehow more than both. "God, I don't even have the words."

"It's not any easier for me."

"Why would it be? You had a head start of, what, a few days? I'm surprised we aren't all out of our damn minds. Or maybe we are, and that's why we're just accepting it." She made that sound again, put her coffee cup on the end table, and rubbed her forehead. "How's that other kid taking it? What's her name, Mack's friend?"

"Sera."

"Right. Sera. She OK?"

"I don't know. I think she is. I think she's been more focused on her friend. I called her last night after Mack woke up and put them on the phone. That was great. For all of us. Needed a win like that." I shrugged. "I don't know, though. I don't know if she's really had a chance to sit and process last week. I'll check in on her tomorrow."

"Good. I was just curious," she said.

I nodded, stood, and stretched, thinking I might actually try and turn in.

Angie took a deep breath, leaned forward, and picked up one of the case files.

"Finding anything?" I asked.

"I don't know. A little bit of yes and no. Mainly no. It's not like I know what I'm looking for." She nodded at the files scattered on the table. "Like, there's a guy who walked off his job at one of the Griffith farms in '83. Mid-forties. Another one's a guy who ran out on a home lease in the early '50s. Found his car but never found him. Basically, there's one or two per decade." She held up and sort of shook the folder in her hand. "Like, this one was a bartender at the Broken Spur who disappeared during the floods in '75. Age fifty to fifty-five. They didn't look too hard for him."

"Fifty to fifty-five? That's a little too old for either of them."

"Yeah, but that rodeo picture was '59."

I had to laugh. "Shit, they could've gone to anywhere and to any time. Do you really think either of 'em would just choose to stay in some version of Westley for ten years?"

"I don't know. I don't know," Angie said. "Literally nothing makes sense. But I can't really rule anything out, either. I don't know. I don't know what I'm saying."

"You should take a break."

"Yeah, but I'm not someone who does that," she said. "Actually, I'm thinking I probably will end up just falling asleep here. Is that OK? If it's not, I'll just leave now and run through this shit at home."

"No, that's fine," I said. "Stay. There are blankets in the cedar chest, and we just got fresh groceries, go ahead and help yourself to whatever you want in the fridge and pantry. Whatever."

"OK. Thank you. You going to bed?"

"I'm going to try."

"Right. Well, good night."

"Yeah, good night. Good luck."

Angie smiled and looked back at the bartender's case file, and I went on down the hall. I made it to the end, checked on Mack again, and then I managed to set one whole foot inside my bedroom. I even turned on the light. Something tugged at me, though. I shut off the light, turned around, and went into Tessa's office.

Since I don't think I went in there the day we developed the pictures, that would have been my first time in the office since the night before the wreck. That's if I'd even gone in there then. When you know it's the last time, you keep track, but when you don't, you don't.

I expected to feel a stabbing pain, but it was more like an intense ache, so maybe that was something. I touched everything that was hers, which means I touched just about everything in there. Every single one of her typewriters. Her shelves and books. The photo of the *Tawny Terror* hanging on the wall. Her chair. Her desk.

Sitting in Tessa's chair at Tessa's desk, I spun around slowly, and I breathed. I just tried to breathe. I don't think I could have done much else, but I breathed like a pro.

I wound up facing the desk, and the typewriter on the desk, and the paper rolled into the typewriter on the desk. I read:

> stopped at the hotel-room door, fist poised to knock.
>
> Through the door came twelve quiet words: "Of all the world's deepest woes, the deepest word went down slow."

The last words Tessa had written. There they were. I reached for the machine to roll the paper out, but then I snatched my hand back like I'd touched something hot. *No, I thought, leave it there. Maybe she'll finish it.*

I looked at the stack of upside-down pages that were right next to the typewriter. God, it looked like she'd almost been done. But since it was a manuscript and not a horseshoe or a hand grenade, I guessed "almost" didn't count.

I flipped the stack over. According to the title page, the name of the unfinished novel was *Beachams Bridge*. That surprised me — not the title, specifically, but the fact that it had a title at all. Tessa always held off on naming her books until after she was done. It was like a title restricted her. Restricted the story. Made it fixed. Permanent. So why was this one different?

I never read all of anything Tessa wrote until it was published. It was always like that. Always.

That night, though, I read *Beachams Bridge*.

***

Breakfast was weird. Angie, Mack, and I stared at our coffees and poked sausages and eggs around on our plates. Going by hours, Mack was the only one who had put in enough time to get a decent night's sleep, but they looked like hell, too. I thought about asking Angie what she'd found, but I figured I either didn't really want to hear it, or she hadn't found anything and would just be reminded she'd wasted her night. I had plenty I could have said, but I didn't want to say any of it. I was still processing it. God, I had so much to process. Thinking about everything arranged in my mental inbox and outbox, I didn't know if we could handle it.

Mack shoved a forkful of egg into their mouth, swallowed it, and set their fork on their plate with a shaking hand. "OK. I'm going to tell you something."

I thought, *Shit.* "Is this what you mentioned at the hospital?"

"This is what I mentioned at the hospital," Mack said.

"If this is a family thing, I don't need to be here for this," Angie said. "Breakfast is good, but I've imposed enough."

244

Mack smiled and said, "Oh, you can't back out of this now."

"Crap."

I asked if Mack wanted to call Sera and get as much of the band back together as we could.

"Yeah, I already did that," Mack said. "I called her this morning, right after I woke up. I needed to take this out on a practice run. It's, um ..." They put their hands against the sides of their head and flared their fingers: *mind-blowing*.

"OK, and how'd she take it?" I shrugged. "I mean, give me a hint."

Mack laughed and repeated the gesture. Then they took another bite of their breakfast. Their obvious nervousness, confusion the stalling, the attempts to keep things light, it all made me think of another time: when Mack came out to Tessa and me as non-binary, before they'd even heard that word. Just like then, I had an inkling of what this might be about. But it wasn't *just* like then. My hunch about my kid's gender identity had come about because I knew my kid. This time, the hunch was because I'd stayed up all night reading an unfinished book.

I put my hand on Mack's wrist — on the arm that had briefly been broken. "Honey," I said, "take your time. Or wait. It's OK."

Mack looked at me. They squinted. "Do you know?"

"I might," I said. "I may have gotten a hint, like, a couple of hours ago."

They clenched their jaw and nodded. God, that kid. That tough kid. How many times could our world turn upside-down before it was right-side-up again?

"Can I ... help?" Angie asked.

"No, I'm fine," Mack said. "It's just ... right before my dad and Jack disappeared, I guess, I made my way into my grandpa's head." Angie opened her mouth. Mack put up a hand and said, "I'll explain that later. But it was him. Actually him. My ... my real grandpa." Mack nodded and took a couple of gulps of coffee. "Just to make sure, though, I stopped by, um … by my mom's place, I guess, on my way back home."

Mack looked at me suddenly, putting it together. "Her book," they said.

"Yeah," I told them. "I read it last night. It looks like it was almost finished."

Mack nodded, and then they looked at Angie, who was doing a great job sitting quietly but was also obviously and incredibly lost. "My mom and I spun out on Echo Creek Bridge," they said, "but Tessa Hatcher wasn't anywhere near that car."

Mack

This is what happened.

I wrapped up my visit with Great-Grandpa WTF — and what a charmer *he* was — and stepped back into the Everystream. This was a few minutes or hours or maybe days before I returned to myself in my hospital room. I really don't know how long it took. I'm pretty sure it doesn't matter, and I know I don't care. I'd been given a new map, and it felt like I needed to do at least a little exploring before I folded it up and tucked it away in the glovebox. There's an old Mitch Hedberg joke: "I wanna hang a map of the world in my house. Then I'm gonna put pins into all the locations that I've traveled to. But first, I'm gonna have to travel to the top two corners of the map so it won't fall down." It was kinda like that.

So I went merrily down the stream, hopping currents, sort of listening for hints, just getting lost in the vibe. Like I said, I don't know how long I did this. I had the odd but oddly definite feeling that I drifted fairly far, and then I looped back. It was like floating on the river with the sun beating down on your face and some sort of totally socially acceptable substance mellowing you out, and then you know you've seen that tree before. And there was something about that tree. That's when I dropped my arms over the side, so to speak, and dragged my hands in the water to slow myself down, and looked for a place to dock.

I disembarked, and the stream and the "tree" hardened before they shifted. Then it was like I was shoved toward yet another set of windows, though not ungently, and then the glass of the windows disappeared. A front-row seat, just like I had in my great-grandpa's head. I braced myself, just waiting for him or someone else to yank me back. But that didn't happen, and exactly like when I rode the currents, I told myself to just enjoy the ride.

These eyes were reading a book, and I recognized it immediately, even without having to look at the author name and title printed at the tops of the pages. It was a yellowed paperback copy of *A Woman Called Kidd,* specifically that absolutely brutal scene where Taija — who one of my moms totally didn't base on my other mom — is killed on South River Road. Not even the target. Just collateral damage.

Eleanor stomped the brake pedal just as the windshield shattered. The car spun. Glass swarmed into the car like glittering locusts. Eleanor's forehead cracked the steering wheel, but she didn't feel it. Because she'd seen Taija. Something was wrong with Taija's arm. Her hand still gripped the armrest, but she had a second elbow now, halfway down her forearm. Her mouth hung open. Her eyes were shut, and her head pressed against the glass of the passenger-side window. *She always looks peaceful when she's sleeping,* Eleanor thought.

The car stopped, and Taija's head lolled, revealing the crimson spiderweb slapped onto the glass. Eleanor heard *plott ... plott* and tracked it to something dripping from Taija's long hair onto the seat. *Upholstery's blue,* she thought deliriously. *Purple spots. Ooh, look at the pretty flowers.*

Eleanor ran her fingers through Taija's sodden hair, smoothing it back from her face, tangling in a snag at the back. A burning river flowed down each of Eleanor's cheeks.

Suddenly, my view blurred, too, but the tears weren't in my eyes, they were in this person's — whoever this was. Rain on someone else's windows. There was a harsh, quivering sigh, shaking this "Attic" or whatever it was, shaking my whole consciousness. Then hands that weren't mine closed that book, turned it over, and touched the author's photo. My mom's photo. And a voice that sure sounded like my mom said, "Just a character to you. Just a character."

Let's say there was a *ka-chunk* then, like a Viewmaster shifting to the next frame, because I don't know how else to describe the transition. Time is irrelevant, like I've said, but that's not all. That doesn't capture it. Words are inadequate, and "time" is just one of them. But we're doing this.

Fingers drummed on an old oak rolltop-desk and then rolled two sheets of paper — the one to be typed on as well as the backing sheet to protect the platen — into an Underwood typewriter from the mid-1930s. I could read the words UNDERWOOD NOISELESS PORTABLE on typewriter's body, right under the space bar. And that was all I read; there was nothing else to read. The page started off totally blank, and it looked like it would be staying that way.

The view spun because the chair did, showing a reeling view of a home-office space that almost looked like it should have. And now we looked out the window, and we took in a view that I'd never seen from my own house but which I'd seen many, many times in my head while reading one of my mom's books. We — as in Tessa, Tomlin, and me — lived on a cul-de-sac, but Eleanor Kidd's remarkably similar house sat on a boring old corner. And I think that's as much as Tessa ever said about it. But now, through Ellie's eyes, I saw the street sign on that corner, marking the intersection of TOMLIN AVE and KEAGAN ST.

Eleanor scoffed. "Nice," she said. "Yeah, that totally makes up for killing her off." The chair and the view spun back. Eleanor's fingers settled onto typewriter's home keys, and they typed this:

CHAPTER ONE: TESSA

    I wept.

    I shifted the car back into park, shut off the engine, and I wept. THE TALK with Nate could probably have gone worse, but I'd dared to hope for better. Maybe things would eventually smooth out. Maybe.

Maybe it was time to break this news to Tomlin.

Maybe.

I pushed myself back from the window, but it was a different window. It was my single kitchen window, which looked out on Sebastian Court — my cul-de-sac. I knew it wasn't the "real world," though, whatever the hell that meant anymore. Despite the details, like sounds of traffic outside the house, the soft hum of the microwave just to the right of me, and the smell of coffee. Medaglia d'Oro instant coffee. That was over to my left, from my mom's steaming cup.

My mom, I thought. I wondered.

Ding. That was the microwave. I ignored it. I'd had dreams like that before: I reach for something like the door of the microwave, and everything else just sort of fades. I mean, I knew that would happen, but it didn't have to happen yet.

"Your coffee's done," my mom said.

"It is," I said. "Yeah, I don't care."

"You don't want it?

"I don't know. I'm not thinking about it. It's not a priority."

"Yeah, but you are thinking about it."

"No, I'm thinking about you," I said. "All the rest of this is just dressing. It's just details."

Mom shrugged and took a sip of her coffee.

"How is any of this ..." I groaned. I shook my head. "How?"

She waggled her fingers just like Jack Beacham had done during our family meeting at Keagans Collections. And also just like Jack, she said, "How do I do this? Nerve impulses, muscle contractions, but what the hell is that? Could you tell someone how to send one of those impulses or how to contract — "

"No, stop it," I said. "This isn't you saying this. I'm thinking it."

"Details," my mom said.

I pressed my palms to my forehead, and I damn near wailed, "What is in me? What is in my fucking brain?"

"Multitudes."

I looked at her.

"Jack hears music, right? I mean, basically," my mom said. "For ... someone else, it's more like speed. A sense of movement. Friction. As far as you go, if I had to put a word to it —"

"Storage. I store stuff," I said, and I was speaking to her, to the kitchen, to the microwave, to the cul-de-sac, to all the Attics, to myself. "No, but that doesn't ... no. There's that view, that clear view of Eleanor Kidd writing, and my great-grandpa, he was up here ..."

My great-grandpa, I thought. *My great-grandpa was Charlie Beacham, which means —*

No. Stop, I told myself. Begged myself. *I'm not ready for this. Not yet.*

"Store it, receive it, *I don't know*, but then I, like, have to process it into some kind of shape I can handle like Attics and boxes and —"

"Like this?" my mom said, raising her eyebrows and gesturing at the kitchen.

"Yes. Exactly."

"Are you?"

"Am I what?"

"Are you handling it?"

"I mean, are you asking me that, or are you *me*, asking me that?"

She smiled. She still didn't lower her eyebrows. I hated myself for projecting that.

I turned toward the microwave, got my hot water out, and stirred in my coffee. I kept my back to her the whole time. When I turned back around, she was still right there. Everything was still right there. I wondered how I felt about that.

"Are we OK?" she asked.

"I'll stay this long," I said, and I tapped the side of my coffee cup.

"I get it," she said. "Can we go to the table?"

"Sure," I said, and we sat at the dining-room table, which looked just like *my* dining room table, and we talked, and we drank our coffee.

Just a cup of coffee with my mom.

Just a cup of coffee with Eleanor Kidd.

***

Angie was the first one to talk. Well, she took a deep breath, pushed her chair back from the table, stood up, and *then* she talked. "I, uh ... yeah, I don't feel like I should be here," she said. "This is ... I'm gonna go."

Mom put a hand on Angie's arm, and Angie patted that hand. "Yeah, I know," Angie said. "It's OK. I don't feel like I have to go. But I do feel like I have to go."

Mom nodded, and she and I just sat silently at the table as Angie both literally and figuratively got her shit together. Literally, it was a coat, a bag, and a bunch of folders. Figuratively, you know, I'm sure we were tough to be around for long.

The silence was broken again by an exchange of fatigued good-byes and by Mom and Angie agreeing that one of them would call the other one soon, either because things had calmed down a bit or because they hadn't. That was good. I liked that. Mom had always had plenty of acquaintances and associates, but besides James, she was kind of short on real friends.

Once Angie was gone, I said to my mom, "You know, this isn't how I expected you to handle this."

252

"Is there a right way to handle this?" she asked.

"OK, so that's an excellent point," I said. "I just mean, I don't know. You don't seem, like, startled or surprised or even, like, thrown off that you …" I just trailed off. We'd covered it, I'd just told it in something like a story, but it was impossible for me to just put it out there. To just *say* it. Learning the truth wasn't the same as knowing it, and accepting it and dealing with it were going to be up at a whole other level.

Mom took us there, though, or she at least brought us closer. "So I wasn't married to Tessa Hatcher," she said. "But I do think, and my heart is telling me this is right, that the woman I was married to was the same one I dated and fell in love with."

"And that was Eleanor Kidd."

"I would have called her 'Ellie,' if I'd known," she said, and her smile sent sad but beautiful lights into her glistening eyes. She shook her head and sighed. "She did seem different when she finally reached out to me after you were born. I just assumed that was why. That and time. And I told myself not to question it because she was happy, and you were beautiful, and she was finally into me, like I'd always hoped she'd be. We'd always been just friends. No, not *just* friends. I don't want to diminish that. But …" She sighed again, and then she pressed her hands together and brought them up to her face and sort of bounced them off the tip of her nose.

"But she never told you," I said, and I instantly wondered why. Not why Eleanor Kidd hadn't revealed her identity to Tomlin but why I would push that point. My mom seemed like she'd come to terms with this impossible situation. Why would I stir things up?

"What would she have said? And I think she was happy, too. I know she was."

I told her I agreed with her.

"Did you read her last book?" she asked. "I mean, what there was of it? You didn't, did you?"

"No, she hadn't asked me to yet," I said.

Mom smiled a little wider, waggled her eyebrows, and got up from the table. "I'll be right back. Stay here," she said, and then she went down the hall and into the office.

And she stayed in the office. For a long-ass time. "Mom? Are you good?" I asked.

"Mack, call Angie," she hollered back, sounding hurt and frantic. "Ask her where it is. Ask her what she did with it."

"Did with what?" I asked, already moving down the hall.

Mom and I almost ran into each other in the office doorway. The whites showed all around her eyes. "*Beachams Bridge,*" she said. "The manuscript. Tessa's book. It's gone."

Tomlin

I sent James another text to assure him that, yes, I was OK, and then I put my phone on silent and set it upside-down on the table, right between my lunch plate and my plastic cup of iced tea.

"You know, you could also put it away," Angie said before she popped a beautifully salted home fry into her mouth.

"What, my phone?"

She shrugged. "It's an idea."

"Oh, I don't have my shit *that* together," I said. "I'm actually starting to think that's not even possible. And it's sort of liberating."

Angie made a sound kind of like "Hm." She went back to her fries, and I got to work on my club sandwich. We got through most of our lunch without talking, though I sort of fed off the background noise of the diner. There's something about that kind of chatter and din that has always soothed me. And Angie knew that. She knew when to help me feel like I was eating alone. She'd become a pretty solid friend.

She is the one who broke the spell, though. She was learning. "I talked to Dylan down at the real-estate office," she told me. "She said she hasn't seen you come in."

"She won't. I'm not selling the house."

Angie nodded, and she looked down at her plate, and then she nodded some more. I wondered if I knew what she was thinking.

"It's all paid off," I said. "Even if he doesn't come back, I'll just need to keep up on the taxes and the utility bills."

"Are you going to move in?"

"No. It's not my house," I said. "Mack might, though."

Angie nodded once more, pushed her plate off to the side, and looked up. "I want to help you. With the taxes and shit."

"Are you sure?'

"Yeah. It's about all I'm sure about."

"Thank you," I said, and I guzzled down the rest of my tea to keep the lump in my throat from rising any higher. "I don't think he's gone," I told her. "I don't. Do you?"

Angie shrugged.

"Also, I just can't handle burying another empty box. I did that a year ago, but it was like I was burying something else and not just Tessa. Or Ellie." I shook my head vigorously. "No. Tessa. She was Tessa. And I *know* we loved each other. It's just a name." I clasped my hands together on the table, I squeezed them tight, and I thought, *Which one of us am I talking to?*

"I get it," Angie said. "I mean, I think I get it as much as I can."

I took a deep breath. It shook all the way in and all the way out. "Well, that's how I feel today," I said. "Maybe don't ask me tomorrow."

Angie said, "I get that, too," and she went quiet again.

She snatched up the check for our meals, which had appeared on the table at some point, and put some money on the table. She stood up, gave my shoulder a quick little squeeze, and said, "You can get the next one."

I nodded, and she left.

I ordered another coffee and hung out there for a while longer. I was getting better at being by myself.

Nathan

I came downstairs and found myself sitting in my favorite chair. "You know, this is some weird shit," I said.

"Yeah, you'll never totally get used to it," Daniel Beacham said. "The Jacks are in the kitchen. I think they're making coffee."

"The Jacks," I said, and I took a few steps to the side so I could see through the dining room and through the kitchen doorway. Sure enough, two Jack Beachams stood bullshitting by the kitchen counter. There was the familiar one with the long coat, the suit, and the ring, and then there was the rookie Jack who had swapped out his well-worn uniform for jeans and a T-shirt from the Daniel Beacham collection. "How was your vacation?" I asked, pinching the bridge of my nose.

"Good. It was good. You do OK here?"

"Yeah, didn't run up too many bills," I said. "Hope you don't mind, but I picked up an Adler typewriter for your shop."

"Ooh. The *Shining* model?" Daniel asked.

"Yep."

"How'd you find that?"

"Oh, had a hunch." I headed for the kitchen. "I'm gonna talk to Jack Sr.," I said. "You just make yourself at home."

***

Jack and I sat out on the back deck and watched the sun set over the neighbor's field. "Pretty," he said, and then he handed back the book I'd shown him. It was a brand-spanking-new hardcover copy of *Keagans Crossing,* Eleanor Kidd's newest book. "I'm surprised you didn't get that autographed. I think she had a signing in Salem just last week."

"I thought about that, but I didn't know the score," I said. "I mean, in her books, Tessa mentioned a rift between

257 "

Daniel and Ellie, and I didn't know how that played out here."

"Hm," Jack said.

Still holding the book, I stood and paced over to the railing. "I didn't want to screw anything up for them. For either of them. They aren't just … characters here."

"Is that what you think I do?" Jack asked, speaking more with interest than irritation. "Just wander between fantasy lands?"

"Well, what side's the right one to be standing on? Who's writing the books, and who's living in them?"

Jack smiled and tapped his damn ring. "Circles and chains," he said.

I groaned and snapped the book like a frisbee. It opened in the air, pages fluttering like it was trying to fly, and then crashed down to the wet lawn.

"Sounds like *you* need a vacation," Jack said. "I thought this might be it."

"I want to go home," I told him.

"We can do that, too." He stood and dusted off his pants. "We can go now. Is there anything you want to bring back?"

"You know, that *is* what I think," I said.

"What's that?"

"Maybe I shouldn't say this, because you are my ride home and all, but yeah, I do think you just hop. You said you got back home, but you got there late. What happened, did you see your girlfriend married? She have a family?"

"I'll take you home whenever you're ready," Jack said. "Just say the word." He kept his voice light and his face was blank. Inscrutable.

I knew I'd ventured into dangerous territory, but I just barreled forward. "You're not connected to anything," I said. "You say you help people, or you close loops, or you get some balls rolling, but there aren't any consequences for you. There aren't. You might occasionally get your ass kicked, but as long as you've got a pulse, you could just lie low for a little bit, heal up — and that doesn't take you long — and then you just go someplace similar and try and try and try again."

Then I asked a question I'd been mulling over for a year. "Why'd you bring me here, Jack? You could have taken me to anywhere or to anywhen. Daniel could've handled Junior. Hell, I bet a lot of Daniels have helped a whole lot of Juniors. I didn't need to be here." I looked out at the grass and pointed at the book. "Was that it? You must've known that was coming out this year. Was I supposed to go to the signing?"

Jack put out his hand, palm up. "Come on. Let's go."

"Right. Yeah, whatever," I said, taking his hand. "Let's go home."

"We will," Jack said, "but we've got a stop to make first."

***

I recognized the bar immediately. It had been a mandatory stop whenever I visited Tessa at college. Well, at least while she was working on her Masters. It had actually been a dry town — a dry *college* town, if you can believe that — until 2002. Even now, eight years later according to that world's clock, it was still the only bar in town. That fact more than anything contributed to its customer base, a fairly even mix of townies, college kids, and professors.

We found Associate Professor Eleanor Kidd at the back of the bar, shooting pool by herself. She grinned hugely when she saw Jack, and she laid her cue stick on the table and stepped forward to give the man a hug. But then she saw me. She froze mid-step, and her smile fell. "Oh, wow. Danny," she said.

"Yeah, sorry," I told her. "This is an unscheduled stopover."

To Jack, she said, "What's going on? You said you'd give me a heads-up first."

"Well, that was the deal with Daniel Beacham," Jack said. "We never really talked about this."

259

She looked from Jack to me and back again, and I looked from her to Jack, two of us trying to figure it out. She got it about a half-second before I did, and then I was the one who got the hug.

"Nathan," Tessa said. "Oh my God, it's been so long."

***

She settled her bill, and then we met for drinks at her place, which was a mid-century split-level not far from the campus. Tessa and I sat on opposite ends of a sectional with a large, low coffee-table between us. She got a fire going in the brick fireplace. Not gas but an honest-to-God woodfire. Jack did a decent job of minding his business behind me. He sat with his whiskey on one of the steps that led back up to the ground floor.

Tessa absently swirled her drink, gently rattling the ice cubes against the inside of her glass. I'd forgotten that tic. "I met Jack when I was volunteering at the air museum," she told me. "My grandpa introduced us. It was right around the time I met Tomlin. It might have been the same day, actually."

"A little after," Jack said behind me. "Henry and I went a few rounds of coffee and cigarettes before he introduced me to you."

Tessa smiled wistfully. "Oh, Grandpa Henry," she said. "I'm always gonna miss that guy." She took a drink.

I followed her lead and took a healthy gulp of my own bourbon. It was one of the higher-end Old Forresters. I hadn't tried it before. I immediately planned on trying it again. "OK, just nutshell this for me," I said. "You're Tessa. You're my Tessa."

"Yours, huh?" she teased, tossing out a smile that I'd really, really missed.

"I hope you know what I mean."

"I do. And yeah, I'm assuming so. Jack's the one who can tell us."

"The song remains the same," he offered from the back.

"Sarge, you want to come around here, sit on the couch?" I asked.

"No, I wouldn't want to intrude," he said.

I couldn't see his smirk, but dammit, I could hear it. I sighed and said to Tessa, "Alright. Keep going. Please."

"Well, Jack offered to take me on a trip almost from the start," Tessa said. "I'm not sure why I held off. I probably still thought he was crazy."

"Yeah, it's amazing what becomes normal," I said.

"Well, my whole normal changed. And you didn't exactly respond too well to my news, so ... yeah. Ellie and I swapped. We both needed some different air. It was only supposed to be for a bit."

"News," I said. "You mean when you were pregnant with Mack."

Tessa put her drink on the table and brought her hands up to cover her mouth. Tears glittered in her eyes.

I went back to my drink.

After a moment, Tessa took her hands away, showing a sad smile. She wiped her eyes, chuckled, and said, "I keep forgetting they're real to you. You've met them. Mackenzie. God, I've always loved that name." She retrieved her drink and knocked the rest of it back in one go.

Confused, I looked back over my shoulder, seeking some help. Jack pointed at me, then at Tessa: *Focus on her*. Then he pointed at himself, then at the ceiling. He stood and took his drink upstairs.

"I lost mine," Tessa said once he'd gone, answering the question I hadn't been savvy enough to ask and wouldn't have known how to ask. "Ours. Our baby. Here. And Ellie surprised both of us by falling in love with Tomlin. So we ... agreed. We made a choice. Each of us stayed on the wrong side of the looking-glass."

My hand shook. Somehow, I managed to get my quaking glass to the table without spilling what remained of my drink. Then again, not much remained. I stood, rubbed my face, and walked around the sectional for no real reason. I ended up getting to the fireplace by taking the long way. I sat on the hearth and said, "Mack ..."

"Hey," Tessa said. "No. I know what you're thinking. Mack is still your child. If you helped raise —"

Fuck. "Daniel, though. That's Daniel Beacham's kid. You and Ellie basically stole —"

Tessa laughed, kind of. It was a single, strong, extremely bitter "Ha." She said, "Yeah, he wouldn't have put up a fight. He was even more of an asshole than you were." Reaching for her drink, she added, "I started writing him on a rough day."

"Your books," I said. "And her books. You're both writing about the people you left?"

Tessa shrugged, and then she nodded. "Yeah, I suppose so. Yes."

"You're writing about things that happened, or are you making things happen? And is it just one of you at the wheel, are are both of you — "

"I don't know. I just write. Both of us, *we* just write. And it's not like all of it lines up."

That got me to my feet. "What about when it does?" I said. "Things happen, Tessa! Bad things happen! Oh, Christ, you're just like him. Just run off to somewhere else when things get tough, and you don't have to live with any of the fucking consequences!"

Tessa stood. Her glass shattered against the brick. Her fingers jabbed into my chest. "Oh, don't you fucking talk to me about consequences! Think about why I'm *here*, Nate. Think about why I *stayed*. I saw something here, fine. But I stayed so some of the people closest to me could maybe have a chance at happy lives. You. Your sister."

"My sister married a lie."

"Oh, fuck you."

"And now, hey, even the lie is dead."

"What? What happened? Oh, did they get divorced?"

"She fucking *died*, Tessa. Oh, I guess the good Sergeant didn't give you that memo. Eleanor Kidd, who we all thought was you, *died,* and Mack damn near died right with her. Our kid. No, wait: evidently, I guess she was Eleanor's and fucking Dan Beacham's kid. A car wreck. She spun out and went right off Keagans Crossing, landed in Echo Creek."

Tessa smiled very, very smugly. I hated it. I'd missed it.

"What?" I said.

"No, I'm sorry. Go ahead. Please, tell me more. No, wait. Let me do it. She hit a patch of ice, and then *whee!* She punched a hole in the wooden sidewall and shot right off the bridge. Eleanor Kidd, done in by a little bit of ice. So, so ironic." She clicked her tongue and shook her head. "Wow. I mean, can you imagine it? Because I did."

My fingers and toes tingled. Actually, everything got a little fuzzy and sparkly. I don't remember sitting back down on the hearth, but there I was, sitting back down on the hearth.

"*Keagans Crossing,*" Tessa said.

"Yeah, I know that. I said that."

"No, I mean my book," Tessa said. "*Keagans Crossing.* Didn't you say you read it?"

"I told you I bought it. I started it. I couldn't get through it." I rubbed my face and sighed. "I don't know. It didn't feel right. It was weird enough to read my own thoughts put down, but my sister's and Mack's —"

Nodding, Tessa spun around and crossed the living room, going over to the floor-to-ceiling bookshelves in that corner.

"What are you doing?" I asked her. "I said I didn't want to read it."

She came back, though, with a hardback copy of the book. It was a different edition than the one I'd picked up. Stamped across the cover were the words *Advance Reader Copy — Artwork not final.* "Just flip to the last page," Tessa said. "Second-to-last, actually. The scene starts there."

I didn't want to play anymore, but I couldn't see a way out, so I took the book, got to the end, and went back a page, just like she said. I didn't even get through the first paragraph before I frowned, and I looked up at Tessa before I turned the page.

"You didn't finish it," she said, smiling that damn smile again.

"Would this make more sense if I'd read the rest of it?"

"Well, yeah, probably," she said. "But lucky for you, the author is available for questions. It's an AMA. Ask Me Anything."

I clapped the book shut and took another look at the front cover, specifically at the author's name. "You wrote this as Eleanor Kidd, but then you bring her in as a character in the book," I said. "Tessa, the character, meets Eleanor Kidd."

"Again," she said.

"Again," I said, not because I understood — I wasn't anywhere close to there — but because she'd sounded so confident saying it. I hoped some of that surety and clarity would rub off onto me.

"Guess what happens at the end of her book," Tessa said.

"There is no end," I said. "Tessa — Eleanor — hadn't finished it when she died."

Tessa sat beside me on the hearth and took her novel from my hands, relieving me of that burden, at least. "Nate," she said, "Jack fixed that. It wasn't as smooth as we'd planned, but he fixed it. Eleanor Kidd isn't dead. She's finishing her book. She's finishing *Beachams Bridge*."

***

We found Jack in Tessa's kitchen, standing by the sink, staring out the window at the network of leaves and branches that formed a screen between Tessa's house and her neighbor's. His empty glass sat on the counter. "This is a nice place," Jack said. "I really think it's going to be." I wasn't sure if he was talking to himself or to us. I didn't even

264

know if he really saw the leaves. It seemed more likely that he was listening to the damn music.

I looked at the framed photos and art hanging in the kitchen and behind us in the hall. Some of the art looked like Tomlin's earlier work. And at first, I thought I recognized both of the women in the photographs. One of them was obviously part of the Eleanor-Tessa set, but the other wasn't quite my sister. "Huh," I said. "You really didn't base Taija on her."

"Yeah, not entirely," Tessa said. "Taija was a lot of people. Tomlin never believed that."

"No, and she still doesn't," I said. "Man. Taija died bloody."

"Yeah, she did."

"And she *really* died here."

"Yeah, and are we doing this again?" Tessa asked.

"No, we're not," I said. "Yeah, that would probably be pointless. God, but all your riddles, Jack. And the manipulation. And the heartbreak. Christ, Tomlin and Mack think Tessa, or the person they think is Tessa, is dead, and —"

"She's on vacation," Jack said. "Someplace safe. She'll be back shortly."

"Oh, will she?" I asked, my rage ignited by what I saw as the sheer, unthinking, self-centered presumption of that. "Right, so she fakes her death, could've killed her kid, breaks her family's heart so she can write a *book,* and they welcome her back with open fucking arms. OK, yeah. Yeah, that sounds good."

"Dodged," Jack said.

"What?" I said.

Jack put his glass in the sink, turned to face me, and said, "She didn't fake her death. She dodged it."

I took a long, long breath. Tessa put a hand on my arm, but I yanked my arm away from her and just said, "No."

"I've watched Taija die," Jack said. "On South River Road, but just as often on Beachams Bridge. And I've watched Tessa die. And Ellie. And Tomlin. And Mack. Many times. Many places. And almost always at the hands of that thing with the shimmering wings and lank, dark hair."

I swallowed. My heart thudded.

"Whenever and however that happens, and whoever it happens to," Jack said, "it's done. That's all there is to it. That story is written. That record spins on. In the beginning, and for the longest time, I respected that. I respected it too much. Like I was watching different versions of the same movie. Taija or Tomlin died, or she didn't. Tessa or Ellie died, or they didn't. Tom Keagan died. I didn't." Jack shrugged. "Variations on a theme."

"You said you respected it 'at first,'" I said. "What changed? What's different?"

"'We passed upon the stair. We spoke of was and when,'" Jack said, quoting my second- or third-favorite Bowie song. He smiled and spread his hands. "I met myself. He'd come from a little further down the road, and he convinced me that I could, that I *should*, have a hand in writing the stories, too. Just like another one of us had convinced him."

"That can't make sense," I said.

"It is," Jack said. "Even now, that's what I understand. It *is*. Chains off of chains."

I looked at Tessa and said, "All because you made a monster."

Her cheeks actually reddened. I took some pleasure from that. "I didn't know any of this then," she said. "I just wanted a strong start to my book."

"And see, that's exactly what I mean," Jack said. "That part was written. And that ... that *thing*, one version of that thing, was coming to Keagans Crossing. I heard it. But it wasn't there yet."

I said, "It wasn't fixed."

"Right," Jack said. "We did what we did, we took its toy away, and it frittered right on off to somewhere else."

"OK," I said, "where it's just going to kill another —"

"No," Jack said firmly, and, I thought, indignantly. "With any luck, no. These are the first links in a new chain. I am not the only enlightened 'me' listening along the creature's path."

"And Ellie is just about done with her book," Tessa said.

I wasn't comfortable with how much I understood. It shouldn't have made sense. I wanted all of it to be impossible again. "How does it end?" I asked.

"Ellie's book?"

"Sure. Yeah. All of it."

"The creature meets an ignoble end," Tessa said, "and then we all live happily ever after to the end of our days."

"Is that from *The Lord of the Rings*?" I asked.

"It's a paraphrase, but yeah," Tessa said. "Bilbo to Gandalf. One of my favorite lines from one of my favorite books."

"Really? It never really did it for me."

"Get out of my house."

"I'd even say the movies were better."

"Jack!"

We laughed. It was a nice moment, but it looked and sounded a lot lighter than I felt. I missed damn near everything. My house — my actual house. My shop. My family, my friends. My life. Despite a lot of things, I'll always think of Tessa as one of my best friends, and I'm glad we tied up or snipped a few of those fraying ends. But we'd both been walking down our own paths for so damn long. "Take me home, Jack," I said. "It's time to go."

Jack said strolled the vinyl floor, squeezed my shoulder, and said, "I understand. One more stop. Indulge me."

Mack

I moved back into the Keagan house so I could be closer to the shop. I stuck with the attic. Like Dad said my first night there, it was "me."

After graduation, we moved the boxes out of the box room and moved Sera in. She kept the ratty chair.

Mom sold the house and found a little place in Portland, and she loved it. It put her that much closer to the art scene there, of course, and it also cut some time out of the drive to Seattle. Both of those things were good, but they were especially great because she had this incredible surge of creativity during that first summer and fall after the wreck, after her brother vanished from right in front of her, after everything shattered and then somehow still managed to flip upside-down. She sold a few of the pieces pretty much right away, and she'd kept that momentum going. People liked her stuff. It was cool. She needed the win. It saved her, which also means it saved me.

Days turned into weeks and months, as they do, and the holidays came around, and then we did all that again. That was life. It was our newer normal.

***

The heater came on just as I put the car into park. I sighed and shut off the engine. In the passenger seat, Sera said, "No! Bring it back!"

"Oh, come on," I said. "The shop has a programmable thermostat, and it stays pretty cozy. You just have to sprint across Main, and then, boom, you're there. You'll be fine."

"Yeah, no," Sera said. "Boom, I'm already here. I don't want to be cold out in the first 'there' on the way to the other 'there.'"

I yanked the keys out of the column, stuffed them into my pocket, and said, "Race you."

Unsurprisingly, I made it across first. I waited on the sidewalk and laughed as Sera made a huge production of crossing that damn street, cussing me out in at least two languages. As she stepped onto the sidewalk, I turned and sort of appraised the store. I like to do that before I open up. I especially like to soak up the beauty of the perfect punctuation on the left-hand window: KEAGANS' COLLECTIONS. I'd insisted on shifting the apostrophe just over two years before, when my mom and I started running the place. I still couldn't officially do anything about the sign for the bridge. Oddly enough, though, some mystery person often *unofficially* did, swabbing an apostrophe up there with some white paint to make it possessive like it should be, dammit.

Anyway, Sera whapped me on the arm because we weren't inside yet, so I unlocked the door, and I got us there. The bell at the top of the door went *ting ting*. I opened and shut the door a few more times, until Sera pretty rudely told me not to. I love that bell.

I looked down as I put my keys back in my pocket, so I didn't see that Sera had stopped just a few feet inside the door. I bonked into her, grunted, and looked where she was looking — at the man standing with his back to us, flipping through the 1970s *Green Lantern* comic he'd pulled off the spinner rack in the "Printables" section Mom and I had put in. I noticed his light-brown hair right away and rolled my eyes. I mean, who else would it have been, reading a comic book all casual-like, lurking like a creeper in my locked store? His clothes did look a little different, though: charcoal-colored pea coat, dark jeans, oxblood Doc Martens boots. "Well, good morning, Jack," I said. "You get a new tailor?"

He closed the comic, carefully slid it back into its polybag, and returned it to its proper spot on the rack. I appreciated every step of that. "Yeah, good morning," he said. "You're opening a little late."

I frowned. This all fit with Jack's M.O., but that wasn't Jack's voice.

"I love what you've done with the place," Not-Jack said as he turned to face us.

I yelled. Or maybe I screamed. I don't know, but in any event, I made a loud-ass noise, and then I ran toward my dad and gave him a big-ass hug. "Oh my God, I can't believe you're back!" I said. Then I pulled away and asked, "*Are* you back? I mean, like, back-back?"

"Yes," my dad said. "Yeah, I think I'm back-back." He looked toward my friend, gave her a little nod, and said, "Hi, Sera."

"Yeah, hey," Sera said. "So, are you going to be needing a job? Because things have been a little down lately, and I don't think they can afford both of us."

Dad laughed and said, "You know, I think we'll figure something out." Then he looked back at me, chewed on his bottom lip for a little bit, and said, "Yeah. So, um ... Tomlin. Jack's with her now, to, uh ... to sort of, well, prepare her."

"Yes. OK, yeah, that's a really good idea. I mean, *I* just about had a heart attack when I saw you, and —"

He tried to hold back a smile and did a really terrible job of it.

"What?" I said. I mean, what the hell else could there be?

"You know, Mack, I am absolutely thrilled you're this happy to see me," he said, "but I'm just gonna put this out there: it is one-hundred-percent fine with me if this isn't the highlight of your day."

***

Dad stayed at the shop. I returned to my shitty car — to *our* shitty car — and drove back through the cold to the Keagan house. I parked right up in front of the workshop. There weren't any other cars there, but if my dad was right, anywhere from one to three people waited for me inside the house. I didn't have any problem reconciling that. As I'd learned, there were other ways to travel.

As per usual, I got in through the sliding door. It still smelled like coffee in the kitchen. I crossed the gulf that was the dining room and made eye contact with the two figures standing between the living-room couch and the entryway that no one ever used. One was Jack Beacham. The other one was my mom, one of my moms, Tomlin. Still-moist clay speckled her hands and forearms like light-gray scabs. We exchanged smiles, but I couldn't call us "happy." At least not yet.

"Well, I suppose I'll leave you to it," Jack said. "Just ... keep your eyes on what's forward. On whatever's ahead of you. And try to keep in mind that whatever she agreed to was probably my idea first."

"OK, so when does it end?" I asked him. "I mean, when does it *really* end?"

Jack nodded slowly and smiled wistfully. "You know, I stopped asking that question a long time ago. But I think I know the answer now. I brought you a souvenir. It's up in your room."

"Jack."

"Say hi to people I know," Jack said.

Whup.

Mom looked at the newly empty space behind her, then she flicked a glance toward the stairs, and then she looked back at me and said, "Hey."

"Hey," I said. "Yeah. So. Any thoughts?"

"Nope," she said. "I don't have a single one. I think I wish Jack had stayed here."

"I don't think he'll ever be gone for long," I said, and I surprised myself by wondering if that was what I really thought. *"I think I know the answer now."* What had he meant by that?

"What are *we* going to do?" Mom asked.

"Whatever it is, it's nothing he could help us with," I told her, and that was something I actually and totally believed.

"This isn't one of his puzzles. This isn't for him. This is ours. This is for us. We got this."

Mom nodded, and then she smiled and touched my arm with one of her wonderfully rough potter's hands. "OK," she said. "Let's do this. Let's go see who's upstairs."

That staircase had never seemed so long or so steep, but we made it up there. As we'd known, but, despite everything, as neither of us had fully believed, my other mother stood in the hallway, perusing the photos covering the southern wall. A woven bag I'd never seen leaned against her foot. Light from that usually worthless window high above the stairway caught the coppery highlights that still ran through her graying brown hair.

My mom. The one who had left. The one who had shattered our hearts.

She took a deep breath, and then she touched the glass covering the photo of teen-aged her and her teen-aged friends hanging out by Echo Creek, and she said, "I don't know any easy words that will put us where we need to be, but I'm here."

That's when she turned to face us, and she saw something in her face that changed hers. It was such an expression of regret. Of defeat. It made my heart ache, and it pissed me off.

"God," she said, "look at you. At both of you. I wonder if I would have hurt you less if I'd told him no."

"Oh, don't you dare say that," Tomlin said. "No, I'm not OK. Mack is not OK. You and me, at least right now, we are not OK. But don't. Don't."

The woman we'd called Tessa Hatcher nodded, and then she hoisted her bag onto her shoulder and rummaged inside it. She said, "Here. I have something for you. I want to show you this."

She extracted a stack of papers and held them out to Tomlin, who made no move to take them. Curiosity rose to the top of whatever the hell else I was feeling, and I grabbed the papers myself. I'm sure I knew, but there it was, typed right on the top page, literally in black-and-white:

BEACHAMS BRIDGE
By Theresa Hatcher
Approx. 86,000 words

I handed it back to her. "Cool. You stuck with the pen name," I said with an unnecessary and unsatisfying amount of snark.

"That's been my name as long as any other one," she said.

Tomlin said, "I know the story." She shook her head and scoffed at her unintended pun. "I listened to Jack. I heard everything he said. I know the *story* is that you wrote that so you could break some chain. But I just can't stop myself from seeing that it is still just a story. Two years. You put us through all of this, and the great grand prize is one of your stories. It's a story, it's a story, it's a story, it's a story."

"This book, *all* the books, let me stay here. This one specifically brought us back together," the woman called Tessa said. She looked down at the typewritten pages she held in her hands. "It made and broke a world, just like it was meant to."

She turned and strode into the bathroom. She dropped the stack of papers into the sink and said, "You're right, though. Let's make this our world now. It has to be."

She stretched out her arm and held her flattened hand above the basin.

And the pages burned.

***

These are the people who were in my house:

Dad sat on the hearth, talking to Angie, who sat on the couch. My mom who died and the one who hadn't both sat the dining-room table, next to each other, technically, but with an obvious distance between them.

Sera stayed in the kitchen, just drinking her coffee and staring at her phone and acting like she was minding her own business.

273

And I stood back by the TV, almost to the stairs, and I wondered if it would ever be totally put back together again. It won't look like it did; I know that. Every one of us passed through a singularity. But it does feel like the side that's facing up is the right one, so at least there's that.

Dad tapped me on my arm, startling me out of my daydreams. I heard the screen door shut and looked behind me. "Hey. Hi. Did Angie leave?" I said.

"Yeah, but we made plans for tomorrow."

"Cool. That's good."

"Yeah, I think it is," he said. "Sorry if I scared you. I didn't know you'd gone somewhere."

"I didn't," I said. "Not really. No Attic or stream for me. Don't have the strength for that today."

Dad nodded. He glanced back at my moms, and then he said to me, "I think we should give them some space. And some time."

"I think you're right, but I don't see things getting all hunky-dory any time soon."

"No, neither do I," he said. "Let's give them a few minutes, though. You want to go for a little drive?"

***

We parked on the shoulder just short of Keagans Crossing. Dad and I walked about halfway down, and then we stood next to each other, resting our arms on the whitewashed sidewall of the bridge and looking out at Echo Creek. The water was murky, like always, but it was at a kind of Goldilocks height: no flooding and nothing morbid exposed in the mud. Just right. I don't know how long we'd just stood there, looking, thinking, not talking. More than a couple cars and trucks had passed behind us.

Dad broke the silence. He said, "This is home, right?"

It seemed like a simple enough question, but there was something odd about his tone and that "right?" tagged on at the end. "What, you mean Westley?" I asked.

"Well, I guess," he said, "but more like Westley versus Chapel Cross."

"Was I ever even over there?" I asked.

"I don't know that," he said. "You could ask your mom."

"I could," I said, but then I shrugged. "No. This is home."

"It's finally starting to feel like it, isn't it?"

He looked back out at the water, and things got quiet again.

"She set her book on fire," I said. "I saw her. She didn't even have to touch it." Those words weren't any less disturbing out loud than when they'd just been banging around inside my head.

"Hm," Dad said. "Well, it sounds like you don't have an empty toolbox, either."

"Yeah," I said, and then I told him something I hadn't told anyone else: not either of my moms, and not even Sera, who would've thought it was cool as hell but still would have kept the secret. "She burned her book, but I have it all up here." I tapped two fingers against my temple. "Or, I don't know, wherever 'here' is. Just from standing next to her and from spending the last couple of days with her."

"And?"

"I haven't ... read it, or whatever. And I don't think I will. She burned it, and I think that's a good thing." I tightened my grip on the railing and rocked back and forth on my feet. "I've got some shit to work out."

Dad nodded, and then he sighed, and then he dug around in a pocket and came out with a ring: a heavy gold one with a green stone.

"Whoa. Did Jack give you that?" I asked.

Dad said, "Nope." He held the ring in his palm like he was weighing it. "Jack took me to the Jack Beacham who was there — well, who was *here* — and he said that my great-uncle left his ring at home when he joined up in '43. My grandpa kept it near-and-dear to him for more than twenty-five years until he gave it to my dad when *he* joined up in '69.

And, for a brief time, my dad was happy with it. He was thrilled. He thought, *Finally, I get something like this from the old man. From his heart. Something without any strings.* Didn't take him too long, though, to realize it came with all the strings.

"When he came back from *his* war — he made it back from his first one — he couldn't keep it on his finger. He'd take it off, and he'd spin it, and he'd just watch it spin and spin and spin. Tables. Kitchen counter. Bars.

"My dad spun his ring one last time on the copper-topped bar down at the Broken Spur, and he asked the bartender what he could get for it. Well, that bartender gave my dad a case of top-shelf liquor for the ring. The bartender slid his new tourmaline ring onto his finger, and he watched my dad, who was already glowing pretty well, stagger out of the bar, lugging that rattling case of booze.

"The bartender knew where he'd be going, and he called the house. My grandpa's house then. He asked if my dad made it home alright. Grandpa's the one who answered the phone, and he said, 'Yeah, he's a little stumbly, but he seems to be holding the couch down OK.'

"The bartender's still worried, though. Like he knew something was going to happen tonight. So he said something to whoever else was working, and he took off down the road, just to make sure my dad's truck stayed parked where it should have been.

"He got to the house just in time to see the truck hauling down the gravel driveway, and then it turned and tore ass down the road. The bartender honked and followed. Both of them were speeding, my dad for his own reasons, and the bartender to keep up.

"They turned left onto Echo Creek Road. And it's raining. I don't think I said that. Sorry. It had been raining hard, and the water was high." He slid the tourmaline ring onto his finger and knocked with it on the bridge railing. "So that's the story."

"Well," I said.

"Well," Dad said.

"Do you know who he was?" I asked.

"The bartender?"

I nodded.

"I've spent a lot of time trying to figure out if I still care," he said. "I'm tired, Mack."

I understood that. "Well," I said again.

"Well," my dad said again.

"But that's not the ring you're wearing."

"This one? No, this is a different ring. That's another story. But it's a short one."

"Thank you," I said.

Dad smiled and turned the ring on his finger. "Jack and I caught up with that Ben Keagan a little earlier. I remembered something that happened between my dad signing up and shipping out, so I helped it happen. I introduced them. And when Ben said he'd give me just about anything for my Best Man gift, I asked him if he'd part with the ring. He'd just had another blowout with my grandpa, so hey, he didn't have to pay for a gift, and he got to give a bit of an F-you to his old man. Just about everybody won."

"You introduced your dad to your mom. To Nana Ronnie."

"I did. Well, there's a 'technically, no' there, but it was close enough for me."

"You got to see your dad again."

"Yeah, and I got to meet someone new. I partied with him, I saw him work, I watched him fall in love. And I took him right up to the bus, and I waved good-bye to him. And Jack ... I will never be able to repay Jack for that."

My heart felt like it was in my throat, but his voice hadn't so much as cracked. It was colored, though, by awe and love and loss. I thought about the "souvenir" that sat on my dresser back at the house, and I wondered how much my dad knew about that.

"You know, the last two years have been *really* boring," I said.

Dad laughed, and then he said, "God, that sounds great."

"Cool," I said. "Let's aim for that."

"You ready to go?"

I nodded and said, "Yep," and then I stepped back from the railing and headed back to the car. I was just about there when I realized Dad wasn't right next to me. He was still on the bridge, still at the railing, still staring out across the water.

I walked back to the start of the bridge, and I said, "Dad?"

"Yeah," he said. "I'm coming." But he only took a couple steps toward me before he stopped again, put his hand back on the railing, and rapped his ring against the wood. He said, "My dad was one-of-a-kind. Well, as one-of-a-kind as anyone is." He smiled like he'd just made a private joke. Then that smile changed, and he told me, "You are, too, Mack, and I am so damn sorry I squandered so many of our years."

I clenched my jaw, and I figured I could manage a handful of words before I totally lost my shit on Echo Creek Road, right there at the western entrance of Keagan's Crossing. So I took a deep breath that shook just a little more than I wanted it to, and I said, "Thank you. Let's go home, Dad."

***

I shut my door, grabbed Jack's dubious gift off my dresser, and sat with it on my bed. The cover art was absolutely stunning. In the top half, a B-17 flew majestically in an almost cloudless blue sky. I brought the book a little closer to my face, so I could make out the nose art. The lower half of the cover was taken up by a too-familiar black-and-white shot of the same plane, blown to hell yet somehow wheels-down in a field of grass. That image was upside-down, so it served like a sort of dark reflection of the picture on the top. The tones were inverted, too, like a film negative, though that photograph had never needed any help to seem otherworldly.

The book was called *The Final Flight of the Tawny Terror,* and its author was Mackenzie Beacham Kidd. My face stared out at me from the back cover, though I couldn't remember the last time I'd smiled like that.

I opened the book to the title page, where Jack Beacham had scrawled this on the flyleaf:

Mack —

Now and again, Ellie or Tessa choose to stay. It just takes one. That's how it always is. Somehow, I've managed to live by this while forgetting it, too. But a wise man or a wise guy got me thinking about consequences. How they give life weight.

At the risk of spoiling it, this story ends where it began. But not how. Ten men walk off the plane in England. The bombardier never does remember how he wound up in the main cabin in those few seconds between calling "Bombs Away!" and when the flak hit. The navigator saw something, but he never tells. Some things are only meant to be known. Felt.

Jim Keagan gets his brother back. Ben Keagan sees both his kids start families of their own. Just one. It just took one domino that knew when to fall.

If you see my face again, and he's heading this way, let him go. He's surely lived a hundred lives and played a thousand songs. So many people don't even get one.

Let this record play. Live <u>your</u> life.

— Jack

It wasn't the first time I'd read that, but it was the first time I had the strength to go further.

I lay back on my bed, and I turned the page.

Author's Note

I began writing this book on 14 July 2020. Just short of a year later, I wound up with what you're holding now, but this story has rattled around my head, taking countless shapes, for a very, very long time. I wrote several chapters as late as the spring of 2021 (the current first chapter was actually one of the last written), but I built several others on the foundations of unfinished projects from as far back as 2006. Other seeds were planted by family stories and personal experiences.

I'm saying it's been a journey. Truly, thank you for joining me for this part of the trip.

I also must say "thank you" to everyone who wandered with me during other parts of the journey, whether they deliberately or inadvertently helped the story evolve to its present form.

First, to the 398th Bomb Group Memorial Association: I am indebted to your incredible collection, including but not even close to being limited to articles, diaries, formation charts, and photographs. Of special note is Allen Ostrom's article "It Was a Fortress Coming Home" and the diaries of Lt. William H. Baker, Lt. Robert J. Beckley, T/Sgt. Oliver W. Bradford, T/Sgt. Ben Core, Lt. E. Dalton Ebbeson, and Lt. Robert E. Weidig. Websites like yours (398th.org) become more valuable every day, as we lose the last living voices of the World War II era.

To my wife, Lori, and our son, Gabriel: I can't imagine enduring this life, let alone the Year of the Plague, without you.

To my LGBTQ+ students, past, present, and future, for inspiring me with your courage as you move through a world that is so often hostile to you simply for existing and presenting your genuine selves. I hope I've taught you half as much as you've taught me.

To my readers and editors: Lori (yes, you're in here twice), Greg Bond, Luke Hudson, Chris Kiesel, Kendall Lavaque, Brianna Myers, Amy Scymanky, and Meredith Work. Your early and ongoing support was vital, and your comments and questions greatly improved the final product. (To those who don't like the book, just think: without these people, it would have been worse.)

To my parents, Bill and Edna Bernard, for more than four decades of love and support. I don't think you've always understood me, but I've never doubted that you were there for me.

To my late grandpas. William John Bernard, you were often an abrasive, obstinate, and generally difficult man. But I knew the guy who endured the horrors of the Korean War as an infantryman in the U.S. Army more than twenty years before you or anyone who could have helped you heard the term "post-traumatic stress disorder." We had some good times, but I often wonder about the man you could have been and the lives some family-members could have had.

Raymond Joseph LeDoux, you didn't quite make it to your sixty-ninth birthday, and that was more than thirty years ago now. I treasure my fading memories. Sitting beside you on the front porch as you chain-smoked Now cigarettes, just watching traffic and counting the bricks in the chimney across the street. Playing cards at the dining-room table, hearing "Rummy, dummy!" when you won and "You cheated!" when I did. Blowing soap-bubbles as we sat together on the low back step.

Wondering about the photo of the blasted and mangled plane hanging on the wall, and knowing, even at that age (I was just short of eleven when you died), that I wasn't supposed to ask.

Here's what I've learned:

On 15 October 1944, in this world, a flak hit devastated the nose of a B-17 named *Lovely Julie* and instantly killed Sgt. George Abbot, the nineteen-year-old bombardier. With no aid from the obliterated instrument panel, Lt. Raymond LeDoux, Capt. Lawrence DeLancey, Lt. Phillip Stahlman, and the other surviving members of the flight crew brought the ruined plane from the exploding German skies to a wheels-down landing at an Allied airfield in England. There were no further casualties.

I enjoy working with alternative realities, theoretical physics, and even "magic," as Henry Clairvaux calls it. But I don't write miracles.

Again, thank you all. This was fun.

Jonathon Bernard
Salem, Oregon
2 April 2021

About the Publisher

At [Blue] [Murrey] Publishing, we take a rigorous, many-eyes approach to literary editing, revision, and refinement, but we also embrace the potential for the democratization of literature provided by e-readers, print-on-demand services, social networking, independent bookstores, and online marketplaces.

We believe that too many wonderful works of literature become forever lost in the increasingly narrow funnel that runs from the author to the agent to the publisher in the traditional model.

We work to ensure that every [Blue] [Murrey] release is as well-written and professionally presented as if it were released by a major, traditional publishing house. Our name must mean something, but so must every author's effort and independence.

Every [Blue] [Murrey] book is published through individual agreements with the author, who will maintain total control of the intellectual property in perpetuity.

In short, we like books, we want there to be more of them, and we hope you enjoy ours.

Email: BlueMurrey@gmail.com
Twitter: @BlueMurrey
Instagram: @BlueMurreyPublishing